A
LULLABY
IN THE
DESERT

MOJGAN AZAR

Building futures, Bridging divides

A Lullaby in the Desert
by Mojgan Azar

© Mojgan Azar 2021

ISBN: 9781912092819

First published in 2021
by Arkbound Foundation (Publishers)

Arkbound is a social enterprise that aims to promote social inclusion, community development and artistic talent. It sponsors publications by disadvantaged authors and covers issues that engage wider social concerns. Arkbound fully embraces sustainability and environmental protection. It endeavours to use material that is renewable, recyclable or sourced from sustainable forest.

Arkbound
4 Rogart Street
Glasgow, G40 2AA

www.arkbound.com

A LULLABY IN THE DESERT

DEDICATION

For the survivors, and for those who did not.

ACKNOWLEDGEMENTS

First and foremost, I wish to thank my husband, who has been beside me with his love and support all throughout our journey.

I am also grateful for the people of Kurdistan, who gave me shelter, love, and empathy over the years. Their hospitality ensured that I felt like a long-lost relative rather than a foreigner far from home. This is the Kurdish spirit, to help those who need it most, especially during those difficult years now behind us and most importantly those to come.

Many thanks to my Iraqi sisters and brothers who helped so many innocents escape a grim fate during those years of conflict.

May peace illuminate the four corners of the earth through actions of people like them.

Prologue

Tehran, 2003

"What does school have to do with girls?" Susan's father demanded, shouting. "A woman's place is in the kitchen, understand?" He pinched her sharply, asking her again. "Do you understand? I can't hear!"

"Yes, yes!" she answered. But he kept pinching her. Susan cowered, eyes to the floor.

"I can't hear! What?" he asked again, relentlessly.

"Yes, a girl should be in the kitchen." It seemed her father wouldn't let her sleep until Susan's skin was bruised black and blue. Susan loved to study, and this was one of the many reasons her father hated her.

Susan's mother couldn't defend herself or her daughter. All she could do was curse him and wish he'd die. If one day she finally left, she would be forced to abandon her dowry, leave what little rights she had behind and lose custody of her children. In Iran, only the father has custody of the children. Only he has the right to seek a divorce.

Every night, Susan went secretly down to the basement and lit a candle. After ensuring no one was around, she would withdraw a stack of books from an antique box she kept hidden down there, arranging them around her in a circle. She'd carefully pick each one up and read it in a whisper. She was careful of each sound she made, checking her breathing, just in case someone was coming.

The reward Susan earned for her interest in learning was the harassment and beatings she received from her father. Her aunt paid for her school, taking care to ensure Susan's father never discovered the truth. Susan's father forced her to earn money by selling knickknacks on the street to pay for her mother's medicines and frequent hospital stays. Her father took whatever was leftover, sometimes beating it out of her. He'd then go and buy drugs, smoking Susan's earnings into thin air.

Susan converted her bitter days and dark nights into a hidden heaven through reading. Sometimes she fantasized about escaping from that house. The hate inside was tangible and it seemed to gnaw away at her. Yet the thought of leaving her mother behind hurt her and held her back.

Susan was snapped out of her thoughts by the sound of approaching footsteps. She stood quickly, hiding the books under the fabric and herself behind some loose planks of wood against the wall. She closed her eyes and covered her mouth with her hand.

"Susan," came a woman's voice. It was her mother, calling carefully. "Susan?" Another step came down the rickety stairs.

Susan peered out from behind the wooden planks. "Mum!" She rushed to hug her mother tightly before looking to see if anyone was following her. "Why aren't you asleep?"

Her mother carefully tucked some loose hair back under her red headscarf.

"The nights you come to the basement, I can't close my eyes, my daughter. I wait for you. I wait until you go under your blanket. I'm afraid that monster will come after you. I couldn't stand you being prisoner in the basement again. You are my life." She had a lump in her throat as Susan hugged her. "Come here, sit, I want to talk to you about something."

They both sat on the floor. Her mother looked around a moment, finding her words, then looked Susan directly in the eyes. "When

I was pregnant with you, I thought a few times about getting an abortion. I didn't want to bring another innocent baby into this world. I didn't want you to become like others, like me. But it was like God didn't want that." She took a breath and continued. "No matter what I tried, I couldn't get the abortion to work. I ate saffron, I jumped, drank liquid soap, I starved myself. No remedy worked. You didn't want to go. But the moment I gave birth to you, the moment the doctor put you in my hands and I saw a little baby girl that was only two cheeks with black hair and those eyes staring up at me..." Her mother trailed off for a moment. "I think if you could speak then, your first phrase would be, 'Can't you see, you couldn't do it? Don't you see I won?'" They both laughed. "Shh! We don't want to wake anyone up." She held Susan's hand for a moment. "You became my whole life. For me, a hope to live, to be alive. You were a quiet baby, easily falling asleep with a simple lullaby."

"Mum, will you sing lullaby for me now?"

Her mother's eyes were welling. She put Susan's head on her chest as if she was still that little baby, caressing her face gently. She began softly singing a Persian lullaby, "La-la- yi. La-layi..."

Susan felt a tear fall onto her forehead. She opened her eyes, looking up at her mother. She wiped her mother's tears with her hands, noticing how her eyes were floating in dark circles.

"Will you forgive me?"

"For what, Mum? Please, never say that."

"I wasn't a good mother to you. I didn't do what I should've done."

"Please Mum, never say that again. You mean the world to me. When I come home and open the door, I see you sitting there waiting for me. Knowing there is someone that loves me, that's everything. I never want to hear that. Please, promise me," Susan said.

"You didn't have a normal mother, and no father. You never

tasted the love a real family can provide. Your childhood was full of harassment from a bastard, full of abuse. He will never give up until he destroys your life, your future and now he's made his decision to..." Her mother couldn't continue.

"What decision? Mum? Talk to me!"

After a pause, her mother continued. "He wants you to marry Agha Masoud, in an arrangement."

"What?" Susan clenched her jaw. "You must be kidding me."

"No! I swear to God. I heard it when I was listening behind a door. He wants to make a deal with him. Your father owes him money and suggested giving you instead."

"Agha Masoud is an addict and he's the same age as my father!"

"Stay calm, my daughter, you are from me, from my blood. If he means to sell your honour, I won't let him. He doesn't want you to study, he doesn't want you to be independent."

"What?" Susan asked. "Mum, what are you talking about?"

"You are a strong girl, I know. You can fight for your honour. It isn't easy for me to ask you to leave your home but staying here will destroy your future. I talked to your aunt. She will keep you for a few days in Bibi's home."

"And after that? After I leave my aunt's and grandmother's houses?"

"It depends on you. You should build your future."

"But what about your medicine?"

"Your future is more important."

"But Mum, I'll miss you. I don't have anyone in this world except you. You're my mother. I'm not brave enough to stay away from you and be alone. How can I?"

"Do you think it's easy for me? I'm sending away a part of myself!" Her mother began to cry.

Susan looked down at the ground and spoke quietly. "You don't want me anymore. Maybe I don't belong in this home. Just like when you were pregnant with me, you wanted to get rid of me then too. Haven't I always done what you asked? I'm the only person in this house who takes care of you. I bandage your wounds with my own hands, I wipe your tears. I've been starving but I told you I was full, just so there would be more food for you."

Her mother held Susan's chin and picked her head up a little, stretching to kiss her forehead. "Forgive me. You gave me life and I appreciate you for teaching me to love. Take your things and leave before sunrise."

"Now? But..."

"Everyone is asleep now. It's the best time. Your aunt will be waiting for you at noon in Laleh Park. Stay near the latrine. She'll find you there."

Susan's face was washed with tears. She took her mother in her arms. They both wept, embracing one another one final time. "When I'm settled, come and find me, please. Don't leave me alone forever. You're my only hope in this world." Susan pleaded softly between her quiet sobs.

"Don't cry my daughter. We'll meet again soon. Be strong for yourself and strong for your mother."

The sky was blue and the streets were bathed with dawn's light. It was almost time for the Azzan, the morning call to prayer. Susan walked with feet that resisted each centimetre of distance from her home. She felt unwanted. Her home no longer had a place for her. She came almost to the end of the street and began slowing her pace. She turned, looking at the small blue metal door, the door to a home she'd lived in her whole life. No one stood to wave goodbye. She left her heart with her mother in that home.

Loneliness called to her now. The street was filled with careless neighbours who wore a smile long enough to get something from one another, shedding it as soon as they retreated behind their metal door. The houses were tightly packed. Neighbours would often listen to a woman's scream or a man's shout, shake their heads but do nothing. After all, family matters were private. Silent judgement was a favourite pastime. But if someone went to their house to propose to their daughter, suddenly their life was an open book, heavily exaggerated and full of flair.

Tehran, with its thirteen million people, with all those towers, all its colourful citizens, with its pollution, lies and beauties, was invisible to Susan and Susan was invisible to it. She always gave love and kindness but got nothing in return. Being alone in this city was a nightmare. The city had twenty-two zones but she only knew Shahre Rey. For her, Shahre Rey was the tiny place she grew up; it was the entire world. It was a place that for her was defined by sadness and pain. She had heard of north Tehran, a beautiful place for wealthy people. She wished she could visit it one day, taking her mum to Valiasr Street for ice cream like the wealthy people did.

Susan took her headphones out of her pocket and plugged them into the MP3 player she'd had for several years. Cars and buses appeared one by one on the street. People began emerging from their homes like ants kicked from their nest. Labourers, employees, managers all wore the same puffy eyes and nervous look that showed how they hated their jobs.

Susan stopped in the middle of the busy street, as confused as a little girl who had accidentally let go of her mother's hand while crossing. She looked around and was met with a sea of angry faces. She didn't know the way to Laleh Park. A woman with a chador was hurrying down the street toward her.

"Excuse me!" Susan strained herself while the woman pretended not to hear her. "Miss!"

"What?" the woman answered finally, perturbed.

"Do you know how I can get to Laleh Park?"

"Where?"

"Laleh Park. My aunt is waiting there for me." Susan thought if she justified herself it might convince the woman that she wasn't just meeting a date or ditching school.

"I don't know, my daughter." The woman pulled her chador tightly around her head with both hands, covering her face and disappearing down the street like a candle blown out by the wind.

"Maybe I should ask a taxi driver," Susan said quietly to herself. She walked along the street, holding her hand up. She saw a Peugeot that might be a taxi. She waved her hand to get the driver's attention, placing her bag down.

The driver stopped the car immediately. He was a young man and the blaring music from his car speakers drowned out the wailing Azzan. He was chewing something in a very dramatic way and Susan could see his throat. His posture in the car seemed exaggeratedly relaxed, leaning to one side, one hand on the steering wheel and the other on the gear. He cocked his head, looking out the window at her.

Susan moved a little closer. "Can you put the window down a little?"

He watched as the window slid downward. "Hello, miss."

"I want to go to Laleh Park. How I can get there? I mean, which bus should I take?"

He laughed, lowering his music and looking at his watch. "Now?"

Susan got the feeling that he was not the right person to ask. She backed away from the car. "Thank you, sir." She grabbed her bag and moved further back.

"Wait!" He rolled the car towards her.

"Thanks, I don't need your help, merci." Susan hurried her steps a little more.

"Come, I will take you to the park sweetie. I'm a taxi driver. I'll take you for free."

He kept rolling his car closer to her, trying to get her to accept his offer. It wasn't the first time a rude man had followed her down a street in Tehran, saying bad words, lecturing her, assuming she was a street walker, a homeless girl or a runaway. This time, the man's assumption was correct. As of this morning, Susan was a runaway.

Chapter One

"Susan!" The manager's shout pierced through the chorus of clinking china and roaring dishwashers rumbling deep in the restaurant's belly. The clamour usually drowned out any possibility of getting lost in one's thoughts, though Susan still tried. She tried imagining the home she had left behind in Tehran more than a decade ago, although that memory was fading more every day. Susan could never keep the manager's panicked shouts out of her head, nor his searching eyes from her body.

"Susan!" he shouted again, forcefully enough to drag Susan back to reality. It was 2014 now and Tehran was a long way away. Susan's manager stood in front of her with his hands shoved in his pockets and a menacing glare fixed on his face. He was about thirty-five years old but his leathery face had aged far beyond his years, no doubt from the diet of cigarettes and sugary tea that he'd depended upon since he was a teenager. Susan's co-workers heard him but didn't want to interfere, Susan tried to ignore him, hoping he'd leave her alone. She tried to plunge herself back into her thoughts, far away from the angry manager, away from this dingy restaurant and away from Erbil.

"How dare you ignore me?"

Susan winced. A soapy tea glass fell out of her hand, exploding into a million pieces. She gasped and looked at the little shards laying between her and her manager. She looked up at his face, trying not to stare at the vein bulging from his neck as his rage grew.

"Yes sir?" Susan's voice quivered, her hands shaking like a willow tree as she panicked in her confusion. She couldn't decide if she should bring a broom to clean up the mess or keep her head down in silence. She glanced over at the plastic broom in the corner, slowly turning on the balls of her feet to grab it.

"Stop!" The kitchen fell silent, as if empty. "Are you deaf?"

"Sorry, sir."

The manager took a step toward her. Susan was keenly aware that she was the only woman in a room full of men with nothing to lose. These men were careless, heartless, tired of the world and tired of life. Every time Susan opened the big iron door and entered the kitchen each day, she feigned friendliness with a meek smile. But now she stood face to face with the greatest menace she knew.

The manager touched the aluminium table beside him with his palm. He squinted at her, as if looking at a distant object, rather than a face full of fear only ten centimetres in front of him. Susan tried to swallow the lump in her throat but it only made her chin quiver. She was sure he could see her nervousness, which seemed to energize him. He raised his hand up to her face, and his eyebrow lifted with it. He smirked as she squirmed.

"Look up." He forced her chin up with his index finger. "You're deaf? Blind too?"

She moved her eyes upward, staring at his hand.

"When you were starving and homeless, I gave you a job."

"But sir..."

"Shh." He put a finger on his lips to silence her. "No need to say anything. Your behaviour says many things."

Susan's male colleagues laughed nervously, observing without protest, as if they were watching a tasteless movie or hearing an uncomfortable joke. One of them took a deep breath, then exhaled. In the same breath he said, "The man has the right to fire her, look how she acts." He continued to curse under his breath, passing judgement.

Susan had worked at this restaurant almost eight months, an Arabic restaurant which employed mostly Arabs. Although she was familiar with the language, Susan wasn't brave enough to say a word. As the only woman, and an Iranian woman at that, it was her job to wash the dishes, clean the floor and prepare utensils.

"Why are you guys standing around? What are you staring at? Don't you have work to do?" the manager asked, glaring menacingly at each witness to Susan's shame.

A young boy working nearby stood and stared angrily at the man. Did he want to speak up, to protect Susan? Could he? She reminded him of his big sister. Susan could see that in the boy's eyes and she felt hope for just a second, maybe there was finally one helpful person in her life. The manager moved his chest toward her, bending his back, so very close that Susan could feel the moisture from his hot breath on her skin.

"I won't repeat it again, sir," she said.

"Look at me." The moment she looked into his eyes, he wet his lips with his tongue, staring at her chest. "I will teach you." He turned on his feet and quickly walked outside.

As he left, Susan was grinding her teeth and her fists were balled against her sides. She looked around at the others silently watching her, staring in disdain, as though it was her fault. To them she was nothing but an object, an object responsible for its own treatment despite the inherent powerlessness of being a woman in Erbil.

"I wish," she thought to herself. "I wish my fear was just for losing my job or starving; instead my life and my body are constantly threatened, no matter how much I've got to eat, no matter how much I'm paid. I wish just saying it was easy. My heart weeps every time I feel these stares."

The weight of the harassment and the fear of rape unsettled her more than anything else in her life. She was living in Erbil, Kurdistan, a place that was surprisingly secure given its location in northern Iraq. Yet, she still felt vulnerable. Susan decided it didn't matter where she was, somehow being female was a curse she shared with women everywhere.

One of the wars nearby was between Iran and the Syrian people and Susan's manager seemed to personify the conflict. Susan was Iran, he was Syria and he was out for revenge. Erbil was a modern city, but some parts were frozen a thousand years in the past. The city lied. It tried to distract people with its shining windows and luxury cars, with men spending thousands of dollars for a dinner, showing off their suits and expensive brands to their wives and their mistresses. All this but only God knows what is going on in their minds. That is, until they corner a woman like an animal and force her to listen to their desires.

Susan wished desperately that another woman would come work in the kitchen with her. There was safety in numbers. To be sure, some women had worked there, but not for long. As soon as they witnessed the behaviour of the men, the sexual advances, the dirty words, the disrespect, they decided the pay cheque wasn't worth the price they paid.

The young boy came to her side and looked up at her. His eyes spoke, connecting with hers in silent understanding. Susan glanced away, and then looked back at him.

"Did you go to Mosul, Faisal?" Susan asked.

"Why should I go?"

"To see your family, silly."

"No." He immediately looked away and began cleaning the table. He made little circular motions, moving his hand fast on the table.

Susan felt sorry for him. His hands should be holding a pencil and paper in a classroom, not cleaning tables in a restaurant while his family lived in poverty in Mosul. He was only thirteen. In Erbil, there were no rules about children working, or if there was, no one followed them.

The other employees all left the kitchen together in a group to go smoke cigarettes in a back alley. Susan watched them go as she clasped the broom, sweeping the floor that one of them should have been cleaning. Faisal thoughtfully came over to her and tried to take the broom from her hand but Susan didn't let go. Faisal let go and shrugged away. He headed outside, behind the others.

"You don't smoke, do you?" Susan wanted to hear him say he didn't.

He paused and turned, looking directly at her with his shining blue eyes. "I've got a lot of problems, but none so great that I need cigarettes to be my therapist."

Now Susan was alone, without the company of her hateful co-workers. They probably thought she was getting paid more because the manager had taken a liking to her. The kitchen fan was deafening. The smell of the detergents and bleach hung around the corners of her nose. The employee time slips were rustling under the breeze of the fan as they sat loosely in their tin on the wall. She noticed the little bits of food stuck to the papers.

She read the first column on one of the time slips. It said START TIME in big letters. To Susan, the start time was her hour for energy. Then she read the last column, moving her finger along the page. In equally big letters, but with a tone she felt was different, the column shouted END TIME. This one was the moment of exhaustion. She saw her name beneath these lines, and she exhaled deeply. She was halfway between energy and exhaustion. It was lunch break.

Collecting some food, Susan absent-mindedly picked up a little yellow soup with her spoon, dripping it slowly back into the bowl. She watched the tiny pieces of something dribble back into the broth. Was this supposed to be food?

"Eat, don't die," she told herself.

She dipped the spoon back into the bowl, this time blowing the broth gently to cool it. She regretted wasting her breath on the dead beans in the spoon. She tore a piece of stale bread with her other hand, nibbling cautiously. It tasted like the plastic bag it came from and her forehead crinkled in disgust. "Eat, don't die."

She was working her way up to her second spoonful when the manager suddenly came out of nowhere and plopped himself in the empty chair beside her. She immediately straightened her back as she slowly spoke, trying to regain her composure.

"Hello, sir." Her shyness and discomfort worked their way through her body, her heart rate racing as if she was climbing the stairs to the citadel. She dared not look at him.

"Eat." His words offered no encouragement. It was an order.

Her shaking hand clenched white with the effort of gripping the spoon as she put it to her mouth. He watched her intently, as if watching his own food, as he slurped his tea and deliberately placed the glass onto its saucer. His face contorted and his eyes flashed. She braced herself.

"This is cold!" He glared at her, blame in his eyes. "Stand up!" He slapped the metal table, sending the little teaspoon skittering off the saucer and onto the floor. Susan shot to her feet like a piece of kindling struck by lightning. Against her own wishes, her attention automatically went straight to his demands, tempered by a lifetime of doing what she was told.

"Bring tea!" Susan tried to take his glass but he batted her hand away. "A new one!"

The other employees returned from outside to resume their act of silent observation, pretending to see and hear nothing while paying attention to everything. Susan reached for the teapot, which felt full. She poured a half glass and then filled the rest with the boiling water from the double boiler. She gingerly placed two sugar cubes on the saucer beside the glass and rushed through the kitchen back to the manager. In her haste, she slid to the floor.

"You're such a loser," Susan's manager spat as she grasped her hip, which had taken the brunt of the fall. He stood over her, hands on his hips, eyeing her like a piece of meat. He muttered something and then left the kitchen.

Faisal ran to her as soon as the manager left. He had been waiting on the side-lines so he could help her but he feared the manager like the rest of the employees.

"This man is merciless," Susan complained as Faisal held her arm, helping her stand on her good leg and pulling out a chair.

"Please, sit. I'll bring some water for you."

Susan put her hand up, stopping him. "I'm good, I don't need it. Are all Arab men the same? I understand, you don't want to say anything because you're afraid to lose your job. But consider me as part of your family."

Faisal only listened and smiled. He brought her an icepack and put it on her ankle. He held it there and became lost in thought for a moment and then looked up at her. "His profession and experience mean nothing if he can't stand to see a woman from a country that he considers his enemy."

"What do you mean?"

Faisal grimaced a moment as he considered his words. He couldn't contain his anger at the manager. "This will stay between us?"

"Sure, of course, you can trust me."

"He was in the Syrian opposition and he lost both his brothers in the war. Then he ran away to Iraq. He hates Iran and Iranians. That's why he always says: 'Iran took our land and killed our people and my brothers.' It isn't only him with a mind full of these thoughts. All Syrians fighting against Bashar al-Assad think the same way. They say: 'The country was collapsing until Iran came to help during the civil war. They killed our sisters and brothers in the name of Allah and won't leave until the last drop of blood.'"

Susan's eyes were welling up. The words she heard were far more painful than the bruise forming on her leg. "Do you think it's right for them to talk this way?"

"What can I say? I'm not saying they're right but you must admit, Iran has played a huge role in what's happening in Syria now. Iran and Syria have one goal and that is to be sure they don't turn out like Iraq. They support each other because Syria was the only one to help during the Iran-Iraq War, and Iran owes Syria for that.

Susan was surprised to hear such knowledge of history and tragedy from a thirteen-year-old boy, but it was not wholly unexpected. The same thing was happening in her country. In Iran, children watched the government's version of the news, which was invariably a fantastic if not fictional interpretation of what was happening. At the same time, parents were always talking about politics, which was a daily topic of conversation over lunch and dinner.

"Can you walk?" asked Faisal. Susan nodded, eager to leave the dirty kitchen where she was growing weary of paying for the mistakes of a government far away.

Faisal's words echoed in her mind as she rode the bus back to her apartment at the end of another long day. "Nobody thinks about me," she said to herself quietly. "Without a mother, a father, a friend, how can I expect politicians to care about my wellbeing?" She looked out the window at the grey buildings and downtrodden faces. "This world with a heart of stone knows nothing of love and kindness. It drags me into these messy thoughts, forcing me to live this unwanted life, while my throat chokes back tears. I am always longing for happiness and laughter. Maybe I'll be alright when God looks at me."

Chapter Two

Susan was living in an apartment on the outskirts of the city, right on the road leading to Mosul. It was in the middle of a highway, lit twenty-four hours a day with unforgiving bright streetlights that flooded her room. A wooden bed beneath the window was draped in a sheet that was no longer white after years of use and across from the window sat a small refrigerator that sounded more like a tractor. If visitors came, which they never did, they would probably wonder how three people could live in a room of only fifteen square meters. There were no shops for at least two kilometres and the place was just as desolate inside as the dirt lot surrounding the apartment outside. In each small room there were three, four or even six beds arranged side by side or on top of one another. For workers like Susan, living their lives like soldiers in a garrison waiting to attain the freedom only death can bring, this was home.

Susan shared her room with two other women. The landlord put them all together to make them feel safe. There were empty rooms on the same floor, but there was always the risk that a drunk man would come in the middle of the night, knocking on one of the doors. How else could the women be safe, except together?

Susan caught a glimpse of her own reflection in the dull mirror hanging beside the bathroom door. She stopped for a moment, observing the dark circles under her big brown eyes and the redness of her skin from the days walking under the bright sunlight. She touched a finger to her cheek, slowly moving it across her skin to her nose, watching the reflection of what seemed to be a stranger staring back at her. She wished for a moment that she could afford those luxurious facial treatments that rich women enjoyed. She quickly shook her head, reminding herself not to dream beyond the possible.

Her long black hair fell around her shoulders like a silken waterfall. She wrapped her hair in her hand and then twisted it gently to one side, wondering if that touch of fashion may bring some excitement to her tired appearance. Instead, a huge wave of sadness washed over her. She reluctantly pulled her hair back behind her head, tying it out of sight.

Her roommates weren't there tonight, so Susan could enjoy a few moments alone. Dropping her bag on the bed, laying down on her back, she began listening to the voices of her neighbours seeping through the wall. Usually the refrigerator was loud enough to block that out, but tonight it seemed they were having an argument. After a moment, Susan realised it was only an animated conversation between some of her Arab co-workers, she didn't need to be worried.

Turning on her side, Susan was reminded of the bruise she had earned earlier. The pain was still there, and it snapped her out of her moment of relaxation. She gently placed her hand on her hip, breathing deeply. Wishing for painkillers she knew she didn't have, Susan pulled her bag toward her and unzipped a pocket, her eyes still forced shut from the pain. She rifled through blindly, wishing her fingers would graze over just one pill. Defeated, Susan pulled the blanket over her face, trying to hide from a world that didn't want to see her anyway and eventually she drifted into a restless sleep.

Suddenly she woke, her body was covered in sweat and she was breathing heavily as if something was pressing on her chest. She looked around in fear, wishing she could see something to remind her this world was real. She could feel tears mixing with sweat on her cheeks. She pressed her head against the wall, hoping the pressure of the cold cement would stop her tears. A hard substitute for soothing kind words and a human touch. She only knew her own pain and, in that moment, Susan wished she could die and escape. Her roommate Narin looked out from under her own blanket but only subtly so that she could pretend that she hadn't seen anything.

When morning came, Susan collected her dirty clothes into a black plastic bag to go wash them. An Egyptian girl named Ament was sitting in the hallway near Susan's room. Ament had long black hair and eyes full of suspicion. She always looked as though she was about to ask an uncomfortable question, with an air of sentimental eagerness, as if she was Nefertiti, Akhenaten's wife. Her pride was a result of her boyfriend getting her a twenty-day VISA to the United States ten years before. Ament touched her hair absentmindedly as she watched Susan walk down the hallway, flashing her classic sarcastic smile.

Susan knew she should ignore Ament and pass by quickly but the pain in her ankle wouldn't let her disappear down the stairs. She took a deep breath and tried to balance her weight on her good foot. She couldn't take it and had to sit down.

"God, how do people live if they can't walk?" Susan thought to herself. "How do they bear it? We used to force my Grandmother to walk fast behind us even as she complained. She was so innocent, she tried to satisfy us and yet she suffered pain much worse than mine. I miss my childhood, when Grandma would hug me so tight in her arms. I wish I never grew older than that moment."

Susan held the railing, pulling herself up. She decided she needed to stop dwelling on her pain and instead appreciate the health she still had. Besides, she only had four minutes left until she'd miss the bus to work. After tightening her sneakers and slinging her bag over her shoulder, she finished buttoning her jacket and rushed down. Midway, she stopped. "I forgot the keys!" The door was locked and there was no one inside to open it. She decided to go to work anyway and hope someone would be there when she returned. She made her way to the bus stop, waiting for it to arrive to shuttle her to the restaurant. It finally pulled up in a cloud of dust. She got on and took her seat beside Faisal, the only person she could trust. She noticed Faisal was wearing a jacket.

"It's the middle of summer, aren't you hot?"

Faisal looked out the window. "I've been getting chills at night."

"Maybe you're getting sick. You might be getting the flu."

"Nobody gets the flu in this weather." Faisal was defiant. "It's a virus that makes you sick, not the weather."

"I can make soup for you if you decide you need it." Susan decided not to argue.

Cars flew past the bus as the early morning haze hung in a curtain over the street. The bus driver almost cut in front of a small car driving without lights and the inevitable cursing and horn honking was accompanied by hand gestures out the window of both the bus and the car, until somehow the bus eventually arrived at the restaurant to drop them all off.

Chapter Three

While Susan struggled to make ends meet in Erbil, something otherworldly was happening less than a hundred kilometres west in Mosul. The second-largest city in Iraq, after Baghdad, became a prison on the 10th June 2014. On that day, a violent organisation declared itself a caliphate from an ancient mosque in Mosul's old city. The organisation called itself the Islamic State but everyone in the Middle East called it Da'esh. In the West, it was called ISIS or ISIL. Da'esh members confiscated all Iraqi government-issued identification cards, replacing them with Islamic State identification cards. Everyone lost their jobs and their homes and there was no money for food, medicine or fuel. Da'esh kept the people on the brink of starvation because it was easier to control them that way.

Prices for essentials increased daily. Doctors and teachers never returned to work and those that did received no payment. Da'esh made their money taxing small street vendors and shop keepers and from other extractions they forced on the people now living under their black flag. The crimes Da'esh committed were more atrocious than anything seen in any movie or nightmare. They demanded submission from everyone, forcing all women to wear strict hijab, throwing those accused of homosexuality from high buildings, chopping off the hands and feet of suspected petty criminals, whipping people who smoked cigarettes and stoning women to death accused of adultery. They celebrated their atrocities in professionally produced videos which proliferated across the internet, which were then picked up by international news outlets, unwittingly helping them instil fear for free.

With each beheading and every new execution, Da'esh tightened its grip on its subjects. The only means of escape were the dangerous smuggling networks, established throughout the many years of conflict the Iraqi people had already faced. Da'esh banned travelling in and out of their zone of control and branded those who tried to emigrate as infidels, which carried the penalty of a gruesome summary execution. If an elderly couple wanted to travel the Islamic pilgrimage to Mecca, they had to ransom the title deed to their property before they were permitted to go. Da'esh claimed their territory was a haven for Muslims and yet they punished those who tried to escape with fates worse than death. Only God knew what happened to the people in Mosul, because the world remained blind.

Meanwhile, the Kurdish Peshmerga began manning a front line between Mosul and Erbil as a last line of defence, with women volunteering to fight alongside their Kurdish brothers. Somewhere between Mosul and Erbil, children looked up at their mothers for water in heat approaching 45 degrees Celsius. Da'esh would have been pleased to let them die in the desert and that knowledge would stay with those refugee families forever, shaping those children. Checkpoints around Erbil were flooded with those that survived and arrived from Mosul and the outlying areas that were besieged by Da'esh. They were welcomed by the Kurdish government, who opened their borders for them, as they had in previous wars, despite the threat of Da'esh sleepers. Within Kurdistan, companies were closing their doors and housing prices dropped. As refugees arrived, the locals who could send their families away did so immediately. The people were filled with fear. The Kurdish Regional Government asked the United States and Israel for help as soon as Da'esh took control of Mosul. The

Yazidis stranded atop the high Sinjar mountain in western Iraq pleaded for rescue as well. Da'esh began enslaving Yazidi women and children while executing all Yazidi men, dumping their bodies by the hundreds in mass graves. Yet these pleas fell on deaf ears, and the Kurds looked eastward to Iran.

During one interview, a Kurdish official said that Iran was the first country to help them and that Iran played the decisive role in defending the Kurds when Da'esh was only a few kilometres away from entering Erbil. Iran sent weapons, equipment and personnel to stop the march of Da'esh, and the Kurds were indebted for this. But for now, Susan, an Iranian living in Kurdistan, remained completely unaware.

Chapter Four

Susan stood contemplating her position at the restaurant. She hated the sexual jokes and conversations she heard in the kitchen. She was also bothered by increasing verbal and physical harassment too, but she had to bear it all silently to protect her honour and her job. Her manager's mood swings, visible from the glaze over his eyes, was another cause for concern. He would reach a boiling point every so often, losing his patience and usually directing his temper toward Susan. As if on cue, the manager opened the door with a kick, hands deep in his pockets.

"Hello, sir."

He responded with a single nod, walking slowly around the kitchen. He opened drawers one by one, and Susan was relieved that she had taken such care that not one thing was out of place for him to complain about.

"What are these papers?" He was holding some slips tightly in his balled fist.

"Ah, those are the entry and exit times for the shift schedule. You asked me to leave them here for you."

"Aha." He pulled his lips tight to one side of his face, looking her up and down. "Do your job."

Faisal was drying glasses nearby, watching the whole thing. He glared at the manager, and his hands slowed. It was clear he felt bad watching the manager degrade Susan. The manager made his rounds and some of the workers seemed genuinely happy to see him.

Suddenly the manager appeared again, grabbing Susan's arms. The hate and disgust shot through her body like an electric shock. "Come for lunch in my room." Afraid of being fired, Susan acquiesced. It wasn't the first time he had touched her. Everyone knew that she needed money for her sick mother and addict father, and it made her vulnerable.

"Sister, what did he say to you?" Faisal asked, noticing her shaken appearance as she stood there frozen. He made his voice deeper, trying to be strong.

"He told me to come to his office during lunch break."

"What do you think he wants to tell you?"

"I don't know!"

Faisal frowned. She immediately regretted her outburst toward him. She lowered her voice this time. "You know this bastard very well." She looked around to make sure no one else could hear. "For sure he wants—." Her voice trailed off as her eyes began to well up. "He's looking for a reason to cut my salary or fire me."

Faisal could see the despair in her eyes. With nothing else he could do to help, he brought her a glass of water. "I never want to see you crying. I'm your brother. I won't let anyone hurt you. Do you want me to go instead of you?"

"No, no, no." She shook her head quickly. She knew Faisal's situation, how hard he worked to care for his sick mother, father and disabled brother. His sister wanted to get married and so he was obligated to save money for her too. Susan swallowed the water. "Faisal, listen to me. If he knows that we don't like him, he'll fire us both. We need our jobs. I want you to stay away from me in front of these people. They're animals, they don't understand anything about a sister, about colleagues, they'll think..."

"It's ok, I understand."

Child marriage is not uncommon in some Islamic countries, where the age of marriage is sixteen for a boy and thirteen for a girl. Susan was concerned about people watching her interactions with Faisal because of this. And there was too much at stake, both she and Faisal were fighting not only to protect themselves but to support their families. Susan fearfully made her way to the manager's office.

Knocking on the door slowly, Susan paused, waiting for permission to enter. The sound of the television echoed in the hallway where she waited, and she could smell his cigarettes and his cologne even in the hallway. If anyone from the Health Ministry checked this place it would be a goldmine for their reports. They'd see the dirty uniforms and shabby equipment, no one wearing hats or gloves and it would all be over. They'd see the gas on all night with zero safety and say "*Inshallah*, it's in God's hands." The unashamed flouting of health standards only demonstrated how people here feared no one. Susan knew that it was only she who was afraid of this world, this place.

"*Ta'al*," the manager called out in Arabic. "Come."

Straightening up and forcing a smile, Susan entered. The room was full of cigarette smoke and an ashtray overflowed on a glass table in the middle of the room. The television was playing some Arabic news channel, showing men in black clothes, long shirts to their knees and baggy pants stuffed in their boots. Some of the men on the television had their faces covered with a piece of cloth, either to hide their identity or to look more ferocious. They held up a black flag with a little white circle in the middle, ringed by the words 'Allah, prophet, Mohammad' with 'No god but Allah' written beside it. The television screen didn't just show a few people but hundreds. All were holding up a mix of AK-47s and M16s, stolen from the Iraqi government when they gave up and fled Mosul. Ultimately the weapons were an indirect gift from the

United States, who had unceremoniously left the country in 2011, leaving their weapons to fall into the wrong hands. The men on the television seemed to stand there with pride, basking in their new power, gained through violence.

Susan turned away from the television. "I've never seen these kinds of faces before."

In response, the manager snuffed out his cigarette into the ashtray, sending up a puff of ashes. Susan felt dizzy from the smell as she stood there, waiting for him to give her permission sit down. Finally, he pointed towards a chair.

"Good afternoon sir," she said, uneasily breaking the silence since he didn't answer her first statement.

"Don't you see what's happening?" He pointed angrily to the television. "They took Mosul!"

"That's Mosul?" Susan stared at the television, watching the female journalist speaking with fear in her eyes as she tried to share the breaking news unfolding behind her. Susan thought it looked like war.

"Yes." The manager stared listlessly at the screen.

Mosul is located deep in Nineveh and even though it's an Arab city, it's surrounded by many small ethnic minorities living in villages, including the Kurds, Yazidis and Assyrian Christians. The news was showing that Da'esh had control of all the government offices, the police station, the airport, everything. The Iraqi military had just abandoned the city to Da'esh and the city was gripped with fear. The news seemed to be unable to keep up with the speed of what was happening, but Susan was no longer paying attention, thinking instead of Faisal and his family in Mosul.

"*Yah, Allah!*" The manager could no longer hide his own fear and sorrow. He stood up and paced the room with heavy steps, flicking the channel to a different news outlet. On this channel, the government building was encircled by Da'esh, with the governor trapped inside trying to get some militia members to take up arms and free him. The manager tried again to change the channel, but they were all reporting the same story. Susan sat quietly, watching it all flash across the screen.

"Meanwhile," the reporter said, "Since Da'esh entered Mosul, over 1,400 prisoners have broken free." The channel changed. "Thousands of civilians flee Duhok to Erbil." Another channel. "Da'esh came to the area with 3,000 militants and this number increases with new members joining them daily. The United Nations noted in 2013 that 8,868 civilians were killed in this area from war or violence, and that was before the advent of Da'esh."

Susan sat on the edge of the chair, thinking the whole time about how to tell Faisal all she was seeing. She couldn't be sure if Da'esh would turn out to be one of the many short-lived but violent groups that had appeared over the years or if this one was here to stay. At that moment, Susan knew the news was bad, but she had no idea how bad and couldn't guess at the impact it would have on the lives of everyone in northern Iraq.

From what she saw on the news, it seemed Da'esh had no mercy for anyone, not the elderly, children or women. They didn't even spare their own families. From the moment they entered Mosul, Da'esh killed innocent people just to make a statement. They kept thousands of women and young girls to be enslaved, selling them amongst themselves for just ten to fifty dollars. They sent the slaves to different cities, to be distributed among the Da'esh fighters. They forced the women and girls to marry the Da'esh fighters, to act as a mate and provide them services, to wake up at four in the morning, to clean and cook for their masters. Da'esh also kept women in one of the villages near Mosul just so some of the Da'esh fighters could come and rape them daily. Susan was in a trance, watching all these stories unfold before her.

"Go, we'll talk later," the manager said.

"Shall I bring tea or water for you?"

"No, just leave. Close the door behind you."

Susan closed the door and went quickly back to the kitchen. "Where is Faisal?"

The men in the kitchen ignored her, continuing their chores as if she was invisible. Susan wasn't allowed to enter the dining area of the restaurant, but she pushed the door open hard and entered anyway. The restaurant seemed different. The televisions were all on, tuned to the news. There wasn't a single customer. Cars passed fast outside; an ambulance siren blared. Buses full of soldiers passed by the window. Susan began to shake nervously.

The servers were standing in a little huddle around one of the televisions. They didn't notice her at all. They were speaking to each other in hushed Arabic, with an urgency of fear.

"Allam," she called out to one of the servers.

He turned. "What are you doing here?"

"Can someone please tell me what's happening?"

"Da'esh took Mosul, and now they're very close to Erbil."

"Are they dangerous?"

Allam smiled back sarcastically. "Dangerous? What are you talking about? They'll kill you slow, they cut heads off bodies. The moment they come to Erbil, they'll take you, they'll take all women with them. You'll become their slave; Allah knows what they'll do to you. We men will be forced to join them, or they'll kill us. They're only thirty minutes away from the city now."

Allam had already made his mind up, and for him the decision was simple. He must have felt absolved of any responsibility, resigned to fate. Although Allam would have no idea, Susan knew how lucky he was not to be a woman in a crisis like this.

There was such little time standing between a decision to flee, to fight or to surrender. The future of millions of people hung in the balance as the self-described caliphate drew nearer. Susan wondered how a group could consider itself a caliphate if they didn't even know God. At that moment, Susan was sure Da'esh would be in Erbil soon to destroy homes, steal what they wanted and force the city into a state of fear and the news paralyzed her.

"What happened? Why is she like that?" Allam said, as the waiters gathered around Susan, arguing with each other.

"Susan? Susan!" They were looking at her as if seeing a discarded piece of clothing on the floor.

"Bring water for her," Allam said. They weren't sure if they could touch her body or hold her arms to lift her to the chair, since they were Muslim. They looked at one another, waiting for the others to act.

Finally, she opened her eyes. "Where is Faisal?"

No one answered. She looked upward with waiting eyes, making eye contact with each of them as they stood there without the slightest movement. Their faces and their eyes made her heart skip a beat for some reason. "Can anyone tell me where he is?"

Allam spoke slowly. "Faisal left. Look, we tried to stop him, but we couldn't. He went to Mosul." A tear began making its way down Susan's cheek as the reality of this sank in.

Chapter Five

For Susan, Faisal's absence was impossible to deal with. She checked the timecards daily, hoping she would see his name. Since Da'esh took Mosul, only half the employees who normally worked at the restaurant showed up for their shifts and Susan faced the choice between a pay cut or leaving her job. The security situation in Erbil was dire, with police, soldiers and militiamen roaming the streets in armoured cars.

One by one, the manager called employees into his office. They went in groups of two or three to wait outside in the hallway. No one spoke; everyone well knew what was going on. Some left his office and went straight to the changing room, solemnly placing their belongings in a plastic bag, leaving the restaurant forever. Others, having no other choice, shook their heads as they walked away, accepting their new salaries – half the original amount. Most of the latter chose to sit and have a cigarette to try ease the pain of losing the fruits of their labour.

All too soon it was Susan's turn to go inside the office and choose between life and death: stay in Erbil or go back to Iran. Her residency and her apartment were provided through her employer, and the law would not allow her to remain in Iraq if she left her job. Nobody could tell what would happen to those who chose to stay in Erbil with Da'esh only ten kilometres away, but the outcome of returning to Iran was clear to anyone. She took a deep breath, stood up and entered the office.

The manager was angrier than ever and fear was written on his face. In front of him on the desk lay a white paper and pen. Susan tried to calm down.

"I was watching the news and they said that fortunately the Peshmerga were able to keep the terrorists away," she said, trying to smile. The manager seemed to ignore her optimism.

"I reduced your salary to 250 dollars a month." His voice was cold. "Do you agree, or do you want to leave your uniform here and go?"

"This is unbelievable! That's nine dollars a day! And for each hour it's only..."

"One dollar and a half. Don't bother with the math. Don't you see the bloodbath going on out there? I know very well about war. Your parents understand losing loved ones, friends, acquaintances, as everyone did during the revolution in 1979. But you don't. Your generation are ungrateful animals."

He stood, approaching Susan and sitting right next to her. The only distance between them now was their clothes. She tried to inch away, toward the armchair on the other side. His hand skimmed across her, as if this was his way of negotiating. A little abuse and a salary, or nothing. Maybe he was concerned Susan would take the second option, which would deprive him of his opportunity to dominate her. He forgot prudence for a moment.

"What do you think?" Pushing the words into her ear as a whisper to a lover.

Susan gritted her teeth. She was boiling but had to remain frozen.

"I know about your family, about your financial problems. Don't let your pride kill them. Don't be the reason they starve." He looked at her hand, grabbed it, and put in his lap. "We can always find a way to make their bellies full."

Susan could feel the colour change in her own face and her lips quiver. Afraid to say any word of objection, she was condemned to silence.

"I will give you a separate room. I won't reduce your salary. I'll keep the same working hours for you. What do you think?" He leaned back, feeling victorious, as a boy feels after trapping a butterfly in a glass. His little soliloquy pleased only him.

Susan felt the lump in her throat growing as she stared at the floor, choosing her words carefully. Earlier, she stood behind the door fearing to lose her job, now the thought of rape terrified her even more. It wasn't fair that the result of her honest hard work should be this. Knowing that even if she got rid of him now and continued working, she'd have to pay sooner or later. Swallowing hard, Susan thrust his head away from her cheek, where he'd been lingering in wait and she stood.

"To whom do I give my uniform?"

The manager punched the chair where she sat moments before and sprung up, blocking the door so that Susan couldn't leave. "You're not going anywhere! You must accept my offer. You have no choice." He put his hand on his jeans zipper, stepping toward her, taking advantage of his opportunity. She stepped backward, against the wall.

"Please, I am begging you, let me go." She stepped backward and her shoulders pressed against the wall.

He continued toward her, deaf to her pleas, a wild animal pursuing its meal.

"Your words are silence here, no one will save you now." He moved toward her and she shrank into the corner, looking around for a knife, a glass, anything to defend herself. There was nothing but the ashtray, overflowing with cigarettes butts, on the desk behind him.

"Please, I beg you, on your brother's grave." Before the last words exited her mouth, she felt his hand striking her across the face.

"Keep my brother's name out of your dirty mouth. He is a martyr!"

She screamed, but no one could hear her.

"Shut up, don't talk. If you'll be quiet, I won't hurt you." He began kissing and touching her as she cried.

Somehow, she found some strength and forced her hand to reach for the ashtray, before suddenly striking it against the side of his head. He cried out, reeling back. Susan sprinted to the door, but the man tore the key out from the lock. He tried to right himself while Susan screamed at the top of her lungs for help from someone, anyone. The keys skittered across the floor. She worked the door open, slamming it behind her as the man writhed pathetically on the floor. She bolted down the hallway, escaping outside.

Once outside, Susan joined the throngs of people fleeing for their own safety on the streets of Erbil – people with a different kind of fear in their hearts. They were trying to save themselves from Da'esh and, at that moment, Susan meant nothing to them. Somehow, she made it back to her apartment, though she'd never remember how.

Chapter Six

Susan frantically packed her things into her bag. "My passport?" she said aloud. She sat on the chair for a moment, thinking. Restaurant policy forced employees to give their passports to the manager, to prevent the employees from leaving without permission. If the manager refuses to give the passports back, there is no recourse. It would be ludicrous to think the interior ministry would help in this situation. It was as if the employers here had authority over every aspect of their employees' lives.

Susan had no other proof of identity, so she had no choice but to return to the restaurant one more time. It was her right to have her documents back, and the restaurant owed her the last month's salary at the very least before she quit. She prepared herself mentally for another argument, even if it got physical; braced for any reaction because she was fighting for her rights.

As she made her way back, Susan wished that Kaka Ahmad, the restaurant owner, would be there. Kaka Ahmad was a middle-aged Kurd, a local from Erbil, with lots of restaurants in the city. Susan had only met him once and he only spoke Kurdish and Arabic. Every time she requested to meet him the manager gave her some excuse about why she couldn't meet him - one day it was because he didn't speak English, the next it was that the manager didn't have his number.

The weather that day was miserable, as summer often is in northern Iraq. It was almost forty degrees Celsius and Susan's black shirt was keeping all the sun's heat, while her mind got foggier as if she was standing for too long in a sauna. She couldn't breathe or think clearly, and she could feel sweat everywhere on her body. The muscles in her legs were spasming, while a headache started throbbing in her forehead, making her nauseous and dizzy. It seemed like the cars flying past her on the street were driving upside down, or she was walking sideways. To steady herself, Susan grabbed a metal railing next to her but yanked her hand back instantly; the metal was searing hot. Looking down at her palm, she saw the red rectangular blister she had just earned herself. "Damn it." She blew on the blister to try to make the pain waft away, but it only throbbed more.

There wasn't a single vendor outside selling water on the street, even though there usually was at this time of day. Sitting down for a moment to catch her breath, Susan observed her new blister. "Welcome," she said to it. She now had a new pain to add to the ones she already felt. "I have no choice but to bear you."

She dialled Allam's number. It rang twice and he rejected the call. She tried once more. Finally, he answered.

"Yes, Susan?"

"Allam I need you to do something for me. I need you to come now to the street behind the restaurant, by the neighbour's generator."

"Which one? The big orange one caught fire. Are you there now?"

"Yes, I am"

"I'm a little busy right now, you should wait."

"How long do I have to wait?" Susan was getting worried.

"Fifteen minutes"

"Okay, I'll wait for you. Hello? Hello? Don't hang up yet."

"Yes?"

"Can you please bring me some cold water?"

A few seconds passed. "Let me see."

"I appreciate it, thank you. I'll wait for you here."

She felt relieved she found someone to help her –a little less lonely for a moment. Even answering her phone call was a big favour, she just hoped she could make it up to him. She looked down at her clothes, soaked in sweat, clinging to her body. "Damn it," she said as she pinched her shirt off her wet skin, waving air onto herself with her other hand. They say the heat makes people depressed and suicidal.

Susan stood up, looking around carefully and absentmindedly wondering why Kaka Ahmad had chosen this location for his restaurant when she felt a scream come out of her lungs and a hand covering her mouth, blocking the noise inside her throat.

"Shut up, you slut!" It was a man's voice.

"Get off me!" She kicked her feet on the ground, trying to get loose. "Get off me you bastard!" she screamed, but her words fell apart as the hand covered her mouth.

The man grabbed her hair in his hand, twisting it, while he punched her head. Susan became dizzy, feeling herself slump to the ground. Allam must have told the manager that Susan called, and he was waiting outside. He'd pushed Allam aside to deal with Susan himself - with his unfinished business.

Susan lay there in the dirt, whimpering. "Stand up!" the man shouted, kicking her in the pelvis. "I'm telling you to stand up, now!" Everything was dark and blurry. Susan couldn't open her mouth. She tried to whisper something. The man grabbed her hair again, using it to force her to her feet. "Let's go!" The man took her bag and tightened his grip on her arm. "If you say one word, I will choke you right here with my own hand." Susan could barely make out the index finger pointing at her face. "Walk properly and act normal. If anyone asks, say you fell down."

Susan moved her head and walked mechanically behind him to the restaurant. As she approached the door, the workers were looking at her with scolding eyes, casting shame at her. They crinkled their lips at her as if they were smelling something rotten. She heard their comments and laughter follow her.

"Look at her."

"She looks homeless. God knows where she must have been last night."

"Look at her, she's wasted, she can't even walk."

Even through her blurred vision, she could feel the heaviness of their stares on her body. Her eyes moved from face to face, finally falling on Allam. He put his head down, pretending to be busy arranging some clean glasses. She was surrounded by a group of men ready to pounce on her or stone her, as if she was an adulterer.

"Let me talk to Kaka Ahmad," she said, finally finding her strength.

The twisted laughter hung around her, as the manager couldn't contain himself. "I am Kaka Ahmad, you can tell me," he said. He sat on the table, looking at her mockingly.

"I want my salary and I want my passport."

"Look what you did to the television set." He pointed at the broken television. It seemed Susan wasn't the only object that got broken earlier as she escaped. "Do you know how much it was worth? You broke it."

"What were you trying to do to me? Wasn't that worse than the broken television?"

"Everyone knows you came to my office, satisfied yourself and locked the door behind you."

"What?" She couldn't believe how he was trying to rationalize what had happened.

She stood up straight. "Now I understand the reason why all

the other employees were looking at me the way they were when I came in just now. What did you tell them?"

"I told them what you did. I told them you came in here and satisfied yourself, and that you wanted to steal their salaries but I caught you."

"You are sick, a sick person, a sick bastard!" She was screaming. "I need to see the owner of the restaurant, now!" And as she made her demand the door opened, with Kaka Ahmad entering the room. He began speaking in Arabic to the manager.

Susan walked toward him. "Hello, Kaka Ahmad." He moved his head in response. "Please let me explain. He isn't being honest with you…" She spoke in Farsi, hoping he could pick out a few words that were understood between her language and his. She took out her phone. "Call someone who speaks Farsi." He turned his head and sat behind the desk.

Susan could just imagine what the manager had told Kaka Ahmad, that she had tried to distract him with flirtation and her body while trying to steal from the restaurant, but he stopped her before she escaped. As Kaka Ahmad considered what he was hearing, he looked at the broken television on the floor, then to Susan, shaking his head. Susan's eyes were full of tears and she sighed in exasperation that her story, the real story, was not being told. Kaka Ahmad said something to the manager in Arabic.

"*La, la, la!*" replied the manager, which Susan knew very well meant "no" in Arabic.

Kaka Ahmad must have told the manager to give Susan her salary and let her go. "We shouldn't give her one cent! Her salary should fix this television."

Susan stood between both men, crying, until the manager threw two hundred dollars on the table in a crumpled pile. "Take it." His voice was hissing with disdain.

Susan glanced quickly at the money. "That's not even half my salary!"

"It's more than you deserve. Kaka took mercy on you—be thankful."

Susan knew there was no way for the truth to be conveyed properly to Kaka Ahmad when the manager was filtering everything. She took the money reluctantly. She felt betrayed, forced to give up her rights and her dignity.

"My passport," she whispered.

"We will call you."

"But I can't come back here, I need it now."

"Where did you put it?" Kaka Ahmad asked the manager.

The manager knew he couldn't say no to the owner. "In the safe box."

"Then give it to her," Kaka Ahmad said.

"Sure, but such an unfaithful woman can never come back here, never!" The manager faced Susan. "Take it." He threw her passport on the floor, forcing Susan to crouch to pick it up. Her eyes were red and puffy, her clothes were dirty. She kept her eyes down as she grabbed her bag and left. On her way out, she could still her the manager and the owner talking.

"Kaka, these people have no god, no religion. I knew what kind of person she was from the moment I met her."

"She's gone now... It's prayer time, are you coming?"

"Yes, Kaka. Let's go."

Chapter Seven

Susan walked down the highway, clothes covered in dirt as cars flew by, their horns blaring every now and then. No one stopped. For one human to see another walking under the burning sun meant nothing to them. Susan was thirsty and her steps slowed. She could feel all the energy leaving her body. Then she saw a small shop from a distance. It gave her a moment of hope, a feeling of brightness in this dark journey. She quickened her steps as she approached.

"May I have one water please?"

The shopkeeper must have been seventy years old. His face was full of wrinkles and his words came out in the shape of the difficulties and pain he felt from past wars. He wore brown traditional Kurdish pants, with a white shirt underneath.

"Here you go," he said kindly. Before he finished his sentence, Susan had already taken the water from his hand. She gulped it immediately without a moment's pause, finishing it. The old man was amazed. He gave her another bottle, this time from the refrigerator. He took a cigarette from his pocket, lit it and left the shop to go outside.

Susan sat down near him, on top of a big metal drum with a small piece of cloth covering it. The makeshift seat was there for the old man to welcome any friends to sit and talk with him. Now it was Susan's seat and she was grateful it was there. She held her hands on her belly and she could feel her hair starting to settle around her as she rested. She must have looked like a mess. The old man took another drag from his cigarette and Susan could feel his eyes on her. She looked up, left a thousand dinar on the table, grabbing her bag.

"Thank you." She started walking, although not sure where to go with the old man watching her.

"Being alive is a difficult job. You need to fight for it every day," he called after her.

The fear of being fired and jobless was now replaced with starvation and homelessness. Fear began defining her destiny. Should she just go with the flow now, or should she surrender to please those who impatiently waited to see her fail? She held her head up and continued walking.

She saw a fish restaurant a few hundred meters away. It had a strong smell. She imagined the smell of fish, entrails and rotten water wafted for kilometres. The fish butcher was cutting the heads of innocent fish, who lay on the table with their eyes staring up into the fluorescent lights. The man moved his knife deftly across the soft fish bodies. He seemed to notice Susan watching him, and he quickened his pace as if making the final strokes of paint on a canvas. Was there an award to be won for fish butchery? His studio was a circular kitchen with a wood ceiling and a big grilling area in the middle. All the fish were arranged uniformly next to each other, waiting to be grilled with their mouths open on the sizzling flame.

"Can I use this water?" Susan asked, pointing at a blue water hose slung into the fish tank. She mixed Kurdish and Farsi, as if this would double her chances of getting her meaning across.

"Yes! Yes!" He said it twice, probably because it pleased him that a woman was asking him for help. He continued putting the final touches on his fish masterpiece.

In the restaurant, a few tables looked full. Three groups of men had all come together and were feasting on fish kebab. Susan grabbed the hose as she looked out into the restaurant, wetting her hands with a little water to clean some of the dirt from her clothes. The man was watching her curiously and he understood now why she asked for water.

"Come here," the butcher called to a nearby young boy. "Bring a clean white napkin from the kitchen and give it to her."

"Which girl, sir?"

"There, behind the fish tank. You'll see her standing there."

The boy nodded and in the blink of an eye he was standing in front of Susan with the napkin in his outstretched hand.

"Thank you, I don't need it," Susan said. She looked over to the man, smiled, and mouthed back a "Thank you," in the way she knew would express her appreciation.

It seemed the butcher understood her situation. "Did you eat food today?" he asked.

"Yes," she said aloud, lying. Susan wanted to tell the truth, but something was stopping her. *How can I know his intention, what if he wants to give me food in order to get something from me? He sees my clothes; he may think I'm ready to accept anything he wants to do to me.* The thoughts rushed to her mind, put there by past experiences. These thoughts knocked her down and it seemed they'd stay with her forever. She took her bag.

"Thank you." She walked quickly to get away, looking over her shoulder to ensure no one was following her.

The butcher looked up and spoke to the empty blue sky. "God save her."

Susan took strong steps, continuing down the road. *I'm proud of you*, she told herself. The fog of war was closing in on the city and Susan fought back her fear. Her own problems helped her forget Da'esh. Going to Iran wouldn't be easy, but she couldn't stay in Erbil now that she lost her job and her apartment with it. She could consider this an internal victory, proving to herself that she was strong. Destroying someone's happiness, their soul, doesn't happen overnight.

Walking determinedly along, it occurred to Susan that she had another choice. People had instilled fear into her and it had taken root until it had hold of her mind, transforming itself into concepts of honour, decency, obedience and especially silence.

Susan knew she was the only person who could support her family back in Tehran. Her father was an addict, comatose twelve hours a day, completely undependable. Her mother's hand was disabled, the result of her husband's violence. It was Susan's hands keeping a roof over her parents' heads and putting food in their bellies. Yet for as long as Susan could remember, her childhood had been filled with her parents fighting, beating each other and forcing her to do things for her father and his addict friends.

The only thing left for Susan now was herself, two hundred dollars and the few dinars she had in her bag. She doubted it was wise to remain in a city from which everyone now fled under the spectre of Da'esh. She could almost smell the blood, disaster and misery wafting across the plain from Mosul into Erbil. She knew that she could stay and be brave or that she could find a new place to live and continue her life but going back to a house vacant of love and life no longer seemed like an option.

Chapter Eight

Susan had no more tears or saddened sighs left within her. She decided to make her way to the most famous street in Erbil. It was the busiest one, with the most restaurants and hotels, making it the best place to find a job - if there was one to be found. The businesses seemed to have changed in the week since the threat of Da'esh had rolled in like a shamal. There were no more than six customers even in the most popular cafes. People glared suspiciously at Susan as they passed her on the street but she no longer cared, her only thoughts were how to find food and to put a roof over her head.

The first restaurant she entered rejected her in one minute. The second restaurant offered her a paltry wage, which they said was commensurate with her messy appearance. The owner, managers and employees all looked at her head to toe, their sneers predicating their rejection. Susan didn't lose hope. She passed each street, checking any place that even remotely resembled a business to see if they were hiring.

"Do you need a worker?" she would ask.

"No!" was the reply.

"I know there is no work because of Da'esh. I don't mind taking a lower salary."

"Leave your number. We'll call you."

The ones who did make an offer had no accommodation to provide. Night was coming and the sun was slipping toward Mosul. She had nowhere to sleep, no friends to ask for help and there was no place to go. She had been walking for hours, but she didn't feel tired yet since her mind was focused by determination. The streetlights started flickering on, the moon sitting like a crystal ball on the black velvet sky.

Susan was approaching Ankawa, the Christian neighbourhood in northwest Erbil. Shops were closing, one after the other. The darkness hadn't yet made her invisible. People's surprised stares didn't bother her. She needed to find somewhere to go. She thought to call her Egyptian roommate. Maybe she had friends who could offer Susan a place to sleep, since she'd lived in Erbil for many years. Susan took out her mobile and called her. The sound of the cars made it difficult to hear. She pressed the phone to her ear. The phone kept ringing but her roommate wasn't answering. It was no use.

Susan looked around. She walked carefully to the middle of the curving highway separating Christian Ankawa from the rest of Erbil. She crossed over and saw that everything seemed closed. Then on a dirt road she saw a small grocery store with its light still on. She walked toward it and could hear children's voices playfully echoing from an alleyway. A big unfinished building adjoined the grocery store, with an old woman sitting in a plastic chair in front, her hands resting peacefully in her lap. Susan could sense she was somehow monitoring the children without moving or even looking at them. A plastic ball rolled up to Susan's foot. The children were visible now, gleefully waiting for her to return the ball. Susan bent over and palmed the ball, holding it out for them. A little girl ran to her and grabbed it and the street was full of their voices once again.

As Susan got closer, the old woman smiled. "*Shokran*," the old woman thanked her in Arabic.

Susan answered with a smile. She looked at the building the woman was sitting in front of. It was a big cement block about four stories high, still under construction. The first floor was covered with plastic and fabric to conceal the unfinished walls, converting grey cement slabs into a makeshift home. A long electrical wire was strung from the adjacent building to this one, disappearing behind one of the fabric walls. Different noises could be heard from behind the multi-coloured fabrics covering the openings and it seemed there were quite a few families settled in this building.

A motorcycle pulled up into one of the openings on the ground floor. It seemed a man had made this his makeshift shop and he probably lived in the opening beside it. He set the motorcycle's kickstand carefully and unhooked a few plastic bags from the back of the motorcycle. It looked like they had food inside and Susan suddenly became aware of her hunger. The children stopped playing and ran over to the man as soon as they noticed his arrival. They encircled him and he gave each one a bag to carry. The kids tried their best to carry the heavy bags, bearhugging each piece of precious cargo.

In the blink of an eye the old woman, the man and all the children had disappeared behind one of the makeshift walls. Susan sat on a large stone nearby. She felt her pulse expanding and contracting her veins and her legs were warm, too warm. Her toes began tingling. Gently, she removed her shoe and then peeled away her socks. The middle toenail on her left foot was split and the dried blood stuck to her sock. She poured some water on her feet and rifled through her bag for a tissue, but there weren't any. As she waited for her foot to dry, she listened to the silence. It seemed like everyone had left Erbil. People were hiding far away from the streets, deep inside their homes as if the house would somehow keep them safe from Da'esh.

The white fabric covering one of the openings on the building moved a little, splashing light on the ground near Susan. A girl popped out and Susan could see her hair twisted in two braids, draped over both shoulders like a harness. The girl's face was indiscernible but her white shirt and jeans easily contrasted against the darkness. She daintily walked out of the room, taking care of each step in her plastic sandals. She was carrying a tray in her hands, with tomato, eggplants and potatoes stacked on top. She didn't dare drop her family's food on the ground, so she walked as though avoiding landmines in the darkness.

Susan tapped her shoes against the rock to get some of the dust off and release the tiny pebbles that had been building in her shoes all day. The girl noticed the sound, scanning the area, until her eyes rested on Susan. Susan had no idea who these people were, where they were from, or even which language they spoke. She wasn't sure which behaviours were acceptable in their culture.

Susan didn't want to scare her, but she knew she needed to stand up. She finished tapping the dust off her shoes and then tried to put them on her feet. The shoes felt like they were two sizes too small. Her feet must have swelled considerably in the few minutes she had been resting there on her stone chair but she forced her feet until they went in. The girl continued staring at Susan, her posture serious but her face surprised, reminding Susan of a stray cat that had been hurt before, hungry but unsure of the danger. Susan was a stranger, an unknown woman with a dilapidated bag, her body draped in dirty clothes. As Susan picked up her bag off the ground, the girl looked behind her at the fabric wall, as if thinking of the best way to run away from the stranger.

She'll call everyone to come after me, Susan thought to herself. *The girl is looking at me as if she was watching a thief in action. What if she is carrying a knife on that tray? What if she thinks that I'm from Da'esh and have come to take her? So many girls have been stolen by Da'esh to be put into slavery. Maybe she'll try to stab me.*

The girl walked toward Susan and Susan took a few steps backward. It was too dark to see anything around her and the girl's face was obscured by the night. The girl picked up her pace. Susan's feet and legs seemed to be so sapped of energy that she felt rooted to the earth beneath her.

"Merhaba," the girl said in a soft, low voice. She appeared to be twenty-one years old and very thin.

"Merhaba," Susan nervously replied.

"Are you looking for someone?"

"No, no, no," came her reply in Arabic. The sound of Arabic immediately brought Susan back to her manager's office. She could see his face with its rabid glare. She looked both ways to make sure there weren't any cars and then started crossing the road back to the Muslim side of the street.

"Wait," the girl said in English. "Where are you from?"

"Me?" Susan was unsure if she should say her nationality or not. What if they knew she was Iranian? She knew neighbours weren't very fond of Iran these days and some people would be happy to leave Persia to the history books. "I'm from here. My name is Susan."

"Where is your home?"

"I live right here." Susan pointed to one of the nearby streets.

"I've never seen you around here. You must be new. My name is Farah."

Susan could tell this family had been living in this makeshift home for a while. They couldn't be Arabs from Mosul, because Da'esh had only taken Mosul a few weeks ago. She felt relief, because she could speak comfortably to Farah. She came a little closer until she was only a few steps away from Farah's tray.

"Sorry, you were making food and I interrupted you."

"No, not at all. Honestly, I'm happy to see new faces around our home. I mean, around our tent. Domestics rarely pass by our home and if someone does come around, it's usually one of those young boys coming at night to smoke shisha or cigarettes out of view of their parents." Farah pointed to a small patch of grass between the buildings. "They turned that place into a park. It's got a little grass and a few trees. That's where the boys go. Honestly, I don't dare go there, even for a walk. And I don't recommend it either. Never take that risk. If you knew what I knew, you wouldn't even come within a kilometre of it."

They both turned their heads toward the now darkened park, silently observing the dangerous blackness. Susan and Farah were strangers but there was empathy between them. It was not easy to trust or believe in someone these days, especially with all the circumstances both faced. Each of them was ignorant to the plight of the other. Still, there was some connection they felt, perhaps because they were both women standing in the darkness with similar fears.

"Sorry," Farah said, breaking the spell. "I should go now. My uncle just got home from work and I need to make dinner for him. It was nice meeting you."

Susan waved goodbye silently. She felt as though another layer of pain had been added to the rest. She empathised with that big family with small children, living in a home with fabric for walls right by the highway and on the Muslim side. It was unfair and she felt hopeless because she was unable to do anything about it.

I wish God would eliminate homelessness, Susan thought to herself. Then she realised she was wishing for a home for this family, as though she had one. She was deep in thought, considering the inequity in the world. She yawned and remembered she needed to find a place to sleep that night. There was nothing else for it but to search for a hotel in the city, hopefully for one with a reasonable price.

Nothing was cheap in Erbil, despite the poverty and the many layers of refugee populations. A simple coffee cost four dollars and somehow there were those wealthy enough to enjoy lobster flown in from Dubai. Yet four dollars was also the income for a refugee and that had to buy food for a family living in one of the camps.

As Susan walked along the highway, hoping to see a sign for a hotel cheap enough, she suddenly lost all sensation in her feet. It was as if she was paralyzed. The streetlights began spinning and she lost her balance. She fell to the ground, breathing heavily, unable to continue any longer. She considered how this abandonment also made her feel free. No one was going to give themselves the headache of stopping for her. Somehow, laying with God's earth beneath her, eyes fixed at the stars and without feet to continue her journey, Susan felt calm.

Even though it was dark outside, it was still over 40 degrees Celsius. The heat encouraged her fever, her dry lips stuck together and she fantasised about a glass of water. Her pain and thirst somehow erased her worry about what people may think of her - just another homeless girl laying on the street at night.

Now I'm homeless, she thought to herself. *They won't call me a slut and they will leave me alone. Who knows? They might give me some bread and put a thousand dinars in my hand.* She looked deeper into the sky, with her eyes half open. *God, I am your guest tonight, under your roof of black night, next to the blue moon and shining stars and the warm, free ground. I will remain here from night to morning. Please don't leave me alone in this darkness. Stay with me. Do you know how it feels?* She smiled. *Maybe even you can't bear it.* She closed her eyes, drifting into the blackness.

She slept through the cars, the honking horns, the loud music. She slept peacefully as though her head was resting on a silken pillow until, suddenly, she awoke with a start. It was still dark. She didn't know if this was a dream and she didn't know where she was.

"Are you alright?" asked an old man standing nearby, wearing local clothes and a mask of wrinkles on his face. "Where is your home?"

Susan was hastily wiping dirt and grass off her clothes, but it was no use.

"Where are you from?" the man asked, beginning to speak rapidly in Arabic. "Where is your family? Are you alone?"

Susan shook her head quickly, not wanting to answer aloud. "Mosul?"

"No, I'm not from Mosul." She knew that the only language she could really speak was her native Farsi. The man's clothes were Kurdish, so she hoped he'd understand even though his opening comments were in Arabic.

"*Irani?*" His wrinkled face turning from exhaustion to worry. Susan nodded nervously.

"Aha," the man said slowly, letting the revelation sink in. He looked her up and down, as if considering whether to buy a bolt of fabric. His stare seemed to reveal his uncertainty. Should he be kind or rude to her? Should he be humane or careless? All humans have these two sides inside themselves: love and hate, good and evil, happiness and sadness, cheating and faithful, brave and cowardly, peaceful and warlike. The negative side of most people seemed to come out regularly when they heard her nationality.

"My home is here and I don't need help." She anticipated

the script every stranger would go through upon seeing this abandoned woman on the street. She felt relieved as soon as she said those words. She took the upper hand from him, letting him remain afraid of her so he wouldn't think to hurt her. By having a family and a home nearby, the man would think twice about doing anything to her.

"Go," the old man said, frowning, waving his hand as if wiping dirt off the table.

She started walking again in the direction of her destination to nowhere. A thought suddenly flashed through her mind, rerouting her back towards Ankawa and the makeshift home where she met Farah. In that moment, Susan felt strongly that her body and her life belonged to herself, and it didn't matter what others thought or said. People's opinions weren't food or water and so she didn't need them. She fixed her eyes on the fabric walls before her. *If they can live in a tent,* she thought to herself, *so can I.*

Coming nearer to the unfinished building, Susan heard no children, no old woman, no Farah. Everyone must have been asleep. She carefully observed the exterior, every opening was covered and she couldn't see inside. She entered the stairway and it was pitch dark inside. Carefully, Susan felt each stair with her foot before committing her steps, until she exited the stairs on the second floor. She paused, listening carefully for voices, but she didn't hear anything. It seemed every person in this building was asleep. She moved one of the fabrics covering a room, her heart racing.

She started to think twice about entering and she began dropping the fabric. But it was too late, a shadow appeared behind the curtain. She sat down on the floor immediately, without thinking. A minute passed, though it felt like an hour. No one was moving. She stood up again. She closed her eyes, breathing deeply.

Do it, she told herself.

She moved the curtain aside again. She saw shoes and sandals strewn on the floor, enough for maybe ten or twelve people. She moved her foot slowly forward, taking her first step into what was obviously the home of a whole family. She felt like she was carrying a ton of bricks on her shoulders. *God help me*, she prayed. *Give me strength to take these few steps*. It was as if God heard her and she could feel his presence filling that unfinished building that so many people called home. Her heart was racing and her breaths were heavy.

The only things she could make out in the darkness were stones and dust gathering on the floor. She found a corner for herself that was relatively clean and she carefully unzipped her bag. She took out two shirts, covering herself with them as a blanket, curled up on the cement and slept.

The noise of a motorcycle yanked her from her slumber. She opened her eyes and the sound of running water became noticeable. It was morning. Opening her bag, which had by now become her pillow, Susan pulled out her phone. It said it was 09:20. She turned her head, taking in the room for the first time in daylight, finding a plate full of bread, cheese, tomato and cucumber beside her and there was a plastic glass with water in it too. She couldn't believe her eyes but was too scared and suspicious to touch it.

She stood and made her way to the open space that was supposed to be a window, looking down at the street from her second-floor perch, high up in the mess of concrete and fabric that had been her home for the night. She saw the same kids outside playing. A boy and girl were holding a broom handle, one on each end, while the others were standing in a line in front of the stick. The first one in line bent slightly, careful not to touch the stick as he passed under it. The boy holding the bar was cheating by lowering the bar on purpose while the other boy passed under it, but the other kids didn't seem to notice. Susan could see his mischievous eyes and little smile from her nest. Three more kids came running to join the game.

It felt like the temperature inside the building was almost boiling. Susan was starving and thirsty and her attention snapped back to the mysterious platter of food on the floor. Overcome, she pounced on it, gulping the cup of water so quickly she barely felt it on her tongue, before tearing at the bread with her teeth and snapping up some cheese with her other hand. Suddenly the plate was empty. She ran her fingers along the plate, checking for crumbs. There were none left. She was still thirsty, but the cup was dry.

Having eaten, Susan became aware of the sweat gathering all over her body. The room felt like a sauna. She didn't need the red mercury of a thermometer to see her temperature; the redness of her skin said enough. She slumped down into a corner, trying to rest her body. She closed her eyes. Sounds seemed to fade out around her and her vision blurred. Her mind was slowing down and letting go of her thoughts. It was not her decision anymore. She faintly sensed the presence of another human being, but her eyelids weighed a thousand kilograms. She could just make out the outline of Farah standing there over her.

Farah was panicking. Not only did she see a stranger in her home, but the stranger seemed to be dying right before her eyes. She bolted downstairs, running straight into her mother, who was caught off guard by the fear she saw in her daughter's eyes.

"What happened?"

"Uh, nothing, nothing," Farah said. So far, she was the only person aware of Susan's presence in the building. She took a napkin and soaked it in water. She called out to her sister. "Haya! Fill that bowl and follow me."

"*Allahu akhbar!*" Their mother looked at the two sisters nervously. "Will you please tell me what is going on?"

"Calm down, Mom. One of my friends isn't feeling well. She needs my help."

"Where is she?" Her mother's hand was floating over her mouth, almost exaggerating her surprise. "Oh God, what is happening?"

Farah stopped her hurried movements and clasped her mother's hands. "Don't worry, Mom. Trust me, okay?"

Farah and Haya bounded up the stairs and rushed down the hall. Susan's limp body was crumpled in the corner. The girls used the napkin and water to wash Susan's face and hands, trying to bring her temperature down. Then they lifted her sleeves to put more cool water on her skin.

"Hey girl, hey you," Farah said, gently nudging Susan's body.

"She needs to go to a hospital," Haya said just as Susan's eyelids parted open.

"What's your name?" Farah asked.

"Sus... Su...," Susan said, barely able to move her lips.

Haya was touching Susan's forehead. "She has a fever."

"Yes, I know this," Farah answered, perturbed.

"Her blood pressure is low, it's dehydration," Haya continued her diagnosis.

"I know! Here, help me move her."

They laid Susan down flat. Haya put a few pinches of salt into the water and then went to grab another litre of cold water from the refrigerator downstairs, where her mother was still pacing madly. Susan could hear the voices from below.

"How is she doing?" the mother asked. "It's a girl, right?"

"She is not doing well. And don't worry, it's a girl."

Haya ran back upstairs. "Drink," she said, as she moved the glass to Susan's lips.

Susan swallowed a little of it, while she laboured to keep her eyelids cracked open. The taste brought a little life to her face, as her forehead wrinkled just a little and her eyes closed in reaction to the salt in her mouth.

"Give her more water," Farah directed.

Susan's hands got a little a strength back and she pushed them against the floor to right herself. She drank some more water, but she felt completely helpless.

"We should take her downstairs," Farah said, raising her eyebrows.

"But..." Haya started to object.

"We must." Farah looked directly at Haya. "Take her arms. She'll die in this heat. Do you want to see a woman die in front of you?"

The girls propped Susan up, helping her stand. The moment she was upright, she threw up everything. The girls immediately sat her back down on the floor. Farah rubbed Susan's back, while sending a worried look to Haya.

"Don't worry," Haya said. "It's normal in this weather. She's just dehydrated."

Susan's body was limp and she was unable to think. She couldn't do anything but listen to the girls and obey.

"How do you figure we'll get her down these stairs?" Haya asked.

Farah stood, positioning herself by the stairwell. "Put her on my back, I'll carry her."

Without a better alternative to suggest, Haya grudgingly put Susan's arm around Farah's shoulder. Farah grabbed Susan's leg, wearing her like a backpack, and slowly made her way down the stairs.

"Did you hear the news?" Haya asked, as they crept down the stairs. "No," Farah breathed, labouring under the weight on her back.

"They bombed the university, the one in as-Sanamayn."

Farah stopped walking. She dropped her head down as her eyes began filling with tears. The town of as-Sanamayn, in southwest Syria, was Farah's motherland. She was born there, she grew up there and she fled unwillingly after the Syrian civil war started in 2011. It was supposedly important to the Syrian regime to recapture this small town from the rebels. It was in the pocket of Golan Heights, Jordan, Israel, Lebanon and Iraq. Some believed it was the most important zone of control since the beginning of the war. Others, like Farah, saw it as a simple town full of people she loved. Farah needed time to process this news but for now she needed to just take one step at a time and get Susan down the stairs. She picked up her head, sniffling a little, before summoning her strength and continuing. She could feel the tears drying on her cheeks as she moved.

"What happened?" their mother said. "*Ya Allah!* What's happening?" She started panicking as soon as she saw a stranger draped on her daughter's shoulders.

"Put a blanket down for her in the other room. I don't want her to be bothered by noises," Farah instructed as she made her way in, gently setting Susan down on the floor. Susan looked like a dead body; her eyes closed and her skin colourless.

"Send someone to bring medicine from the pharmacy," Farah called to Haya.

"But we don't have any money."

"Here," Farah said as she opened a drawer. "Take this, it's my savings. Go, bring whatever she needs to feel better."

"It's better if we take her to the hospital."

"No." Farah shook her head. "We'll take care of her here at home. Here." She handed Haya the money.

"Why are your eyes so red?" Haya asked, inspecting Farah's face.

"I'm just worried about this girl."

Haya knew Farah was lying, but didn't push her, instead putting her sandals on and making her way out.

"Bring some fruit too! I can see she hasn't eaten in days." Farah turned to Susan. "What's your name?"

"Susan, my name is Susan."

"How did you find this place?"

"I don't know..."

"How do you not know?" Farah needed to be sure this wasn't some kind of trap. "You were here last night, near our home. We spoke then and you said you live around here. And now, this morning, you're camping out on our floor."

"I was just looking for a place to sleep."

"You?" Farah looked at Susan, her eyes incredulous. "Looking for a place to sleep? You don't look like you sleep in places like this. A homeless girl speaking English; that doesn't make sense."

"Same as you," Susan said quietly.

"So where are you coming from? What are you doing here?"

"I lost my job and they kicked me out of my accommodation. I couldn't sleep on the street anywhere, until I found this area last night."

Farah listened carefully, peering at Susan's face to see if she was being honest. "Where were you working?"

"In Sahand's Restaurant, on 100 Meter Road."

"Where is that?"

"Hundred Meter Road," Susan repeated. Her mind wasn't working properly and she couldn't seem to remember the details.

"There is no restaurant by that name."

"I don't know," Susan said, rubbing her forehead. "Maybe it was another street."

Farah seemed to doubt Susan's story. It was unusual for a woman so beautiful to have no one. A moment later, Haya entered the room carrying a plate with fruit and medicine, breaking up the interrogation.

"These will make her feel better," Haya said. She set the pills one by one in Susan's mouth for her. Farah was staring at Susan, barely noticing Haya taking care of her. By now her mind was far away from this room, far from their strange guest, and far from 100 Meter Road. Farah was thinking about the bombing at the university in as-Sanamayn and she wondered how many of her childhood friends, aunts, uncles, anyone, had died.

"Thank you," Susan said as she sat on the floor with her legs tucked tight under her. Haya whispered something indiscernible to Farah and then left the room. Susan tried to stand but Farah stopped her.

"Stay there." Farah reached her hand towards a piece of loose wood that was near the wall, in case she needed to defend herself. Susan backed up against the wall.

"I know you're worried. You think I might be a criminal, a murderer, a terrorist. Maybe you think I'm a street girl. You have the right to think that. Maybe I would think the same if I was in your shoes. A stranger coming in my home, slumped on the floor and barely alive? Yeah, I'd have questions, too." Susan held her hands up in front of her face. "Look, I don't have any weapons or anything dangerous."

Farah searched Susan's bag to see if there was anything suspicious inside. It was true; there was nothing interesting. Susan's only possessions were her mobile, some currency and old clothes stuffed in her bag.

"Can I stay here one more night? Tomorrow I'll go find work and a place to stay."

"Stay here?" Farah asked, looking around as if seeing the terrible living conditions for the first time. She was unsure if it was a good idea, but Susan was homeless.

Haya popped back in. "Are you seeing the news?"

"No, not yet," Farah said. Haya could tell it was not a good time to talk about what she was seeing on the news. By now Farah was deep in thought again, transported to as-Sanamayn and its growing list of victims.

"Farah!" her mother called out. "Farah, come here. Who is that girl?" her mother pressed again. "What does she want from us? She's behaving like an addict. She can't walk, and it seems like she's high or in withdrawal."

Haya shook her head. "*Wallah,* I don't know either."

Farah came to them, her shoulders slouched. Haya looked over at her mother blankly, indicating she shouldn't say anything. She went to Farah.

"What should we do with her?" Haya asked. "Don't you want to say that she is staying here, in this little space? We don't even know how she got here, from where, or who she knows. Maybe someone is following her. Maybe she killed someone or saw someone kill someone. Maybe she stole something. Or..." Haya paused, preparing to drop the larger issue. "Maybe she's working with Da'esh."

Farah put her palm on her forehead, breathing deeply. "I don't know. Maybe you're right. Where is she now?"

"She's in the same spot," Haya said. "She's laying down. I think she's an addict."

Farah didn't want to make that assumption. "What if she needs our help? Don't you remember our own escape through the desert? We had no shoes, no nothing. That heat was hell. Nahal's baby died. I lost Ahad. I don't want to bring guilt upon myself by rejecting someone who needs help now just like we needed help then."

"Well, you need to do something before Uncle comes back home. You know what will happen if he sees a stranger in the house."

"It isn't just his house." Farah motioned around the room. "It's ours, too. We found this place together, and so we'll all make decisions together about what goes on inside."

Farah and Haya went back to check on Susan. She was sitting there on the floor, as if waiting for the prison warden to open the cell. She had heard everything, but she was too weak to speak up and defend herself.

"Do you have a number we can call to have someone come take you?" Farah asked.

"No." Susan's eyes filled with fear. She knew it would be impossible to convince a refugee family, who already had nothing, to let her stay with them. Farah stood there, observing Susan. Her eyes travelled up the wall, resting on some point beyond it as she remembered her own plight two years before. She knew how Susan felt, because she had spent many nights sleeping on a roadside in the Syrian desert.

"You can stay," Farah decided. "I'm not sure if I can keep you here more than two nights though. As you can see, there is barely enough here for my family, let alone a guest."

Susan bolted up and hugged Farah. "Thank you." Her arms tightened around Farah, her energy returning for a moment in her gratitude.

"Mom," Farah called out, with Susan's arms still around her. "Susan will stay with us for a few days."

"But—," her mother began.

"Don't worry," Farah said, interrupting her. "I take responsibility."

"What will you tell your uncle?"

"I'll talk to him," Farah said. Then she looked at Susan. "Bring your bag."

Farah's mother looked at Susan resentfully as she walked by. Susan felt ashamed. She wasn't wanted here, and she was taking away their peace with her presence. Reluctantly, she followed Farah. They entered another room further down the hall. It was six meters, and one of the walls was made of produce carton boxes all the way up to the ceiling. The boxes were lashed together tightly with a cable. The other three walls were covered in fabric.

"This is my room," Farah said. "I sit here and read sometimes. No one else comes in here – it's too hot."

Susan watched Farah rifling through some fabrics on the floor. This room was more than enough for Susan, and it was better than the dirt outside. She had no questions and no complaints. "Take this," Farah said, holding out a lumpy rag. "You can use it for the floor when you sleep. I'll bring you a pillow, too." Susan laid the rags down neatly. The room was like a prison, but it was all she had. "I know you're hungry. Sit here, and I'll bring you some food when it's ready." With that, Farah disappeared behind the fabric curtain, gingerly hooking the cloth to a nail in the wall to keep the room's privacy intact.

Not long after, a man's voice came wafting through the fabric; he was speaking Arabic. Susan listened carefully. She heard women's voices too, and it sounded more like an argument than a conversation. Susan noticed herself trembling. She recognised Farah's voice speaking strongly, confidently. The voices grew in intensity, lifting from loud to shouting, and finally to screaming.

Susan remained on the ground, holding her head in her hands, covering her ears, but she could still hear the shouting. It reminded her of her father's fits and forced on her the memory of the night he sent his friend to her room in exchange for a packet of drugs. That was the night her mother finally stood up to her father, earning herself the permanent paralysis in her hand. Despite the blood, the man still came to Susan's room.

Suddenly, the curtain moved aside, and Susan snapped back to the present. The outline of a huge man framed the doorway. He had a black shirt, jeans, a wrinkled face. His ears seemed too dark compared to his face, and his eyebrows were so thick they must have obstructed his vision. His eyes seemed to be completely black, except for the fiery glare where the pupils should have been. He reached out, yanking Susan to her feet by the front of her shirt. She could hear the fabric tear as her body became weightless.

"Who are you working for?" he demanded in Arabic. He was winding up his fist as though he was about to hit her. Susan clenched her eyes shut and tried to turn away. She couldn't make a sound. Her lips quivered, and tears began flowing down her cheeks.

"She doesn't know Arabic," Farah said, suddenly entering the room. She lowered the man's arm. "She doesn't understand what you're saying."

"Are you stupid?" he asked, swatting Farah's arm away. "How does she not know Arabic? She's acting. How stupid you are."

"She's Iranian. She speaks Persian." Farah stood between her uncle and Susan, defending a stranger from her own family. "I talked to her in English. She understands it."

"I know someone who speaks Farsi," he said, pulling out his cell phone. "I'm calling them now."

"You don't need to call anyone."

"Why should we trust an Iranian? These people are the reason our lives are in ruins. They've destroyed our livelihood, killed our people. All our misery flows from Iran. You're a child. Don't you see the news?"

"You say I'm a kid, and don't understand. I listened to you once. Now we're homeless, a thousand kilometres from home." Farah turned to her mother, who had followed her into the room. "Say something mom. Are you happy? You took my life away and forced me into this hell!"

Haya stood, listening and watching, her back to the wall, quietly sobbing. Their mother stood silently, motionless.

"Enough!" Farah said. She turned to Susan. "If you want to hurt us, if you're a spy or a thief, if you want to kill us all, do it! But promise to kill me ten times!"

The room was silent for a moment. Susan stood in the middle of the room, surrounded by a family that seemed more at odds with one another than with her. Susan was their excuse to tear each other apart, to finally confront the animosity fermenting within. Susan said nothing, obliged to listen, a witness to the remnants of a war far away.

One by one, they left the room in silence. Susan was invisible, but this time she welcomed it. The shouting man, the crying sisters, the total loss, all flooded out of the room and swept away. As time passed, Susan could hear the clinking of dishes and hurried movements of food preparation, but not a single word escaped. Their dinner was a funeral feast, as it had been every night since the family fled Syria. Susan made herself small in the corner of her new cell. She became aware of her hunger, but she felt ashamed to feel in need when the family helping her had lost so much.

The fabric door peeled back, and Farah entered. She was carrying a tray with a small plate of rice and bowl of beans. There was a little water in a cup on the corner of the tray. She set it down on the floor without coming too far into the room.

"Susan, take your food."

Susan pulled the tray toward her, into the depths of the room. She drank all the water in one gulp, placing the glass by the door in hopes that someone would notice it and refill it. The heat in the room hung about her like a blanket, making it difficult to breathe. She thanked God anyway, because she was grateful to be breathing at all. She moved the curtain covering the door, and to her surprise there was a full glass of water waiting for her. She smiled, drinking the second glass gratefully, making sure to keep just a little in case there would be no more tomorrow. Susan rolled onto her side and laid her hand on her belly as she had always done since she was a baby. She felt both unwanted and thankful.

Chapter Nine

Susan awoke earlier than usual, and breakfast was waiting for her near the curtain. She reached and dragged the breakfast tray toward her, looking around as she did. She listened intently. It seemed as though the house was empty. The heat in the room was stifling, making it difficult for her to breath. She peeled back one of the fabrics covering the far wall, exposing the room to the chilly air outside. The fresh air entered the room, and Susan closed her eyes and smiled as the wind danced over her face.

Susan tore off a piece of bread and spread some cheese inside it. She was so grateful to have something to eat, and even more grateful that someone was willing to give her some of what little they had in her time of need. She raised the bread to mouth, savouring the smell. Just as she was about to take a bite, the huge outline of a man appeared behind the curtain. In an instant there were two burly legs in front of her face, standing over her. She saw the plastic sandals, the faded pants, the stained shirt of a labourer. As she slowly moved her eyes upward, the face became clear: Farah's uncle. His eyes were filled with hate, burning a hole in her. She stood immediately, as though his presence commanded it, still gripping the bread in her hand.

"Bring that," the man said, pointing at Susan's bag. The room was small enough that he could have picked it up himself. Susan silently obeyed. "Come out."

Susan carefully stepped over the tray of uneaten food on the ground and exited the room. The man grabbed her bag, unzipped it, and then paused to observe Susan's expression as he rifled through her belongings. His face was twisted in hatred, as if the muscles needed for a smile had been absent since birth. He threw her clothes to the ground, as if impatient with gravity itself. He was digging inside the bag, his anger growing as he failed to find anything incriminating. Susan had learned her lesson already; her passport was safely stored in her pants.

The man stopped for a moment, dropping the bag by his side. He bent his neck to the side and squinted, as if something flashed in his mind. He lifted the bag back up again, unzipping the side pocket. The first cloth he removed was Susan's underwear. Susan had used that cloth to cover some of the papers she was trying to keep hidden inside. He muttered something unintelligible, shaking his head. He picked another item out, this time a bra. Susan felt ashamed to see a strange man holding her underwear in front of her face. She looked first at the wall, and then at the floor.

Farah appeared in the hallway. She froze for a moment, then ran toward her uncle and Susan. She was in shock as she stared at her uncle holding Susan's bra between his thumb and forefinger like a discarded banana peel.

"What are you doing, Uncle?" Farah demanded.

"I have to know who she is. I need to know where she's coming from."

"Here we go again, you checked all of her stuff already, and found nothing. She doesn't have anything dangerous. For God's sake, leave the poor woman alone." Farah snatched the underwear from his hand and carefully put it in the bag. As Farah spoke, Susan became aware of the pain in her leg from her fall at the restaurant only a few days ago. She tried to turn and pick up her things, but her balance was off. She sat on the floor instead, gingerly holding her ankle. She began picking the clothes up that were strewn about, placing them one by one back into her bag.

"I'll figure this out!" the man said, leaving and taking his anger with him.

"I don't know if I can say he has the right or not," Farah said, kneeling to help Susan. Susan was silent, folding a pair of underwear.

"You know he's the man of our house," Farah continued. She looked around at the cement walls in the hallway, which looked more like a military barracks than a home. "If we lose this, we'll have nothing left at all."

"He has the right," Susan said in a whisper. Susan knew that was what Farah needed to hear to justify what she had witnessed, even though she knew they both felt it was wrong. Susan reached for her bag.

"No, stay sitting," Farah said. "I'll bring it to you. I think your foot hurts, right?" Susan nodded.

"Sit here." Farah glanced at the tray, still filled with breakfast food. "*Allahu Akhbar!* You still didn't eat your breakfast?" She slid the tray toward Susan. "Have it. I'll bring you tea."

Farah returned in a moment with two cups of tea and sat beside Susan. Farah could feel the shame Susan felt to be eating in front of her. Farah took a piece of cheese. "I'm hungry, too."

Susan felt a little more comfortable, but still sat silently.

"Do you know how to cook?" Farah asked.

"Yes. I used to cook for my dad and his friends."

Farah looked away wistfully. "Since we escaped from Syria to Erbil, I'm cooking a lot. Not working, not studying, just cooking. My mum is getting old and depressed, and she never feels like cooking for us anymore."

Susan related to Farah's description easily. She was reminded of her own mother who, seeking relief from her burdens, had unloaded her difficulties upon her daughter. She visualised her mother in her mind's eye, waving goodbye. Susan's eyes began watering. A single word illuminated a world of sorrow.

Farah could see that the topic of Susan's mother was too sensitive to discuss. It saddened her deeply that they couldn't talk about what was clearly weighing heavily on Susan.

"You didn't eat anything."

"Thank you, I'm good." Susan looked away from the food.

"Did I say something wrong?"

"No, I just have a fever and I lost my appetite."

"Can I get you more tea?"

"No. Thanks, though."

Farah looked at Susan for a moment, trying to find a way to keep her talking. "It seems like your injuries might be getting worse. How did your feet get hurt so badly?"

Susan pulled the extra fabric from her pants down over her ankles, covering them. "It was nothing. My shoes are just uncomfortable. And I fell down."

"Aha, I see." She raised her eyebrows sceptically. "I have betadine in my room. Can I bring some for you? If you leave it this way, you'll get an infection."

"I don't know how to compensate for your help, for everything you're doing for me." She reached out and held Farah's hand, squeezing it.

"Well, you can try be honest and trust me. How about that?" Farah went out, returning swiftly with first aid supplies for Susan and wrapping her ankle with a bandage to keep the swelling down. She gave Susan a pair of rubber sandals. "Here, wear these. This house has got dirt everywhere."

Susan took the sandals but kept her eyes on Farah. "How old are you, Farah?"

"Me? How old do I look?"

"Am I measuring by your kindness or your appearance?"

"But I was rude to you earlier," Farah said, playing idly with a small pair of scissors from the first aid kit.

"No. You gave me a place to sleep. I understand the apprehension you feel, letting a stranger in your home. It's your right."

"I'm twenty-one."

"So, we're almost the same age."

"How old are you?"

"About the same age as you."

"For God's sake, look at our lives. Instead of studying and planning for our futures, we're sitting in an unfinished skeleton of a building, worrying about our next meal, Da'esh, and homelessness. We've become puppets to the superpowers. They kill our loved ones, destroy our homes, and displace us. We are welcome nowhere, and it us who are the terrorists, so they say."

"Well," Susan said, smirking. "In the end, we're all guilty and we're bound to go to hell."

She began to relax a little with this companion to her misery. Some of her fear faded into the background as she considered this stranger, another human being, caring for her health. Maybe there were still some good people left in the world. Who else does one human being have except another? Susan wondered how many of the billions of people on this earth really understood the value of human life, and the impact a little kindness could have on strangers.

Farah left for a moment and returned with a photo album, smiling sheepishly. She sat down and placed her palm on the cover for a few minutes, going through the photos in her mind before sharing them. She was wondering whether it was the right time to share something intimate with Susan, to share her own story of difficulty. Maybe it would help build trust between them. She opened it to the first page.

"Here." Farah pointed to a faded Polaroid. "You can see I was four years old. My father just got back from Europe and he brought a new camera. This was the first photo he took."

Susan smiled at the picture of a little girl with golden hair and pouting lips. "Here are my mum and dad. They're in my aunt's engagement ceremony."

"The woman in this house is your mother? The same person that's in this picture?" Susan couldn't quite believe it, the woman in the picture was gorgeous and self-assured. She looked nothing like the worrying old woman downstairs.

"After Da'esh killed my father, my mum changed overnight. She aged a decade in a week. She loved my father, she always said he was the best thing that ever happened to her every breath she took was for him. Our life then was beautiful, peaceful. Then the war started, and we were forced to leave our home. They captured my father; I don't know why. He never did anything wrong but they still sawed his head off in front of all of us - a warning to obey. My father paid with his life, and my mother practically gave hers up because of it."

Susan leaned forward and embraced Farah, and though Farah refused to cry, Susan could tell the sadness in her heart was far deeper than she'd ever express. People pretend to be strong by not crying, and by training the mind to prepare for the next difficulty. Susan hoped Farah could someday be honest with herself. But then again, Susan needed to be honest with herself, too.

"I'm sorry," Farah said finally, breaking Susan's train of thought. "I wasn't talking about nice things. Honestly, my life has been devoid of beauty for years." Her breaths were measured, careful, as though she'd practiced for years to keep her emotions in check, ignoring her heart's thrust in her chest.

Susan was torn, both wanting to improve Farah's mood and craving her own shoulder to cry on. But she felt that if she opened her mouth, she'd just be stealing the opportunity to vent from Farah. Sometimes people sought to top another's misery as if it was a contest, and Susan did not want to do so. Instead, Susan searched for some magic words that would help Farah feel better. The quietude and solemn atmosphere in the unfinished building made everything worse. Her eyes scanned the room, looking for inspiration to help lighten the mood. Her eyes fell upon a bookshelf in the corner, partially covered by fabric. The bookshelf was made using three slats of wood for shelves, with grey concrete blocks as its walls, and the books were all arranged neatly. Susan could tell someone cared deeply for this humble little shrine.

"Whose books are those?"

Farah smiled, turning her neck slowly toward them. She put her hand on the floor and pushed herself up, leaving her misery there behind her. She stood in front of the shelves, tracing each binding with her hands, caressing them as though they were silk. Her hand paused on one, she gently pulled it out with her thumb and forefinger and dusted the cover gently. Susan looked on, imagining that, for Farah, the sentimental value of this book must exceed any monetary value of any book anywhere. Susan was not wrong, each morning after waking up Farah would take this book out, open it to the first page, and read the note that her lover had written to her. She'd run her fingers over the letters, knowing that once his pen, his hand, and his body were connected to this page. She'd close her eyes and, for a moment, become the happiest woman on earth.

Susan was curious to know what about this book transformed Farah from the verge of tears to a beam of sunlight. She squinted her eyes, trying to make out the faded title.

"*Through the Looking Glass*?" Susan quietly mouthed. She was careful to pronounce it correctly, not wanting to reveal that she had not heard of the book before. Farah held the book out to Susan with both hands, urging her to take it.

She took the book carefully in her hands. She hadn't read a book in years. She tried to remember the last time a book had taken her attention. It must have been on Enghelab Street in Tehran, a street full of many books. It was difficult to walk out of that street empty handed. This book had a blue cover, and there were fantastical creatures illustrated beneath the title. Susan cracked the book open and began flipping through the pages.

"This book is English." It was the first time Susan had really seen an original English-language book, and she had instinctively opened it from the wrong end.

"Yes. Ahad gave it to me." She said his name with love, softly, as if no other word contained such beauty.

"Ahad?" Susan could guess now why the book was so valuable to Farah. It was silk, it was love, it was a priceless treasure in the Louvre. It was the only thing Farah had left.

Farah was looking at the other books on the shelf while Susan studied the little book. It was clear that Farah's only friends were the pages resting peacefully on the shelves she made for them.

"So," Susan said. "I never read this book. Can you tell me what's in here? Whatever it is, it must be special to you. I can see it."

"This book is about a little girl's childhood, turned upside down."

"Is the reason for her suffering due to a man?"

Farah smirked. "Of course."

Susan thought for a moment of her own experiences in Erbil. Her dealings with the restaurant manager rose in her mind, becoming real again. These memories would go with her to her grave. Some children's lives are destroyed by abuse, rape, or war. Susan and Farah had both had their share of all of these.

"Children always suffer," Farah said. "People are killing children for the simple reason that those children aren't from their own blood. The building was full of silence and where there was silence, memories always flooded in.

Breaking their moment of reflection, a siren rang out in the distance, screaming quickly closer until it seemed to stop right in front of their building. Farah pulled the fabric from the window slightly back, peering outside carefully. She saw a black car with a lightbar flashing menacingly on the roof and a steel brush guard on the front for smashing cars out of its way. The side of the vehicle said "Police" in big letters. This must help civilians know they aren't being captured by Da'esh when men in black uniforms show up at their doorstep. These days it was not easy to tell if a man in a black outfit and carrying a gun was a terrorist or a policeman. It was wise to fear them both.

"Why are they here?" Farah whispered, half to Susan, half to herself. "The *mukhtar* who sits across the street all day would know everything happening in the area. They should talk to him if they need something."

Farah watched as all four doors opened at once, while Susan watched the worry on Farah's face. From their perch by the window, the girls could see the policemen walking around the building, observing the exterior carefully.

"Hm," Farah said quietly. "What do they want?"

"Who are they?"

"It looks like Asayish, the Kurdish intelligence agency. They've never come here before. Even if they come to Ankawa, they usually cruise past and are gone quickly." Farah paused, thinking for a moment. "Actually, they did come here once. They were checking identity cards. It was a few years ago, when we were living in a tent nearby. They asked my mum some questions, looked us over, and then never came back."

Susan placed the book on the floor and stood up, making her way to the window to observe the situation beside Farah. They watched the four policemen inspecting the ground outside the building. One spoke into a walkie-talkie while his other hand was authoritatively perched on his black utility belt. He was observing some children running around the corner of the building and looked surprised to see kids playing outside in the 40-degree heat.

"Do you know why they're here, Farah?" She felt a panic taking over her body.

"I don't know, maybe they're checking on neighbours, maybe there was a fight, maybe someone called the police."

"They'd call Asayish for a family fight?"

"Maybe."

"No, no, maybe they're here for—." Susan trailed off.

"For what?" Farah let the curtain drop down and squinted at Susan.

"No, you must be right," Susan said, gathering her composure, trying to act naturally. "They must be coming for the neighbours. But are there any neighbours here?"

"Anybody there?" A man's voice travelled up the stairwell from inside the building, echoing down the hallway. "Hello? Anyone home?"

Farah started putting her sandals on, but Susan grabbed her wrist.

"What are you doing?" Susan asked. "Please don't go.".."

"I know what I'm doing. Don't tell me what to do."

"Please," Susan felt a lump in her throat growing, causing her voice to falter.

The man's voice sounded louder and closer.

"Go to the room you sleep in," Farah instructed her as she began to loudly descend the stairs. "I'll go see what they want."

Susan did as she was told, and went to her sleeping room, closing the curtain behind her and pushing her body up against the wall, listening carefully. She covered her mouth to quiet the sound of her heavy breathing. As far as she knew, the only people in the building right now were Farah, the policeman, and herself. She closed her eyes and began to pray.

Farah made her way down the stairs but stopped abruptly at the bottom as she almost ran into a small man with a belly protruding ahead of him. Farah was shocked that the man had entered her home uninvited. Sure, it wasn't a real house with a front door but it was someone's home nonetheless. As she talked to herself, she noticed two other policemen rifling behind a wooden palette that functioned as a door. They were looking for something. Although the way they handled Farah's and her family's property threatened what dignity she had left, she knew she couldn't object.

The policeman with the belly was studying her. He pulled his belt up with two fingers, then put both hands on his hips.

"Is your father home?" the policeman asked.

"My father is dead." Farah stared intently at the man.

The man dropped his authoritative pose and clasped his hands together over his belly. His eyes dropped a little as he frowned. Farah was shocked at the policeman's candid display of emotion.

"I'm sorry, my daughter."

"Thank you."

"Is there an elder at home?" This time he used a friendlier tone.

"No, my uncle is the elder of the house, but he's at work now."

Susan was listening to the exchange from behind the curtain upstairs, slowly rocking forwards and backwards, trying to savour the few moments of peace she estimated she still had left. She waited for an arm to reach through the curtain and yank her to her feet.

"How many people live here?" Susan heard the policeman ask.

"There are nine of us."

"In here?" The policeman raised his eyebrows, moving his head around to confirm he was looking at the same building as Farah.

"Yes." She knew this wasn't his first time in a Syrian refugee's home. There were two million of them in Kurdistan. Surely, he was taking a moment to count his blessings.

"When will your uncle return home?"

"I have no idea. Maybe after sunset."

The potbellied policeman motioned to the others, who were presently inspecting a pile of sandals. They left the building and headed back to the car, dejected that they found nothing incriminating. Farah stood in between the shell of a building she called home and a shiny police car full of powerful men. Other cars passed by, slowing as they realised there was a police car parked there. Farah was unaware of anything else around her.

Once the car had disappeared, she ran back up the stairs to find Susan. She looked in each room along the hallway leading to Susan's room. She was nowhere to be found. The curtain acting as a door for Susan's room was blowing gently in the breeze. Farah heard a vehicle engine somewhere nearby.

"Susan?" Farah called for her cautiously. "Susan?" Her legs felt weak as she took a deep breath. She moved the curtain aside that was covering the opening to Susan's room. She closed her eyes, and then slowly opened them again. There was nothing left. No bag, no shoes, no Susan.

Chapter Ten

It was another boiling July day in Erbil. Sometimes it felt as if the days were competing to be the hottest ever. In the afternoons, the earth seemed to inch closer to the surface of the sun. No one walked outside on days like these, not even domestic workers. The city became nocturnal. The wind made it worse; it was like opening a convection oven. But one needn't step outside to feel cooked. Besides the faucet water coming out warm enough to make tea, the government rationed electricity in the summer so that unless residents kept a generator it could be hotter inside the building than outside. To make matters worse, the combination of poor-quality electrical systems and overworked generators ensured fires were common.

Despite the heat, some women were forced to wear hijab, like the abaya or chador, to protect Islam. Somehow the logic was that their health was less important than the danger their bodies posed to men. The long black sleeves were there to protect the religion, not the women. Some women in Erbil could choose what they wore but a woman in a sleeveless shirt would be the object of every male eye. The two categories available for a woman wearing comfortable clothing was either expat or slut. Female expats were then divided into two different groups: Eastern and Western. Western expat women were brushed aside as normal and outside the conception of modesty. Somehow, they didn't cause men's heads to explode into a sinful lack of self-control the way an Eastern woman wearing shorts was supposed to.

Either way, it was the woman's fault the men reacted that way, according to the men. An Eastern woman, from Iran or Arab countries, was socially barred from wearing the same clothes as a Western woman. The assumption would be that she was a prostitute, or at least available for sex. Men in Erbil were excused of their self-control and judgement, so there was no support for their prey once they became a victim.

In the centre of Erbil, a taxi driver barrelled down the street. His thick eyebrows seemed to cover most of his eyes, while his nose stuck out like a mountain peak between the dark valleys of his eyes and his long hair covered the back of his neck. He was wearing the traditional tan baggy Kurdish pants and shirt. He kept shifting his body weight in the seat trying to get comfortable, with one hand resting on the steering wheel and the other draping out the window. Behind him, Susan fanned herself with a notebook, but it just seemed to move the hot air around the back of the car. She felt like she was burning up in the heat of the sun and the taxi was a greenhouse. Why wouldn't the taxi driver turn on the air conditioner?

"Kaka?" Susan asked the man respectfully in Kurdish.

"Yes?" he replied, looking at her in the rear-view. His laboured response clearly showed the heat had sapped his energy.

"AC, AC," Susan gestured to the middle of the dashboard, trying to show him what she meant. "Hot, hot, turn it on."

"No, gas is too expensive." He glared at her in the rear-view mirror.

"But I'm paying you. You're taking my money. This isn't a free ride."

"No, impossible. Ahvaz, Ahvaz." Ahvaz is a city in southern Iran, near the Lur Desert, known to be one of the hottest places on earth. Clearly, he was trying to blow her off by minimising the heat in Erbil in comparison.

"What does Ahvaz have to do with turning on the air

conditioner?" But Susan knew she couldn't argue with a local man, and she stopped trying to stand up for herself. It was futile and wasn't worth being dropped in the middle of nowhere. Instead, she focused on the road so she could tell the taxi driver where to stop so she could meet the smuggler.

She turned and watched out the window as a group of kids were playing soccer on a patch of dirt. They had separated themselves into two even teams, and they seemed to be unaware of the heat. *God save them, where are their mothers?* Susan asked herself. By now the taxi driver was babbling about something in Kurdish, and Susan was barely aware of it. Maybe he was trying to take the opportunity to talk to the only female passenger he'd had in a long time. A feeling of dread crept over her. How long until he would figure out she was Iranian? He would lean his seat back and start touching himself, grinning in pleasure, knowing he couldn't be punished since Iranian women had no rights here. Rape, aggression, assault: these were not only physical experiences but emotional traumas too. Women here had to carry the assault, disrespect and violations of their privacy with them, lest they be shamed for trying to seek justice. Be quiet and say nothing. This was a rule Susan learned early on.

Susan noticed groups of men sitting together here and there on top of boxes and coolers as the taxi sped down the street. There were no women to be seen. Susan double-checked the address she had written on a slip of paper in her hand. The taxi was getting close. She saw the cafe ahead, with its brown chairs and tables visible in the distance. After sunset this place would be full of men smoking shisha and playing with their mobiles, ignoring the glasses of Iraqi tea getting cold on the tables beside them.

"Stop here."

"You want me to drop you off here?"

Susan was unsure if the driver was worried about her safety or worried about losing his audience. She expected him to ask for more money, even though he refused to turn on the air conditioner. She would pay a price for taking away the two free ears that were forced to listen to his nonsense. She took out two blue five thousand-dinar bills, and then held them out over the centre console to him.

The taxi driver kept both hands firmly in place. He looked down at the bills dangling over his shoulder, then scoffed. "It's too little."

"This is what we agreed in the beginning." This was not Susan's first time in an Erbil taxi. She dropped the bills in his hand, got out, and closed the car door. The street was lined with men. Shop owners and the unemployed mixed together here, and it seemed like everyone was sitting outside the stores instead of working inside them. People were just waiting around, but for what? The street was quiet, and all eyes were glued to the strange woman walking alone, as if she had just arrived from Mars. Men were subtly adjusting their clothes, fixing their hair, perhaps hoping she'd be interested.

As she approached the café, Susan noticed a layer of dust that no one had touched for years. No one cared about customer service, or even life and death, in this kind of place. A scraggly tree branch was hanging behind the roof, but that was the only sign of nature anywhere. The smell of tea blew across from the café. Tea was the only thing Susan could never refuse, no matter the weather. The idea of it lightened her steps.

Susan entered the outdoor area of the cafe, which was a spacious seating area with probably a hundred chairs and tables. She passed a man shifting nervously in his seat, and another patting his hair down. She held the smuggler's photo in her hand. It was a man with black, shoulder-length hair, wearing a full beard and moustache. The face was self-assured, the eyes were suspicious, sceptical. Susan was trying to act normal as she caught a glimpse of the man sitting across the huge patio. It was him. She made her way toward him, trying to remain calm.

"Mustafa?"

The man nodded. "Come inside." He stood up, fixed his pants, and grabbed the ancient Nokia phone off the table. He looked around the area, looking straight through Susan as though she wasn't there, and then he went inside. Susan followed. He pointed to a table near the cash register. "Sit. Tea or coffee?"

"Tea please," Susan looked around. There was no one else there except the man, the cashier, and Susan.

Mustafa hadn't taken his eyes off Susan. "You from here?"

"Yes," Susan said, forcing a smile. "I'm a resident here. I think you know Abu Ahmad. He gave me your information, told me how to find you." Susan knew Mustafa already knew she was coming, but she just wanted to start a conversation to get rid of the awkwardness.

"How old are you?" he asked, ignoring her attempt at small talk.

"I'm twenty-four."

"You're still young,"

"Yes, I think most of your customers are my age. Most of the young people in my country just want to leave."

"Your country?"

Susan stiffened. She was unsure whether she should speak about Iran, her real country. She was born and raised there, but if she spoke her mind there it would mean death or prison - while if she told outsiders she was Iranian they'd reject her.

"Where do you want to go?" He must have been busy and wanted to get straight to the point.

"Europe, or Britain." She looked out the window. There was no one else around besides some young Arab men with strange looks, surveying one another, all certainly up to no good. They all seemed mischievous, walking with a nervous gait. Some stopped in front of the cafe, looked right and left, then scurried away. Susan wondered what kind of crimes they had committed or were planning to commit.

"Europe? Which country?"

Susan squirmed in her chair and scratched her head with her index finger. She knew this meeting was sombre, but for a moment she got a little excited. It was like she was sitting in a travel agency talking with an agent, planning a holiday.

"Well, I want to go to Germany, I guess." She had been warned that she could go to northern France and take a boat to Britain, but it was too risky. She could get left in France, or the police could discover her in Britain and deport her. Worse, she couldn't swim.

Mustafa eyed her for a moment as he leaned on the back two legs of his chair. He seemed to listen to her, but he also seemed to be a thousand miles away.

"Aha," he said finally, nodding slowly.

"So, can you tell me, what's the best way to get there, what the timing will be, how long it'll take?"

"Germany is good."

Susan wanted to understand every word correctly, but Mustafa's English was poor, and she strained to listen, as though she was borrowing two more ears.

"Very good," he continued, speaking as though he was complimenting a child on their kindergarten art project.

"Yes. For sure it's good. They accept a lot of refugees. I heard they accepted something like 216,000 already." She had done her research as soon as she had hatched her plan to leave Iraq and go to Europe, looking for the best places to go, the places most open to refugees and asylum seekers.

"What?" he asked, his face contorting strangely as a smirk flashed across his face. "No!"

"What do you mean?" Susan asked.

Mustafa moved his head closer to her. He picked up his empty coffee cup and saw there was nothing left. He didn't want to have wasted his energy, so he tried to drink from it anyway. Mustafa took a deep breath, leaning precariously back on his chair. He looked at Susan with a penetrating gaze. "So, do you have anyone here? Father? Mother? Brother?"

She shook her head and looked down at her feet. "I have no one. I'm alone."

"Good." He pulled a cigarette out of his pocket and the cashier appeared like a fairy out of nowhere, lighting the cigarette for him. The little boy disappeared again. Mustafa inhaled deeply from his cigarette, satisfying his craving and relishing in the searing feeling in his throat that made him feel alive for a moment.

"How much will it cost?"

Mustafa looked at her, appearing unable to comprehend her question. "I said how much will charge to send me to Germany?"

"Aha," he said. He pushed the cigarette into the ashtray and then grasped at his beard to comfort himself while he thought her question over. "Five thousand."

"That's not what Abu Ahmad told me. Come on, five thousand dollars?"

"No *habibi*," Mustafa said, laughing contemptuously. "Five

thousand euros."

Mustafa picked up the cigarette and filled his lungs. Then he looked at Susan and blew the smoke out in her face while still holding her gaze. Susan felt sick to her stomach and wanted to vomit. She waved her hand frantically back and forth to get the smoke out of her eyes and mouth. Susan needed this man right now, so she had to control herself and say nothing or else he would certainly regret wasting his time on her. The price he quoted was way too high. More importantly, it was more than Susan had. Still, she was optimistic that she could negotiate the price.

"They told me three thousand dollars."

"Who told you that?"

"Abu Ahmad, the one who sent me. He said that he was even thinking about taking his own family to Germany now because of the situation here."

Mustafa sucked his teeth for a moment. Once the debris was free, he straightened himself in his chair. "*Habibi*, it cost five thousand." He held up his hand with all five fingers extended. "See? In Euros."

Susan had forgotten she was negotiating with a smuggler, not an immigration attorney. She grabbed her bag and stood up. "Sorry, I don't have that much."

A man outside looked in, and observed Susan standing. Mustafa looked at him, and they seemed to reach an unspoken understanding.

"Sit. Maybe there is another way."

"What way?"

"Two more coffees!" Mustafa shouted, ignoring Susan. There was no one around, and it seemed like he was ordering from a ghost. He stretched his neck and clasped his hands across his belly. Then he fixed his gaze again on Susan. "There is always a way to solve any problem."

The little boy appeared from nowhere with the two coffees. He looked at Susan demurely, and Susan looked into his eyes. He reminded her of Faisal, the shy little boy she missed every day.

"Go!" Mustafa ordered, as if the boy was a dog waiting for scraps. Then he pushed one of the little Arabic coffee cups toward Susan. "Help yourself."

"No thank you," pushing the cup back toward him. "I'm not really thirsty."

"Drink it, don't worry about the price," he said. "Just drink it."

Susan slowly took the cup, noticing the man outside watching her too. Mustafa looked at him again, silently negotiating. Susan could feel both sets of eyes on her as she sipped the coffee. It felt like they were sapping away her energy, somehow reducing her humanity. Susan tried to think of the little boy, who only appeared when Mustafa needed service. She cleared her throat.

"Can you tell me your final price please?"

"The same price you said. I'll send you for three thousand, no problem."

"That's great!" Susan said, her eyes blinking quickly in disbelief. "Thank you. God bless you and your family."

"Do you have your documents?"

"Um, let me see," Susan said. She rifled through her bag, which for a moment felt so cavernous that a camel could get lost in it. "Ah, here is my residency card."

Mustafa took the card and then looked at Susan, comparing the photograph with the woman in front of him. He read the card carefully, his eyes resting on one part in particular. "How much cash do you have on you?"

"Two thousand." Susan knew his eyes were stuck on the word

"Iran" on the card where the country of origin was written, and she wondered why he didn't mention it. Susan took a crinkled envelope from her bag and handed it to him. "Give me a little time and I can get the rest."

Mustafa opened the envelope and craned his neck a bit to see if the stack of bills looked right. The man outside stood, pulled out a cigarette, and disappeared. The little boy was watching from the kitchen.

"I'll tell you when you'll leave. For now, this will stay with me."

"But how will we go? Which way?"

"Don't you want to go to Germany? It's the greatest industrial power in the world!" he mocked.

"Yes..."

"So, I'll send you there, *khalas*, that's it."

"No, I want to know how far it is, what I need to pack, things like that."

His laugh echoed throughout the empty cafe. The boy was no longer watching. Susan stared at him, unable to stand up for herself because this man now controlled her future. Mustafa took a tissue from the box on the table and flattened it out between the two of them. He put the pen in his mouth and tore the cap off with his teeth.

"Our first destination is Turkey." He put a small dot on the tissue. "Where is our first destination?"

"Turkey." Susan answered with a touch of excitement.

"Good job." He put another dot a little distance from the first one. He scrawled *Younan* in Arabic, which Susan knew was Greece because the spelling was the same in Farsi and Arabic.

"Then we'll go to *Younan*."

"Aha. So, what way will we take?"

"Sea."

Susan squirmed. She couldn't swim, but she didn't want to tell him. "Will you give us life jackets?"

"Yes, of course. It's a seven-star cruise! You'll travel in luxury." The man really seemed to be enjoying playing with this helpless woman. He looked her up and down, searching for her response.

Susan forced a smile. She hated that he was making her life into a joke. The life she had dreamed of for years was now in the hands of a sleezy criminal, enjoying himself at her expense.

"Next destination," he said, drawing a line to connect the dots together. *Maqduniye*! Where?" he asked her, verifying if she was paying attention.

"*Maqduniye*," she answered robotically. She was glad the name for Macedonia was again the same in Arabic and Farsi. She didn't want to ask any more questions than necessary from this man

"Good *habibi*."

Susan cringed. She hated when strangers spoke to her in such a familiar way, using pet names reserved for families and lovers. She felt nauseous again.

"The next destination is a little harder. Where is it?"

"Where?" Susan asked, raising her eyebrows in frustration.

Mustafa drew another line slowly across the tissue, clearly enjoying his moment of artistry. "Serbia." He circled the dot he just made. "You should be careful here, though."

"Why, what should I do?"

"They'll tell you when you arrive, don't worry."

"Look, how many days will it take?"

"Maybe a month. Maybe a year."

"So, you're saying you can't guarantee it?"

"No, of course! We have a special five-year warranty just for you." He laughed devilishly, pleased with himself.

Susan was getting more perturbed as the conversation went on. She wanted to slap him across his open mouth but she took a deep breath, calming herself, waiting for him to finish laughing at his own joke.

"Where is the next destination after Serbia?"

"Ah yes, next..." He pressed the pen hard on the napkin, causing it to tear as he drew the line. "Damnit!" He threw the tissue, cursing at it as it floated to the ground. He swallowed the saliva that had erupted in his outburst, and then withdrew a new tissue. "So, from the beginning..."

"No, no, I got it, all the way up to Serbia. Please continue."

"The rest?" Mustafa looked at her, shocked that this woman's voice that was earlier so silken and quiescent was now striking him with irritated boldness. He sat back in his chair for a moment, staring at Susan to ensure it was the same girl.

"Yes, please. It's getting dark and it will be hard to find a taxi soon, so let's just get on with it."

"Your next destination will be Hungary." He decided to ignore her moment of strength.

"Tell me more about the journey. Will we take a boat the whole way?"

"Well, yes, but there will be places with mountains and forest. You'll also have to give your fingerprints along the way, but they'll explain all that to you."

"Who?"

"My colleagues."

Susan didn't have the energy to push him further. "How about the weather along the way? Is it cold there? Snowy or rainy? I need to pack properly."

"It depends when you go."

"The sooner the better."

Mustafa sat there for a moment, stroking his beard. He pulled out a new cigarette despite the first one still having plenty left. He clenched the new cigarette in his teeth and lit it with the cherry on the old one. "Yes, I think it'll be cold. Is this your number on this slip of paper?"

Susan nodded. His nonsense answers were worrying Susan. She did not like to hear that everything would be clear later, no one had a name, and no place was certain.

Mustafa picked up one of the three remotes on the table and switched the television on. "Looks like they'll invade Iran, too," Mustafa said as he shifted his attention from Susan to the news. The idea of Iran being invaded seemed to please him as he smiled absent-mindedly.

Susan didn't want to talk about politics and she certainly didn't want to reveal anything about herself to this man. She knew from her childhood that saying anything bad about the government could mean the end of her life. And worse, talking about Iran outside the country seemed to make people suspicious of her, as though she was a spy by birth. She pretended to be totally disinterested in the images flashing across the screen.

"I'll get my stuff ready and pack, and then I'll wait for your call. I need my identification card."

"Did you give it to me?"

"Yes, my Kurdistan residency card. I gave it to you a few minutes ago with my money."

"Yes, yes," he laughed. "I'm kidding. I have it, but I need it to finish some paperwork. I can have someone deliver it to your house when I'm done. And you better gather the rest of the cash or you can kiss your trip goodbye."

"I'll come tomorrow and take my card after you're done." She didn't like the idea of some stranger handling her only non-Iranian identification card. And now she needed to find a way to raise a thousand dollars in a city where that sum could support a family for six months.

"Great. Be here at this time and on this date," he said, absent-mindedly flicking a torn piece of napkin with some writing on it at her. "Don't be late."

Chapter Eleven

Susan was supposed to meet a friend for dinner near Erbil's old citadel in the city centre and she was running late. She pulled her white shirt over her chest and wrists, ensuring it was covering everything, so no one could accuse her of seducing anyone, and tied her hair back with her black hair band. Next, she carefully applied colourless lip gloss from one side of her mouth to other and gently touched both lips together to ensure it was evenly spread. She started applying her eyeliner but absent-mindedly drew a curved line slightly off centre from her eye.

"Damnit!" She threw the eyeliner to the side of the mirror, ran the tap and splashed water over her eyes.

Susan was the only one who could motivate herself. She would beat herself up over the slightest mistake, labouring over small details and holding herself accountable even when things were outside her control. She had often wondered why she was so hard on herself. She looked at herself in the mirror, doubting how she could ever survive an unending series of internal conflicts with this soft face staring back at her, with its big eyes, nose like a little pea and that silky hair.

Flicking off the light switch in the bathroom, she hurried out, grabbing a tissue from a table nearby, drying her face. She decided to teach herself a lesson, and not wear makeup. Susan remembered briefly when Farah had cleaned her face with a wet cloth, and it seemed like ages ago. Could it really have only been a few months? She wondered for a moment about Farah's family but quickly put it out of her mind, dropping the thought and the towel. She sat on the edge of her mattress, wishing for a comfortable bed she could roll around upon freely, wrapped up in her dreams.

The blaring fan in the bathroom was still going, and it sounded like it was getting ready for lift off. The landlord had wired the electrical system poorly and had forgotten to install a switch for the fan. It spun day and night. Sometimes Susan would close her eyes and imagine the sound as a rhythmic song and remind herself of the Persian saying that if one can't cut a hand, then kiss it.

The laughter of her Syrian neighbour pierced through the walls just loud enough to compete with the fan. He usually sang along at this time of day and whenever he did, he seemed to fill the entire building with the smell of his cigarette smoke. For him, singing and cigarettes were intimately connected. Susan had complained about the noise to the Syrian manager several times, but he was useless. Susan knew the story about the manager, he had raped a girl that was living in the very room Susan now occupied. That was how Susan got such a cheap rate. Apparently, the girl didn't tell the police because the man threatened her family, so she just packed her things one day and left in silent shame.

Susan locked her apartment door behind her and made her way down to the ground floor. As always, a group of six or seven guys were sitting in the lobby, smoking and drinking coffee in silence. They always gave her an uneasy feeling, especially as their eyes followed her out the building. They looked at her like she owed them something and Susan had decided that only criminals acted like everyone else owed them something. As she walked past, feeling their eyes on her, she couldn't help but compare these men with the Syrian or Iranian governments. Iranian people often question why the government spends so much money in Syria, while sixty percent of Iranians live in poverty. At the same time, people outside Iran become immediately suspicious and distant after hearing someone has Iranian nationality. They associate the ordinary citizens with the government, when the citizens want nothing less than to be free of it. Like all Iranians living outside the country, Susan was a victim of politics and criminals in power, criminals just like these good-for-nothing men always watching in the lobby.

Susan shouldered her bag and pretended not to notice them. They were too absorbed anyway by their cell phones to really give her any attention beyond their stares. *Once I'm outside, I'm sure they'll say 'Look what she's wearing! She moved her ass while she was walking. She must be going out to find a man'* Susan thought to herself.

Outside, cars wove around one another without indicators or regard for road markings. It seemed the taxi drivers depended on God, not their steering wheels, mirrors, or seatbelts, to ensure they survived the night. The light turned red at the intersection in front of the building, and Susan saw a little boy with half his body peeking out through the sunroof of a car stopped there. The driver seemed to be his father, who was talking on the phone, while a woman seated beside him glared at Susan until the light turned green. The driver started going, but then struck the brake. The little boy in the sunroof lurched forward. The woman giggled in excitement, and stared back at Susan, then they drove away. Susan was hardly surprised; this was typical behaviour from some people in Erbil. It wasn't just the locals. Expats picked up the behaviour too after a while. Susan started walking down the road toward the citadel to meet her friend. The air was getting colder and colder, as the year turned its back on autumn. During the day a shirt was enough, but these nights it would be too chilly to get away with leaving a jacket at home. Soon, it would be cold enough to need a thick shawl.

Erbil was the kind of place that grew on a person for no explicable reason. Maybe it was the Kurdish people. They were the only truly nice people Susan ever met. They were helpful to strangers, spoke respectfully, and offered genuine friendship. Their openness and acceptance of other cultures and the outside world must have made it easy for Westerners to call Kurdistan their second home, especially in contrast to the dangerous streets of Baghdad.

Susan knew some Kurdish people who, flush with oil money from Kirkuk, had bought luxury cars not for themselves, but for friends and family as gifts. One Kurd had given property to a friend for them to set up a home and business. Their generosity and smart use of oil wealth had made many previously uneducated and unemployed people into local celebrities and wealthy businesspeople. Many residents were known for throwing ostentatious parties, inviting people of all backgrounds. Sometimes those parties were like attending the United Nations, one could find Iranian, American and Russian people all socialising as if their countries were the best of friends. The Kurds had that effect on people.

Susan, on the other hand, was an Iranian living in Kurdistan. She was a friendly stranger. She never thought of herself ending up with a rich man or being his lover like so many young women did. She didn't know how to ask for help, because she was always the one helping others. She didn't know how to depend on anyone else. Still, she knew Kurds would be there, too. They had been living together in tribal groups for a long time, defending their right to exist from all sides over the centuries. They always ensured every person around was invited to weddings, funerals and parties, in good times or bad. They would share everything together because community was the only thing they had. Susan understood them.

She neared the citadel, a huge brick amalgamation of buildings gathered in a spiralling shape around each other, united this way for at least the last seven thousand years. Shops were everywhere, with little alleys, tunnels and walkways crisscrossing in every direction. The covered bazar sold everything from antiques to *zataar*, and everything in between. Men, women and children scurried in all directions over the ancient stone streets. The old cafes thronged with equally ancient Kurdish men wearing traditional dress as if they had stepped out of a history book. At one cafe, a group of men were intently listening to a man on the second-floor balcony telling a story. People were buying different types of *chookhe*, *pantol*, and *sarveen* in front of the bazaar. Everywhere was a flurry of tradition in Erbil's citadel. The Kurds were proud of their history, and they literally wore it on their sleeves.

Susan loved watching the Kurdish warrior dance, which was a real sight to behold. Women and men would hold each other's hands, dancing together in a big group, with the first and last person holding a trinket symbolising equality. The group would make fearsome sounds to inspire their cohorts and shun their enemies, while they would stomp their feet in unison on the soil, showing that the land was theirs.

Susan had a definite attachment to Erbil, despite all its problems. She knew that when the time came for her to leave, her tears would flow freely in remembrance of the meat and chicken *lafas*, for the boiling summer heat, the Kurdish language, the admonition of *sarchawa*, the random police checkpoints, the power outages and the self-proclaimed taxis who drove by their own rules. She'd even miss the two-faced expats that would be her best friend one day and forget her existence the next. Today was different than usual. She felt like a tourist walking through the old city on holiday. She paid attention to the sites, smells and sounds around her, gently stepping down the cobblestone sidewalk. The smile on her face was one of discovery but also reminiscence. All she needed was a Canon DSLR around her neck and she'd probably look like one of the United Nations expats totally in awe of this other world.

Cars slowed as they passed her, honking their horns abruptly to let her know they could give her a ride. Some of the drivers stared hungrily at her, trying in vain to mask their intentions by smiling or avoiding direct eye contact. Susan didn't care; she was used to it.

Erbil was beautiful in its own way. She pulled her mobile out of her bag and zoomed its camera in on the meter-long stone slabs layered on top of one another to form a unique architecture only time could construct. She took the photos so she could have them for a time in the future when she was far away from Erbil and missing the predictable chaos of this place. Soon, all she'd have was a collection of memories.

Moving slowly on, she walked down the sidewalk towards the restaurant. Big pieces of fabric hung over the tops of all the buildings like colourful clouds, adding to the feeling of a rich heritage. Behind the buildings there were some little hills with grass that had begun to turn brown, getting ready for winter. Susan remembered how green they were earlier in the year. Their colours were nature's smile.

Remembering the time, Susan doubled her speed and soon reached the crosswalk by the restaurant. Looking around, she saw Anas parking his car. Susan breathed heavily from her little sprint but she was relieved that they had arrived at the same time. *I shouldn't go inside before he does*, she said to herself. *I'm a lady, a man should wait.* She leaned against the wall outside, watching Anas trying to cross the street. Cars were flying past as though there were no pedestrian for miles. Susan thought to herself that this was the only situation where it was better to be a woman: cars would certainly stop for her. Unfortunately, a male driver wouldn't do anything for a woman unless there was some benefit in it to him. Maybe Anas was lucky he had to wait.

Susan was deep in these thoughts when the sound of a horn pierced menacingly into her ears. She saw Anas arguing with a taxi driver, who was hanging halfway out his car window. They were shouting simultaneously at one another, unable to understand each other. Susan ran towards them, she didn't want to hear another news story about road rage here in Erbil, where it was not uncommon to be shot by one of the drivers who would then flee.

"Anas! Anas!" Susan shouted. People had stopped their cars and were forming a small crowd around the arguing men. They were probably waiting to see if someone would be punched, shot, or who knows what. This was entertainment for them. An old man standing in front of the shop nearest the taxi came over and blocked the road, and then forced the driver back into his car. He shouted something at him that must have been convincing, and the taxi driver sped off angrily. The customers at the restaurant were watching through the windows, enjoying their kebab and the show. Certainly, some were disappointed they hadn't seen anything more interesting happen, like death or injury. Susan and Anas entered the restaurant, and everyone craned their necks and fixed their gazes on the pair as if some Hollywood stars had decided to stop in for a shawarma.

"People in this city have no idea that there is a war going on less than a hundred kilometres away," Anas said. "That guy was more concerned about his beard and moustache than about what's happening in Mosul right now."

"Come on," Susan said, flashing a smile. "It's done now."

"This restaurant is beautiful, isn't it?"

Susan looked around and nodded. The furniture had the sheen of something brand new and there was the smell of fresh paint in the air. The restaurant had a palette of rose and burgundy and all the wooden objects were a light brown. The leather chairs in the lounge area and the carefully planned colour scheme left no doubt in Susan's mind that both the restaurant's interior designer and the furnishings were from either Turkey or China. There was a big wooden table near the kitchen's swinging doors, covered with small red cloths, velvet swatches and *termeh* fabrics. On top were elegant silver samovars arranged carefully by size, the steam from the boiling pots wafted gracefully upward.

"It's my first time here, it's a nice place."

Anas was playing with his phone. Without looking up, he said, "The food is good, too. Sometimes we bring the *Farmandeh* here for lunch."

It was not uncommon to see diplomats and generals or others with high positions in the Kurdish government having meals around Erbil. It is unsurprising that even the *Farmandeh*, someone so powerful here, would come have lunch in a normal restaurant. Sometimes the elite would go smoke shisha on the weekends at the busy cafes like everyone else, faces stuck in their phones, glances stolen at women passing by and even sneaking some alcohol. The only difference would be the flock of bodyguards scanning the area ominously. Some of the most powerful people in Erbil needed bodyguards for their bodyguards.

"By the way," Susan said. "How is the situation here?"

"Difficult, much worse than people think. Every day we are losing soldiers. Da'esh is godless, faithless. It doesn't matter to them if they kill children, women or the elderly. They thirst for blood, like animals. God should keep us from knowing the extent of their barbarity. What you see on the news is only a sliver of their true crimes against humanity, but especially against Yazidis and Shi'a. You could never imagine the things going on in Mosul, Sharqat, Tal Afar." Anas straightened himself in his chair. "Long live Barzani! We are fighting alone."

"What do you mean, alone? The US isn't helping? What about other countries?"

"Well, yes they give us weapons and training but should we wait for them to fight for us? Should we count on them? This isn't their land. It's ours. We have martyrs, and they died for this country, for Kurdistan. We Kurds have been fighting for our rights and dying for our land, both of which we still don't have. On one side there is Turkey and Iran, on the other Iraq." Anas was deep into his diatribe. "Don't we deserve a country?"

Susan knew Anas had been out on the frontlines near Mosul for the past two months, far from the relative safety of Erbil. He had been living ten kilometres from Da'esh and had seen things Susan couldn't imagine.

"The Iraqi military got millions of dollars," Anas continued. "They gave it all away to Da'esh. Where do you think Da'esh got all their weapons and military equipment? It was left behind when the Iraqi army fled the cities. Only the Peshmerga can stand up to them. It wasn't just the Iraqi army either.

Da'esh destroyed museums, destroyed history. And they sold stolen antiques on the black market. In the middle of this all, it's just us, the Kurds. When a wolf comes to speak to you, it's because he wants something, Susan *khan*."

The waiter approached their table, interrupting the politics lesson. The smell of the food preceded the waiter. There was a big tray with fresh lamb brochettes, still sizzling from the grill. Susan's stomach growled. The *kebab* was resting on top of a fresh piece of flat bread, with the usual side of red onions covered in paprika, two charred green peppers and some other herbs that were so fresh they were probably picked that morning. Susan's favourite part was the grilled whole tomato.

"Coca? Fanta?" the waiter asked.

"For me just water please," Susan said.

Anas furrowed his brow, considering his options carefully. Finally, he looked up at the waiter. "Coca." He looked at Susan and grinned. "*Nooshe jan.*"

That phrase was their green light to start eating. The conversation could wait. Susan and Anas shifted their full attention to the food, tearing away at the lamb like prisoners enjoying their last meal. Susan hadn't had the chance to eat at a real restaurant in a long time, longer than she could remember. She'd been eating boiled potatoes and eggs that she'd cook on her little propane tank beside her ragged mattress. Anas, too, had been forced by the necessities of life at the front lines of war to eat very little. He had been living in a tent at an austere outpost north of Makhmur, without the familiar comforts of tasty, greasy, sour *dolma* and *kebab* from his home city.

Anas tossed the fork aside and began eating with his hands. The fork was standing in the way of the bites he wanted to take. The meat and the onion and the pepper all combined in the mouth with all the flavours of lemon, spices and meat juices perfectly balanced as they went from chewed to swallowed. A starving housefly was buzzing around the window next to their table, trying frantically to either escape or eat. Anas shook his head, his mouth too full to answer. Susan was getting full, but she couldn't pass this opportunity to eat well. She had the last bite of the lamb in her hand, and she rested for a moment, gathering the strength to stuff herself with it. She wiggled in her chair, hoping to shift the food around that she'd already consumed. She finally forced it down and smiled at Anas. Anas leaned back in satisfaction, slurping his tea, he winced a little from the heat but quickly recovered.

"It seems like Da'esh has really gotten to you," Susan said, now able to pick up the conversation.

"It's pretty terrible over there. I remember a little boy that was left for dead in the desert with his family."

"What happened?"

"We were searching the area at night. It was in a residential area. A few stray dogs were mulling around near what looked like a body. We thought it might be a martyr from our Peshmerga, killed by Da'esh, so we went to check it out. We shooed the dogs away and got close enough to see that it was a young boy, not an adult." He took out his phone and started looking through his photos. His eyes were glossy, he was getting emotional.

"They executed a lot of old women and little kids, ten or twelve years old. Da'esh fighters would leave the bodies in the streets as a message. Usually the victims were just trying to flee. Those bastards would steal all the valuables from the bodies. On the little boy's body that was laying there we found a photo in the pocket. We think it was the same boy that was laying there that was in the picture, but we couldn't tell because his face..." Anas trailed off and looked back at his phone, thumbing through the photos. "It seems that Da'esh relishes death and destruction. They are murderers and thieves. They'd sell each other for a pack of cigarettes."

"That's awful. I have no television in my room to follow the news but it seems that everyone is talking about Mosul and the

Yazidis trapped in Sinjar. I don't know what kind of religion Da'esh follows. What religion is this that calls for spilling people's blood in the name of God and enslaving innocent women?"

"Here," Anas said, barely listening. "I found it." He slid his phone across the table to Susan. "It's the picture I was looking for. The one from the boy's body."

Susan held the phone in her hand, staring at the photo. Shaved head, bright blue eyes, innocent face: she recognised Faisal easily. The phone slipped from her hand and the room spun. She tried to fix her eyes on Anas to balance her vision, but it was no use. She was in shock, disbelieving what she had seen. She felt the tears on her cheeks but they didn't feel like hers. Anas picked the up the phone, and took a second look at the photo, trying to understand.

"What's happened to you *keche*?"

Susan struggled to find her words. "I'll use the bathroom, sorry."

She ran out, slamming the door behind her. Leaning against the wall, she slid to the floor, mourning little Faisal, the innocent boy who had treated her like his sister, worried about her and stood up for her. The little boy whose mother and disabled brothers depended on him to survive. He had been the hope for all of them. Now he was gone. She wept as her mind's eye cycled through the memories she had with Faisal, coming to the citadel one day and buying gifts for Women's Day for their mothers and sisters. He was young but he was brave. He wanted nothing but happiness for his family and those he cared about.

"God knows what those bastard *kuffars* did to his brothers and his sister!" Susan mourned to the empty room. Her eyes were red and swollen. She wanted to stand, but her feet felt like bricks. She talked to her reflection in the mirror, half her head visible above the sink as she sat there on the cold floor tiles.

"Susan?" Anas' voice came through the door. He knocked gently. "Are you Ok?"

"How can I be Ok?"

"I'm worried about you. Do you need anything?"

"I just need you to drop me off. Can you?" Susan emerged from the bathroom clutching tissues in her hand. Her eyes were puffy and glistening.

"Yes, sure. Why are your eyes red? What's wrong?"

"Nothing."

Anas knew not to ask anything more. He put his arm around her shoulders, and they walked together back to his car. As they started driving, Anas put on some music to help Susan get her mind off whatever was bothering her. The sound of *I Am Missing You* by Sivan Perwer came through the speakers, beautifully sung but painfully poignant for Susan. Sivan Perwer was a Turkish-Kurdish singer famous for his love songs. While Anas was thinking about how special it was to the Kurdish people that Sivan Perwer won an art award from French President Chirac, Susan was thinking about how special Faisal was to her. His face was in her eyes even when she closed them. Every little boy she saw out the car window reminded her of him and she wished they were him. She closed her eyes again and tried to push her despair down deeper, further from her mind.

"Sorry I couldn't stay longer," Susan apologised.

"No, it's fine." Anas was still confused about Susan's changed mood. "Just take care of yourself. You told me you were leaving Erbil so I wanted to see you, but..." He trailed off.

"But what?"

"Well, did you make your decision? I mean, are you sure?"

"If I wasn't sure before, now I'm one hundred per cent certain.

Look where we live. The world has dumped its poverty and misery in our little region. Maybe we're cursed, the Kurds, Persians, Iraqis, you, me. Who knows if a person you meet today might be dead tomorrow? Da'esh is just over the horizon. They're so close, and yet we are still hoping they won't make it these few extra kilometres. They're genocidal, they're psychopaths and the world doesn't care. It was difficult for me before the war started but I had no idea what else I would have to endure. You know how it is for me, being Iranian. We're hated by our country because we refuse to be slaves. Every other country hates us because we are from the same country as the government from which we've run away. Anas, I have nothing in this life except a backpack with some worn out clothes."

"Don't say that, Susan. I'm your friend. I'll do whatever I can for you."

"You've already proven your friendship to me, Anas. You're a real man, a man I can trust but you've got your own family and responsibilities. I've got my responsibilities, too."

"Susan, listen. Your life is hard not just because of your circumstances, but also because of your pride. You've got to let other people in, let them help you. You're my friend and if I have something you need, I'll share it with you. But it's like you curse me every time I offer something helpful for you. Please don't let this pride destroy you."

Susan looked out the window. "Thanks for the lunch today." She got out of the car and started walking down the roadside. Anas watched her walk, helpless to stop her. Susan's life was a long series of unplanned farewells. She never knew when a meeting with someone would be the last.

She walked aimlessly down the street, staring at the photo in her phone that she kept of Faisal and her together at the restaurant the day before he left forever. She had no tears left for him and crying only seemed to make him persist more in her mind. She could hear his gentle voice, reassuring her. "You're my sister, Susan. I'll always have your back."

Why was it that good people meet the worst fates? It seemed like the poorest countries were bearing the worst of the violence, with new groups emerging every year claiming to be more brutal than the ones they crushed or absorbed. They all had one thing in common: targeting ordinary people in the name of an idea they claimed came from God. Susan thought of the children in refugee camps and the families like Farah's left behind. Their lives were sickness, danger and fear. Their biggest dream should be to have a nice toy, not to maybe have water that day. Susan kicked a piece of gravel across the street. A little girl popped out from an alley, apparently aroused by the sound. She had a head of messy yellowish hair and was carrying an armful of tissues wrapped in plastic. She came up to Susan's side, tugging at her shirt. She was barely up to Susan's hip.

"Buy one for God," the little girl said, matching Susan's pace as her oversized plastic sandals clicked beneath her feet. "Please sister, buy one."

These days it was easy to find children sitting around the corner, selling something for a pittance. Most of them were Syrian refugees, but really, they could be anyone. Sometimes a mother would be sitting in the shade nearby, dressed head to toe in a smothering black baya, somehow more religious through her poverty.

Someone shouted and the girl got scared. She cowered behind Susan, still gripping a piece of Susan's shirt. Susan stopped and took the little girl's hands in hers. She turned them over, looking at the rough calluses covering her palms. Wear and tear like this would be common for a construction worker or a soldier, not a little girl. Susan patted the girl's head, ignoring the grease that she felt on the strands. This girl was beautiful, but she was trapped behind a shroud of poverty.

"Where is your mother?"

"I don't have one, I have an uncle."

"An uncle?"

"Yes," the little girl said cautiously, as though someone might be listening. Then she looked up at Susan and spoke loudly. "Give me a thousand, I haven't eaten yet."

"Look, I'll give you a thousand if you tell me who told you to sell these tissues."

The girl looked around nervously. Susan could see fear in her eyes. Someone must be watching from a dark alley or a building somewhere. Susan couldn't be sure but she scrounged in her pocket and found a crinkled thousand dinar note. The little girl was miserable enough, she didn't need a beating for Susan's concerned curiosity.

"Promise me you'll buy some food for yourself, please."

At that moment Susan noticed a man in ragged clothes sitting against a trash bin sitting across the street, watching the two of them intently. Susan looked down at the girl, to see if she was looking at the man, too. When Susan looked up to see the man again, he wasn't there. Susan took the little girl's hand.

"Come. They have tasty sandwiches at this restaurant here. It's called Lafa." They walked together up to the open ordering window. "Here," Susan said. "They have chicken, meat, all kinds of things. Which do you like?"

The little girl put her finger on her mouth and looked up innocently but not saying a word. It seemed she didn't know the difference between chicken or beef, and especially not the different ways they could be served. She stared at the chef behind the window, who was furiously chopping away at something.

"Look, look at the pictures up here." Susan pointed to the menu on a lightboard above the window. "Which do you like?"

The girl pointed with her chin in the direction of one of the pictures. The cashier rang up the order and Susan paid. The little girl was hungry but shouldn't go home empty handed either, as Susan knew she was on the clock.

The cashier glanced up from his register at Susan. "These days they come here in a car, get dropped off on the street and at night they collect the kids and the money together. They take all of it."

"Where do they live?"

"Well, I heard that in one room they'll put twenty, maybe thirty kids together. They promise to feed them and give them shelter in return for selling this junk on the street."

"So, where are their families?"

"This one you're holding onto now?" He scoffed. "*Wallah*, I don't know. She has an addict uncle but maybe it's her father. You can't be sure. He leaves her on the street all day and at night he collects her and her money. Last winter she sat and waited for him for two cold nights. Nobody came. She slept here near the back door of the restaurant since the wall was a few degrees warmer than the freezing sidewalk. We didn't know where she lived, so we couldn't take her anywhere."

It seemed the little girl had chosen this area of the street and this restaurant storefront as her own. She was like an abandoned kitten with no owner, prowling the streets, hungry and cold. She relied on the kindness of strangers to leave her a little food or water because her family had decided long ago that she wasn't worth their care.

"See here?" the cashier asked, pointing to a tree across the street. "The man would leave her on the street and then he'd sit under that tree, just watching her all day."

The cashier handed over a shawarma and the little girl started munching away while she watched families coming and going from the restaurant. A father and mother were inside with a girl probably the same age as the little one standing nervously by Susan's leg. The father was helping his daughter with her iPod, while the mother was putting the menu down in front of her at the table. Susan looked down at the little girl by her side, saw the longing written on her face and heard her whimpering quietly. This beautiful life the family had was a hell for the little girl, because she'd never reach it.

"How is your food?" Susan asked, trying to distract her with something positive.

"It's delicious! Thank you, miss. But my uncle is going to be mad if I don't go back to work."

Susan wished she could take the little girl with her but she knew it was impossible. Instead, she kissed her on her matted head and watched as she ran off down the street. Susan felt even more determined to leave. All the sadness and unfairness around her convinced her to make the decision that could cost her life.

Chapter Twelve

Susan rifled through her bag to find the crinkled napkin with the smuggler's number on it. She found it and tried calling. No connection. She tried again, double checking the number. A third time, nothing. *Maybe this isn't his number?* Finally, her phone rang through WhatsApp while she looked through the other papers in her bag.

"Hello?"

"Did you call?"

"Excuse me," she said, only half recognising the voice. "Who is this?"

"Mustafa."

"Ah, ok. How are you?"

"Fine, thanks. Why did you call?"

"I want to know the details about my departure time."

"Next week, Friday,"

"Where should I go?"

"I'll let you know where. Listen, you didn't tell anyone, right?"

"About what?"

"The trip. Don't be stupid."

Susan detested him, his behaviour, his tone. She didn't expect a smuggler to be civilized but he could at least be human.

"No," she lied. Susan had told three people that were close to her but she feared what would happen if Mustafa knew she didn't follow his instructions.

"Listen. Don't bring anything unnecessary with you. You're not going to be on a luxury cruise liner. It's a plastic boat full of forty people. Do you understand? It's not a trip to Hawaii."

"I understand." She was already annoyed and wanted to hang up. "You get the rest of the money?"

Susan looked at the little book she kept in her bag that had a secret compartment. There was some money in it but it was only about half of what she still needed.

"Yes, it's ready." She hoped he couldn't tell she was lying through the phone. "How are you going to guarantee I'll reach my destination? I heard some travellers like me have left money with a *hawaladar* while they travel and then the smuggler gets the money once I arrive safely."

"No, no, no, *habibi*," his voice rising. "Whether you arrive or not, whether you live or die, it doesn't matter. I get paid. The price you got is a crime, you're basically stealing from me. I'm doing you such a big favour. If you want to find a *hawala* or an exchange, be my guest. Get your full five thousand euros ready and then some more."

"But you know I can't afford that."

"Ah, you want to have your cake and eat it, too. Too bad."

"What I've given you is my entire life, everything I have, just to reach Europe."

"Not my problem. Your problem. I am not worried about what is or is not in your pocket. I'm worried about what's going into mine. I'm busy now. We'll talk Wednesday. Don't call me. I'll call you. Don't miss my call. Women are always drama. You have one chance. Don't blow it. Bye." The phone beeped three times. He had hung up on her.

Susan had to steel herself for worse behaviours, worse words and worse people. She knew she was unprepared for the journey but she knew she had to do it. She didn't know who would be with her on her journey, whether there would be food, water, or shelter. She tried to imagine the procedures she'd endure crossing all the borders that lay ahead. It frightened her to think that it was Da'esh laying between where she now stood and her destination. That was her true obstacle to survival. Her only wish was that there would be at least one kind soul along the way to give her hope.

Susan had to work to collect the rest of the money she owed Mustafa. She found a hotel where she could work double shifts doing housekeeping during the day from eight to five and then from seven to midnight, when she would host in the restaurant in the lobby. Although the salary wasn't enough to make her target, she hoped customer tips would make up the rest. Susan had never done housekeeping before but she kept that detail from management. Once she was hired, she watched what felt like a million videos on her phone about how to clean toilets, make hotel beds and prepare a room for guests. She also visited an old Bangladeshi friend who worked at the same hotel to ask his advice. She shadowed him on his shift so she could get enough knowledge to make it through the days she had left to raise the money she needed.

The hotel customers seemed to be Europeans and Gulf Arab businessmen but there were a few American oil company employees, too. Many of these foreigners not only lived long-term in the hotels but they also kept their offices in them since the amenities out in the city were apparently not up to their standards. The British even had their consulate inside the hotel.

A tall man with blonde hair and a big gap in his teeth spotted Susan from across the lobby and flashed a bright smile. His coat alone probably cost more than Susan could make in six months. He waved at her in a friendly way. Susan was still shocked by the behaviours of Westerners. It was such a contrast to Middle Eastern men in this region. It seemed that Westerners smiled out of courage and pride along with a certain oblivious feeling toward the intricacies of other cultures. They wanted everyone to be like them but then they'd feel uncomfortable if those alien people decided to migrate to their country. Susan wondered what the source of that friendliness was that cut across cultures. If a man from her culture acted like this, she would be obligated to show offense or else her honour would be questioned. But when the foreigner does it, it seems acceptable. Susan smiled back at the man as he turned away.

"I think he likes you," the Turkish chef said, watching the interaction from behind Susan. He was standing very close to her. Susan could smell the cologne he was wearing, the onions he'd been cutting and the breath coming out of his mouth. Susan felt sick and took a few steps away from him. She looked him up and down, signalling silently that he was too close to her and turned back to the food labels she was sorting through. The chef's assistant was busy setting up all the dishes around the buffet and two other assistants inside the kitchen were flipping sizzling meat. Everyone was scrambling to quickly fill all the plates, bowls, and platters for the onslaught of guests who would be down shortly to enjoy their free food. The cold items in the buffet were Susan's favourite to look at. There was grilled mahi, pecan-crusted shrimp and, best of all, smoked salmon thinly sliced. Susan relied on a more experienced assistant nearby to help her arrange the labels, she hadn't heard of many of these dishes before and she could not risk messing up.

Susan spent as much time as she could around the cold items because the smell of the salmon would waft upward and it almost felt like she was eating it. She was only torturing herself though, because her growling tummy would never be satisfied. It was forbidden for the staff to eat any of the food, even when the leftovers were completely untouched. The previous day, she was in the kitchen fixing her uniform and apron when a waiter pushed the swinging doors open with his back, carrying in a huge tray full of untouched dishes from the buffet, full bottles of squeezed juice and fresh yogurts topped with sliced fruit. Now it had to go to the trash and Susan realised that in this place, the trash was more deserving of the food than she was. She snuck a peak of a plate hidden beneath a pile, it had a juicy steak, dessert and fruit. The waiter had snuck this one off for himself and he planned to store in the cabinet to have a luxurious illegal lunch later.

Susan was eying a plate of ribeye steak, cooked rare and with a dainty dish full of *au jus* tucked against it. A bowl of mashed potatoes was snuggled beside these, completely untouched. The waiter noticed Susan and he set the tray down. He was very young, his body barely filling the uniform he had to wear. He looked around and then leaned over to Susan.

"Take it," he said quietly. Susan looked at him and said nothing. She was unsure if this boy would report her to management. "No, really, it's for you. Look at the marbling of the steak. The Italian chef made it, not the Turkish one. These ones taste really good."

Susan looked around, adjusting her uniform then watched as the little boy in his oversized waiter's outfit started slicing a little cube of the meat from the corner.

"Take it." He held the fork up to her as a drop of steak *au jus* fell onto the floor between them.

Susan was pleasantly surprised by his kindness. She took the fork and tasted Brazilian steak for the first time in her life. The hotels in Erbil flew frozen steaks like this in on special chartered airplanes to keep the foreigners satisfied. Whether it was steak from Brazil, fish from Dubai or oranges from South Africa. Westerners and Gulf Arabs would not go hungry while staying in the fancy hotels in downtown Erbil. The Italian head chef at the hotel would then whip the delicacies into a beautifully presented dish. The foreign guests would often simply take a few bites and then push the plate across the table for the waiter to take. Susan couldn't believe how delicious it was.

Suddenly, the food and beverage director slipped into the kitchen out of nowhere. Susan blinked in disbelief, still chewing. He was tall, young and well-dressed. He stopped right inside the doorway, staring at both Susan and the little waiter. His mouth was slightly open, perhaps more surprised to see them flouting his rules than were to be caught. He had a hint of pity in his eyes, as he stared at the two hungry human scrounging through a plate of discarded food in the same way a passer-by may notice a homeless person rifling through a garbage can. The only difference was that these scavengers wore uniforms and they were his.

The director stood there with one hand in his pocket and the other adjusting his tie as if he was having trouble breathing. He was a big fan of Al Pacino and the movie *The Godfather* and it seemed like he was always trying to emulate Michal Corleone. He tried his best to forge his staff and his hotel into some semblance of the power structures in his favourite story. He liked to be called "boss" and he felt satisfied by the deference his staff felt obligated to render him. He rewarded the informers and punished the weak. He revelled in other people's fear and he didn't seem to see a difference between a person's fear or respect. The female staff from the Philippines and India were safe from his attention, since they didn't fall into his category of beauty. However, the rest of the female staff lived in constant fear of his inevitable rebukes, always living under the threat of termination. One week a young Filipina woman might be receiving the employee of the month award and the next she might be on the first flight out of Erbil. They all lived by the whims of the director and no one was safe.

"Eat," the director said quietly, almost without emotion.

Susan's hands were shaking, and the meat slid down the prongs of the fork. The little boy in the waiter's clothes was looking at the floor. The service elevator opened and another waiter stepped out, whistling a tune, oblivious to the scene he was stepping into. His face flushed and he stood still, understanding he was now witnessing something consequential.

"Eat," the director repeated. Something about him reminded Susan of her old manager. Where the previous one was a dog, this one was a wolf.

Susan obeyed. She chewed slowly, as the flavour of Brazilian beef transformed to bitter venom. Both waiters continued staring at the ground, like inmates after the suppression of a prison riot.

"What are you doing here?" the director asked the waiters. He pointed at the door. "Go back to work."

Susan swallowed the meat and, with it, her hope. The two waiters, her witnesses, were gone. Susan was alone with the director and could only hope that he'd just fire her so she wouldn't have to suffer a worse fate.

"So, what were you celebrating back here? It wouldn't be a party with only two of you. You should've invited the rest of the wait staff. The four of you could've really enjoyed the free food."

"But sir..."

"Don't talk."

The memories of the previous manager and this director were blurring together and she felt powerless. Susan wanted desperately to stand up for herself. She wanted to stand tall, close her eyes, and open her mouth to shout to the world the injustice of it all but she stayed silent because she needed to make it through just four more days before she would be on her way to freedom.

"Go see Mr. Khan."

Mr. Khan was the human resources manager and had come to Erbil from Bangladesh many years ago. The longevity of his career was the result of his merciless ambition. Susan silently looked down at the floor and made her way to the stairwell to the basement, down to the heart of the hotel. The human resources office was in a cement hallway that looked like a German bunker and was lit by a flickering fluorescent light that was probably just as old. There were other offices along the way, including the tailor's shop and the dry cleaners. The whole place smelled of bleach and damp. Susan stood in front of a door and read the little plastic sign which shouted in bold letters: MR. KHAN – DIRECTOR OF HUMAN RESOURCES. Taking a deep breath, she slowly pushed the door open. The young waiter was standing against the wall, hands clasped over his crotch, his eyes cast down to the floor. He didn't look up when the door opened. Mr. Khan was sitting confidently at his big desk with his hands steepled together like the roof of a house.

"How was the food?"

"It was shit," Susan said, boldly trying to resist the inevitable direction she knew the conversation would go.

Mr. Khan laughed but his fingers stayed glued together. He finally released his hands from each other and picked up a pen. He signed a few of the papers in a conspicuous way, then slid one in Susan's direction and the other towards the young waiter.

"So," he said, as though narrating a children's story. "This is the consequence of eating shit."

Susan stepped forward and eyed the papers. "These are too long. Can you just tell us what they say? Are we fired?"

"No, no. I am a fair man. Each of you will pay fifty dollars, American. It's a simple fine, very lenient considering what you did. If you don't have it now, that's no problem. We will deduct it from your salary. This is normal."

The little boy in the waiter's clothes scrunched his face and scoffed at the papers. He threw them down on the desk. "This is more than I'll spend on food for the whole month! I didn't even taste the damn food. That's enough. Sir, you have to know it was—," the boy's words faltered under the heat of Susan's glare, which switched his speech off like a mute button. Susan couldn't believe he was about to implicate her when it was his fault that they were in this situation in the first place. The boy snatched the pen off the desk, scribbled his name on the paper and left the office in silence.

Susan was shocked at how seriously everyone had taken this situation. The papers in front her looked more like a mortgage contract or a nuclear agreement than a fine. How did these managers have the time to draw up such elaborate statements but not to plan the proper quantities for food preparation each day?

Mr. Khan raised his eyebrows and pointed at the paper with his chin. Susan felt the weight of obligation and necessity weighing down on her. She counted only four days in her mind. Four days left before being released from this five-star prison into the dangerous freedom she so desperately sought. She reluctantly signed the paper and walked out without a word. Taking her bag from her locker, Susan made her way upstairs to the nicer bathrooms in the lobby.

She looked at herself in the mirror, reflecting on her plight. It didn't matter that she got charged fifty dollars for having two bites of steak. While working here she had smiled, been patient and saved more money than she needed to pay Mustafa. Taking out her money, she split it into two piles, one of dinars and one of American dollars. The dinars amounted to about one hundred American dollars but she couldn't exchange it once she left the country since Iraqi dinars weren't accepted in the global currency system. She put the little stack of dinars in her purse. She still needed to eat. Susan also decided to give a sheaf of dinars to the restaurant where she met the little girl, so that she would have a sandwich each day for at least a while.

She cleaned her little black backpack in the sink, taking care of it like it was an expensive handbag. She carefully sewed a small tear in the fabric and then sorted through her things to ensure everything was in order. While she was preparing herself in the bathroom, she noticed a plate near the sink with a half-eaten boiled potato covered by a used napkin. A cockroach scurried out from under the napkin as if it noticed her stare. Susan took a paper towel and caught the roach underneath without a thought. She knocked the whole ball of roach, napkin, and potato into the trash bin. Like the cockroach, the people working at this hotel were feeding off everything around them and offering nothing to the world outside.

Susan made a promise to herself at that moment that she'd never lower herself to be like them, no matter what. Since childhood she had no voice and her entire upbringing had taught her that women have no right to complain, to wear what they wanted or to make their own decisions. Being an Iranian woman meant being open to harm in all directions and safe in none. Strangers knew they could take advantage of Susan because she had no recourse, not from her family, her society, or her government. She knew this pattern of mistreatment had become expected and she wanted rid of it. What caused this hate? Was it the media, religion, or just plain bigotry?

Chapter Thirteen

Susan made her way to the location she'd agreed to meet Mustafa and looked at her watch. It was already getting dark and the electronics shop she was standing in front of had just pulled its shutters for the night. It was close to the cafe where she'd met Mustafa but she couldn't see it from where she stood. She was relieved that she wasn't late but she felt uncomfortable standing out in the open as night approached. Her black sweatshirt covered her body but she still felt exposed. She put the hood on over her head and tucked her hair under it, like a makeshift hijab.

She set her bag beside a trash bin, knocking something over behind it. A stray dog poked his head out from the alley across the street, probably awakened by the sound. He pranced over to investigate the stranger in front of his territory. Susan put her hands in her pockets. The dog stopped in the middle of the street about a meter from Susan and the two looked at each other without moving. The dog seemed surprised to see her standing there. Maybe he had never seen a woman on this street before. Susan wouldn't have been surprised.

The dog was sniffing around, trying to figure out if Susan was a threat or not. She whistled to the dog and he looked up at her. At the same time, a little boy sleeping in a truck across the street poked his head up out of a flatbed. Susan felt better knowing she wasn't the only human on the street. The dog sniffed closer and became very interested in Susan's bag. Maybe he was looking for the little bag of biscuits and cold cuts Susan had saved for her journey. Susan tossed a piece of Turkish sausage near the dog to show him she wasn't a threat. The dog was already getting his muzzle into the meat. He seemed to eat it in one bite. Susan looked down at him thoughtfully, if this dog had been born in the West, he would have been someone's best friend. But he was in the Middle East. Dogs here could be severely beaten or chained up for days but that was the least of their problems. In Islam, keeping a dog is considered *haram*, impure. With the dependence on a single phrase from the Quran, some people in Iraq would go around injecting dogs with an acid solution or simply shooting them. People used religion to justify anything, especially the worst things.

The dog appeared to feel safe, laying down beside Susan and curling his tail around his body. He laid his head down on his paws and Susan could feel the warmth of his body against her legs. Suddenly the little boy in the truck threw an apple core at the dog, striking him right on the head. The dog yelped and ran away, leaving Susan feeling strangely bereft.

Twenty minutes had passed since the arranged meeting time, Susan had no choice but to wait. It was normal in the Arab world to make an appointment, get a response of *Inshallah*, God willing and then expect a variable meeting time of perhaps hours off schedule. This Middle East clock was both faster and slower than international time. Sometimes people purposely showed up late to give the appearance that they were so busy and important that they couldn't possibly be on time. Other times, the person who called the meeting would force the client to stay in the waiting room for an hour despite having no other people waiting, letting the feeling of importance marinate for a while. This was a constant friction point in Erbil, where many Westerners came to do business and expected their contacts to value punctuality the way they did.

Susan looked down the street at a children's game shop. Some little boys appeared and disappeared inside, their muffled laughter fading into the sound of heavy truck motors revving on the main highway behind this neighbourhood. The shop owner was sitting outside on a dilapidated plastic chair. His finger was resting on his nose and he seemed to be clinging to his last days. He shouted something to the children inside but in vain. His voice was too weak and his words too garbled to have any effect. Susan looked down at her phone again, checking the time. Another twenty minutes had passed without a call.

Susan stepped behind an electric pole to conceal herself a bit. She started noticing a few figures in some second-story windows coming and going. In another part of the street a man had come to a window to smoke a cigarette and Susan could have sworn he was watching her. Suddenly, the light from a vehicle of some kind splashed onto the street. Susan stiffened herself against the pole and tightened her hood. She squinted and could see the outline of a motorcycle approaching. The sound got closer and closer until it stopped directly in front of her. The smell of gas and cigarettes caught up and washed over Susan. She coughed, trying to fight it from entering her lungs.

"Hey," the man on the motorcycle said. "Hey, you."

"Yes?"

"You're Susan?"

"Who are you?"

"I'm your seven o'clock appointment."

"From who?"

"From Mustafa."

"Where is he?"

"He's busy. Can't come." The man scratched at his beard as though he was noticing it for the first time, then spit on the ground between

Susan and his motorcycle. He stared at Susan while he pulled a cigarette out of his pocket and stuck it in his mouth. "Get on."

"Where?"

"Right here," he firmly patted the rest of the seat behind the part he was sitting on. "On the bike."

"Where will you take me?"

"Girl, I'll take you all the way to Germany." He laughed as he clacked his lighter. "Come on, I don't have time to waste on you."

"Look who's talking!" Susan said angrily. "You made me wait an hour!"

"You coming or not?"

Susan reluctantly got on the motorcycle and hooked her bag to the back. "You still didn't say where you're taking me,"

"I'm taking you to the rest of the group."

"Rest of what group?"

"Yes, your team, your travel buddies." The motorcycle sped up, and the smoke from his cigarette was trailing directly into Susan's face.

"Can you please not smoke? It's going right in my mouth."

"Shh, watch it." He looked at her in the little rear-view mirror by the handlebar. He revved his engine and purposely hit a bump to give Susan a jolt but he lost his cigarette in the process.

"Listen. My health is not that good. Please drive carefully."

"Just sit there." Susan couldn't tell if this meant he understood.

As the motorcycle sped up, Susan relaxed a little and steadied herself on the motorcycle seat, grasping the little metal rail she sat on. She watched as they passed all the *mukhtars*, some sitting in their plastic chairs, some framed in their windows or some standing with a tea glass in their front doors, each watching over his territory. The scents of smoke, *shisha*, and family dinners all mixed in the air to compete with the ever-present fumes from diesel and burning trash that defined Erbil's summer evenings. Susan's hair flitted around her face and for a moment she felt free. She enjoyed the feeling of moving forward, leaving difficult memories behind her and taking a leap of faith into the unknown.

The motorcycle drove for at least thirty minutes down the highway. The scenery had given way from densely packed buildings to sparsely populated patches of open dirt, with streetlights illuminating the clay earth only every so often. Susan was no longer in the city limits of Erbil and she didn't recognise this place at all. The darkness had fallen fully, the stars sewn into heaven's blanket above her.

Big tanker trucks carrying oil from Kirkuk were flying past as though the motorcycle wasn't there. Susan gripped the seat carefully as gusts of wind caused the bike to wobble each time one went by. She could make out some yellowish lights on the horizon but between the road and that infinite edge there was nothing. She reminded herself that being in a desert outside the city shouldn't bother her if she really was prepared to travel a thousand kilometres across the Mediterranean Sea in a tiny boat. This was just the beginning.

Suddenly, the driver turned sharply and cut along into an expanse of dirt that seemed to stretch for miles. There was nothing around, no lights, no trees, no people. Susan could only see five meters in front of her from the motorcycle's shuddering headlight. The arms of darkness otherwise embraced her. Eventually the motorcycle slowed and came to a stop in front of a big walled compound. The cement was all a light creamy colour and was chipped here and there from the unforgiving desert weather. The motor switched off and Susan heard only silence. She felt for a moment as though she was visiting a cemetery or some isolated shrine.

"Is it ok?" Susan asked, unsure of where she was or what to say.

The driver didn't answer, instead knocking the kickstand down and hopping off the motorcycle. He walked up the cement stairs to the metal door and tapped his key on the metal three times in a rhythmic way. The door opened almost immediately and a little light came through. Susan tried to make out the figures but she could only see the edges of shadows. She hugged her bag tight against her chest. A cricket chirped close by and the sound startled her.

"Go inside," the man said to her.

Susan dutifully dismounted the bike and walked toward the doorway. As soon as she stepped inside, she was shocked. The floor was almost filled by families with their little children moving in a sea of clothes and faces. Susan was in awe that the children were as calm as they were as she looked around at all the faces, many of whom didn't even notice she was there. Her eyes came to a little baby wrapped in fabric, who happened to open her eyes suddenly. Susan smiled at the little baby girl but the girl only stared in wonder at this new stranger.

"A car will come at midnight," a man called across the room. He had one hand on his hip and the other was loosely holding what looked like half a broom handle. "Are you listening?" he asked in Arabic. He started moving the stick slowly in little circles. "Do you understand?" he asked again, this time in Kurdish.

Everyone nodded. It was easier to move at night since the only people awake at the checkpoints were the ones looking for bribes. Susan sat herself at the end of a crowded hallway, next to a woman with two young children. The children looked a little dazed and the mother seemed exhausted.

"Salam," Susan said. She could feel worried eyes on her from around the room and she thought it best to break down a barrier with at least one of the people who now shared her fate. She felt ashamed for a moment for looking around at the faces, looking instead at the worn-out plastic rattan rolled out on the floor beneath her. The woman held the two children a little tighter, but she forced a careful smile.

Susan wondered what kind of people there were sitting around her, where they had come from and what made them decide to leave it all behind. She wondered if they knew each other or if they were all little groups of strangers whose lives had all aligned in this little building. Would these people become forever changed from who they were yesterday? This was no place for ordinary people. From their clothes, Susan could tell they were from many backgrounds. There were little groups of Yazidis, Sunnis, Shi'a, Christians, Assyrians and Turkomans. They all shared one thing in common: their desire to escape from the oppression and the violent death they'd surely endure if they remained in Iraq.

A young man who Susan assumed was a guard was walking among the families seated. He was thin, maybe twenty years old with a pistol strapped to his belt that seemed too heavy for his pants to carry. His face was covered by a black and white checked *keffiyeh*. He appeared to be the only relaxed person in the room. Resting one hand on the back of the gun while he walked around, he seemed comforted by the authority the feeling of the cold metal transferred to his body.

Susan was getting a better look at her surroundings now that the initial shock had worn off and the mundane feeling of waiting took its place. Most of the men were no older than thirty or thirty-five. A group of five women sat together and one of them had three toddlers clinging to her at different angles. In all, Susan estimated there were probably a dozen people in the room awaiting their next move. Everyone looked tired, as though this was not their first stop.

One young man took out a book from his backpack. He put the backpack behind him as a little pillow, so he could read more comfortably. The man beside him shifted dramatically.

"Watch it, Heja!" the man exclaimed, perturbed.

"Sorry," Heja said, adjusting his backpack and going back to his book.

Another man down the hallway was biting his nails while his leg anxiously bounced off the floor. He was looking all around at everyone but really at no one and his behaviour seemed to make the people around him nervous. A little girl sitting amongst a ring of children in the far corner of the main room raised her hand when the guard passed by.

"What do you want?"

"He's not feeling ok," the little girl said, referring to the man with the restless leg. "Can you give him water or something to calm him?"

"Water?" The guard looked incredulous.

Susan noticed some of the people around the little girl tucking their water bottles away to appear as though there was none to give, just in case they were asked to help a stranger. The guard rolled his eyes and walked over to the anxious man.

"What's your problem?"

"Nothing." He appeared more nervous than before.

The guard gave him the cigarette he was smoking. The man took the cigarette gratefully, taking a big drag. As he exhaled his body was visibly calmed. The man must have lived off a diet of cigarettes and he hadn't eaten in days. The cloud of smoke began settling in the room over the head of the little girl who had just expressed concern about the man. A mother covered the little girl's face with a piece of fabric. Susan heard a lighter clacking elsewhere in the room, and then another. The smell of the cigarette had triggered everyone's addictions. The guard shooed them outside.

"Go smoke in the courtyard." He seemed to be the only one allowed to smoke inside. About half the men got up and made an exodus to the courtyard to pray to their nicotine god. A woman motioned to the guard to close the door to the outside but he stood there in the doorway, simultaneously keeping an eye on the men outside and everyone else who stayed behind in the room.

"Can you please close it? My little Fatima has difficulty breathing in the first place," the mother said.

"Yes, please close it," Heja said, offering a show of support to a stranger.

The guard glared at them but remained motionless. After all, he was a smoker, too. One of the men outside offered him a new cigarette, which he took without taking his eyes off the mother who asked him to close the door. A few lighters clacked in assistance, their flames glowing brightly. It was interesting how these men had prioritized new lighters among their essential supplies over warm clothes or new shoes.

The children were getting agitated from all the waiting. They started running around, touching the walls, trying to release some of their pent-up energy. They ran by the mother, who held a baby in her arms. She didn't seem to notice them at all. She was focused on the baby girl, who looked to be on the verge of sleep but was fighting to stay awake.

"Stay away from those smokers," the mother said to the children running around. "That means you, Fatima!" She singled out the more active of the two as they dutifully regrouped and came to sit with their mother. Everyone seemed so young to Susan. They could have been university students or artists somewhere if only they hadn't had this accident of birth. Most of the adults sitting around had their phones out, aimlessly flicking through one app or another to pass the time or perhaps to avoid the possibility of uncomfortable small talk with strangers. These phones were the only valuable items anyone in this room owned.

As people flipped through news stories on their phones, Susan wondered how they felt looking at the world through their vantage point as stateless, homeless refugees. Did they really understand how different their lives were from the carefree children running around parks in Berlin or by the beach in Barcelona? The advertisements on the websites were the strangest element of all. The people sitting in this room couldn't possibly understand the context of those smiling European families with clean clothes and straight hair telling these refugees to buy an Alexa or drive an Audi. Worse, these people had left their homes to save their own lives and the people in Europe and America feared them as though the refugees were the murderers, not Da'esh. Indeed, Susan imagined most of the families in this room had decided to leave because it was better to arm a child with an education far from home than to let Da'esh enslave the girls and make the boys into murderers, or worse.

All the politicians alive now would be dead in a hundred years. Children like these sitting on the floor could have the opportunity to provide a world of freedom and comfort for their own children. But those politicians seemed to be clinging to life, refusing to believe there was a future beyond their own and that death would come sooner or later. People wished they would just die already, instead of making a heaven on earth for themselves at the expense of everyone else who was living in hellish conditions from Iraq to Syria, from Iran to Palestine. What could these politicians teach the children?

They would be shaped by a lifetime of violence, destruction and despair. It was hard to imagine this was the reality.

Technology linked the world with the internet, worked miracles with medicine and solved the greatest paradoxes with science but bombs were still falling, bullets were still flying and lives were still ending, perhaps faster than ever before. It only took one Bin Laden to oversee an attack that killed three thousand innocents in a flash and only one al-Baghdadi to forge Da'esh into a force of evil like no other. Susan lamented the many young boys growing up in an environment defined by war, learning that the only way to be heard was to make the loudest noise and to silence everyone else.

Little Fatima walked over to Susan. She was skinny, too skinny for her age. Straight away Susan worried she wasn't eating enough but then again, no one in this building was.

"I wish I could bring my teddy," Fatima told Susan in Arabic.

Susan looked at Fatima, and then to her mother. "Sorry, I don't know enough Arabic to talk to her."

"It's ok," the mother said. "I'm Malika, and this is Fatima, my daughter. She's a good child. My little baby here is Lina." She motioned to the smiling baby in her lap.

"Fatima. That's a beautiful name."

"She was just telling you she wanted to bring her stuffed animal with her. She's telling everyone how she misses her teddy bear." She turned to Fatima. "Speak Kurdish, *habibti*, so the nice lady can understand you."

Fatima plopped down by Susan as though they were sisters. She scratched at the plastic rattan with her fingernails, staring at the floor but seeing something in her mind.

"I want my teddy. But Da'esh destroyed our home. My teddy stayed behind. He couldn't come with us. They put him in the dirt."

"Aw." Susan was unsure what to say. "You'll find another one."

Fatima exhaled in exasperation while Susan stroked her hair. Malika adjusted the fabric around the little toddler she was holding in her arms, reassuring the baby that she wasn't going anywhere.

Malika held her baby Lina's hand in her fingers, smiling down the baby's beaming face. "These three are my everything." Lina moved her hands and legs in the air happily, as if she understood her mother's praise. "*Habibti*, you brought happiness to all our lives." Malika kissed Lina's cheeks, listening to her daughter's joyful babbling. "I've lost a lot, and these three are all I have left." The baby smiled at her mother, beaming from the gentleness and care Malika wrapped around her. "Lina is a gift." She cradled Lina carefully in her arms, and Susan could see the connection between mother and daughter that was made of pure love.

"Aren't you scared of bringing them with you?" Susan was worried. "I mean, you are..." She stopped herself.

"These three are everything I have in this life," Malika replied, caressing her son's hair. "Once Lina was born, I told myself I would need to be even more careful, because it's not easy to raise girls in these countries. They have no rights, almost no existence because they are women instead of men. It is the best decision I could make to bring my children with me. *Inshallah*, we will begin anew as a family, far from this war and bloodshed."

Heja was now watching Susan and Malika, listening intently. He looked away when Susan saw him. One of the girls nearby had been listening, too, and she turned to look directly at Fatima.

"Good that you only lost your teddy," the girl said, gnawing away at a piece of chewing gum. "You still have your dignity. Lucky they didn't rape you."

Fatima said nothing, instead digging more feverishly into the rattan with her finger.

Susan looked at the girl and wondered what these people had seen, what they had been through and how they had suffered. What kind of life had they been through for that girl to suggest that raping a child was such a possibility?

The men who had been outside smoking started trickling back inside. They looked relieved, their stress and uncertainty temporarily ameliorated by the nicotine. It would come calling again soon enough. The guard followed them, resuming his monotonous patrol from one side of the room to the other. He noticed something and seemed to anchor his walking path to that side of the room more than a few times. Susan realised the guard was noticing the girl with matted brown hair who was staring into the distance in silence.

Despite being a smuggler overseeing a dozen people like slaves, the guard must have still had a little humanity in a corner of his soul. He was trying to find a way to speak to the girl, to comfort her somehow. The girl with the chewing gum noticed his attention. She sprang up and whispered something in the guard's ear. The guard nodded, pulling out a cigarette for her. She stuck the cigarette in the corner of her mouth, lighting it absentmindedly while she stared at the girl with matted hair who remained unmoving. She squinted as she took the first drag, blowing the smoke straight up to the ceiling.

Susan looked at the time. It was almost midnight. Malika took out small sandwiches from a backpack between Susan and herself. Everyone seemed to hear the crinkling of plastic wrapping that certainly meant food. Like zombies, half the room turned to see where the sound was coming from. Malika hastily gave Fatima one corner of a sandwich and then tucked the rest food away into a black plastic bag, hiding it from the prying eyes. The little girl excitedly danced as she took bites of the sandwich. The room full of observers each turned back to his own misery as the group finished watching the sandwich disappear into the girl's belly. Malika looked down at the ground, ashamed she had nothing to offer these hungry people.

Across the room, the girl with the chewing gum and the cigarette was gesturing wildly at the guard. They were arguing about something. The guard grabbed her by her sleeve and pushed her. "Sit! Sit down, Rima!"

"You can't tell me what to do, Amer!" Rima cursed at him and frowned, elbowing her way between two people as she sat.

The sound of a vehicle engine filled the room. A car must have pulled up outside. The engine sounded like it was labouring to stay running. A knock came from the door, in the same rhythm as the one the motorcyclist gave when he dropped Susan off earlier. A man wearing a *dishdasha* entered, followed by Mustafa. Their faces were grave, their movements mechanical. The room fell silent. All eyes were on the two men. It was time to move.

"Listen up," the man in the *dishdasha* said in Arabic. "My name is Abu Bayda."

"Do you know English," Susan asked the little boy sitting beside her.

"Yes," he whispered. "I can translate for you."

"This is not a vacation," Abu Bayda continued, his *dishdasha* moving with his gesturing hands. "You're a bunch of people running away from your homes. You're choosing to become criminals, outside of the law. Whatever Amer says, you will listen to him," he said, pointing at the guard. "Ala, our driver, will take you to a certain location and we are doing so on someone else's orders. Don't ask questions because we have no more information than this. It's for your security."

Amer nodded his head in confident approval, looking around the room at each face to ensure they understood.

"If you still owe us money, you must pay before you move, otherwise, start walking back home. God save you." Abu Bayda paused, thinking his check list through. "Also, place your cell phones in the bag by the door before you leave. It's for your own safety. And one more thing, you might need to show your identification card at a checkpoint. Don't panic. Show it like normal. If you don't have an identification card, Amer will give you one. Memorize it, become that person. Don't be an idiot. If the police take you, we cannot help you."

Mustafa smirked. Susan bristled at his apparent contempt for other human beings. "You!" Abu Bayda pointed at Malika with her three children seated beside Susan. "Tell your kids to keep their mouths shut. I don't want to hear a peep out of them. If they cry, whimper, whatever, we will leave you along the way."

His words reminded Susan of the speeches she'd seen from Da'esh videos before they were about to kill one of their prisoners. It seemed all humans were cut from the same cloth and would become evil at the first opportunity. Abu Bayda looked around the room.

"And men, control yourselves." He was pointing at the woman with his chin. The men laughed, some more earnestly than others. He then rested his eyes on Susan. "You! *Irani*. Come here."

Susan grabbed her bag and stood. The man motioned for her to follow him and she walked outside with him into the courtyard. Mustafa followed, too. He was sipping tea from a paper cup, balancing a cigarette in between his fingers and the cup.

"You got the rest of the money?" Mustafa asked.

"Yes, I have it." She was annoyed that he didn't even say hello before demanding something from her. She grabbed the little envelope out of her bag and handed it to him. Abu Bayda grabbed it, took the cash out and began counting. It was clear he was higher in the smuggler hierarchy than Mustafa. He muttered incoherently while he counted. Mustafa sat down on a wobbly stool, watching Susan's crotch the whole time. Susan felt like insects were crawling on her.

"Listen," Mustafa said, still staring at her legs. "We took a big risk taking you with us. You should be very careful. You're Iranian. They're looking for people like you. We've never moved an Iranian before. If they find out your nationality at one of these checkpoints, your head will be cut from your body before you can figure out if it was Da'esh or someone else. Do you understand? Trust no one." He finished his cigarette and flicked it into the darkness. Maybe even one of the people in your escape group may betray you. Don't tell anyone your nationality. Speak no Farsi. Become someone else. All our lives depend on it."

He rifled through his pocket and pulled out a stack of identification cards. He sorted through them for a moment under the light bulb hanging from the wall. The cards all had blurry faces that could really match anyone. Some of the cards were blank. He picked one out that looked something like Susan, or at least like a Middle Eastern girl through a blurred lens.

"Here, this looks like you. Take it. She's you."

Susan took the card and squinted at it. The photo was foggy and the woman's facial features were too soft to be anyone in particular. Susan read the name aloud. "Yara Asfour"

"Yes, very good."

"But she's not Kurdish. The name looks Arab. I can get by in Kurdish but not Arabic."

"Tell them you're a Syrian Kurd. Forget it, it's not important. They'll tell you."

A LULLABY IN THE DESERT

Before Susan had time to ask who *they* were, Mustafa was standing up and moving towards the truck parked outside the compound. The others were placing their phones into the black pouch by the door. Reluctantly, she looked down at the identification card and began memorizing everything she could about Yara Asfour.

Chapter Fourteen

The rickety old truck was stuffed with people. The back had been covered with cloth and there was a kind of frame keeping the fabric in place, making it twice as hot inside than it was outside in the desert heat. Women sat in the far back, while men were stacked like sardines toward the front. Susan estimated the truck was designed to hold a maximum of twelve people but it probably had two dozen squashed in as it bumped along over neglected roads into the unknown.

Abu Bayda, Amer, and Ala sat in the cab up front and were dressed to look like a regular family just traveling from one place to another across the desert. Ala, the driver, wore a black *dishdasha* and had a beard with no moustache. He looked scary to Susan but she knew he had a good chance of passing through the checkpoints with such an appearance. Amer, the young guard that had been patrolling like a hall monitor earlier was now seated in the middle between Abu Bayda and Ala. Beneath their feet lay a prayer rug, a spare tire and some tools. No one in the back could see through the fabric but they could hear the smugglers chattering up front. The refugees had gone from a stationary prison in the compound to a moving prison in the back of a Bongo truck.

Everyone seemed to relax a little now that the guards were in a separate space and the fabric around them blocked out the outside world. Some of the refugees began speaking quietly amongst each other. Malika held her kids a little looser but didn't quite let go. Her son was probably less than ten years old, though he had his arms crossed and was watching over his sisters as if he was their father. A little light attached to an exposed wire hung from the top of the cabin, casting a yellowish glow over everyone and air was stifling inside the cabin. Heja would periodically open the fabric to let in fresh air even though they had been instructed not to do so. The fumes of brunt petrol would waft in but at least it was cooler.

Rima was now seated next to another teenaged boy who seemed to take a liking to her. Susan watched the boy lean over to the Yazidi girl.

"What's your name?"

The Yazidi girl ignored him. Every time the truck went over a bump, she discovered that the boy miraculously moved closer. She looked around haughtily and ignored him completely. The boy looked down at his feet while she edged away and said nothing.

"Ashwaq, don't let him bother you," the older Yazidi woman said to the girl in Kurdish, so the boy wouldn't understand.

"How can he not bother me, Dalal? He's practically on top of me."

Susan thought about how silly such a game was. Men in the taxis in Iran would do the same thing except they weren't innocent. They thought they were slick. They would spread their legs wide, forced the woman sharing the taxi with them to be in contact with their body the whole way. Then the men would lean over and invade the woman's space completely. Susan didn't miss that at all.

Little Fatima was sitting in between her mother's legs, napping while sitting upright. Her head bobbed with the rhythm of the truck. A particularly large bump pulled her out of her dreams. She looked around with eyes half open.

Susan smiled at her. "Come here," she said. "Sleep in my arms." The mother mouthed her thanks to Susan and stretched a little as Fatima got up and went to Susan, hugging her tight like she'd known her for years. Susan put her scarf around Fatima's head to muffle some of the roaring engine sound coming from the front of the truck.

Susan continued to be fascinated by the different lives all brought together in this stuffy truck. She watched one of the men on the other side of the cabin who sat beside a teenaged boy. The boy would periodically reach out to find the man's hand and he would lean over to listen to the boy speak. Two other boys were sleeping against each other in a corner. As the night went on, they kept each other warm while the wind whipped through the fabric walls. Susan became aware of her own chills and wrapped her scarf more tightly around herself and Fatima. She looked down at Fatima, a harmless, innocent child deprived of her home, her life and her precious teddy. Maybe she was dreaming of her life before the storm. She nudged her head gently against Susan's chest, then tightened her little arms and muttered quietly.

"Do you have a cigarette?" Rima asked loudly to Heja. She seemed to want everyone around her to be involved in her request. Heja shook his head, frowning.

Susan couldn't believe how selfish this girl was, wanting to smoke inside a confined cabin with children and with air saturated with gasoline fumes. But Rima wasn't alone in her selfishness. A man gave her a cigarette, quickly followed by his lighter. Heja glared at her as she blew smoke throughout the cabin.

"Switch places with me," he said to Rima. "The smoke will bother the kids."

She glared at him, offended. "Nah, I'm fine." Her words were tinged with disdain and hung in the air along with her smoke.

Something about Rima made people nervous and no one dared speak up, even though children were suffering because of the smoke she bellowed in their faces. It seemed she was looking for a fight and her fellow passengers were too exhausted to grant one. The little boy coughed, choking on smoke. Malika glared at her, sending a silent message, but Rima leaned back, seeming to enjoy her cigarette even more. She grabbed a bottled water from Ashwaq, downing the whole thing in dramatic fashion. She put her cigarette butt into the water bottle and put it back on the floor beside the two Yazidis.

"Who gave you permission to drink my water?" Ashwaq demanded.

"Permission?" Rima asked, laughing.

"Yes, permission." Ashwaq retorted.

Rima and Ashwaq acquiesced, glaring at each other silently with burning eyes.

Malika looked down at her little baby. "Sleep, my dear Lina."

"Did we arrive?" Fatima fidgeted uncomfortably, perhaps jealous of her mother's attention to her infant sister

"Soon, sweetheart. Soon." She kissed Fatima's hands. "Close your eyes and count to a hundred."

"A hundred?" Susan asked, playfully interrupting them. Malika and Susan both smiled, sharing a sparkle of hope in their moment of levity.

Everyone's shoulders bounced along in unison as the truck barrelled along down the highway leading west out of Erbil towards their future. Growing tired, Susan looked down at the worn-out watch on her wrist but it no longer seemed to be working. She didn't want to totally lose herself in her sleep in a truck full of men separated only by the distance between their clothes. Heja pulled the fabric aside to steal a glance of the outside world passing by in streaked shades of black and grey. They could have been on the moon and Susan wouldn't have been able to tell.

Trying to stay awake, Susan watched Ashwaq tuck her legs under her after placing her bag between herself and the man beside her. She was staring straight ahead as if sleep would never find her. It was clear this woman was not only worried by the men in her vicinity but also by the men in her past, and perhaps those who awaited her in the future. Ashwaq didn't dare let her guard down. Susan wondered what she had been through, and perhaps what they would all go through together now that they shared their fate in this war.

Susan was getting hungry but little Fatima was sprawled peacefully across her chest. Susan didn't want to disturb her sleep. Carefully leaning forward to retrieve a sandwich from her bag, she stopped when Fatima shifted suddenly. She could wait to eat. Susan let her fatigue wash over her as her eyes became heavy. She leaned her head back against the metal pole and began letting herself fall asleep. With half open eyes, she watched the boy across from her fumbling with his bag.

Just as her eyes were falling shut, the truck stopped suddenly, thrusting everyone forward on top of each other. Fatima immediately began wailing loudly. No one knew what was going on, why the truck had stopped. The smugglers in the front tightened the fabric separating their cab from the cabin in the back. The cabin was a smothering cell and the darkness amplified the notion that they were all in trouble.

"Shh, keep calm," Malika whispered to her children. But now little Lina started crying, too. Rima cursed under her breath and stared at anyone making the slightest noise. Everyone looked around nervously, waiting for something to happen.

Without warning the fabric was torn away from the metal frame around the truck cabin and light poured in. Some smiles appeared with the dawn light and fresh air but all hope vanished the moment everyone saw what was unfolding before them. Abu

Bayda was standing behind the truck. He looked like a ghost or a movie villain. Susan felt her heart thumping in her chest.

"Get down from there!" he shouted. "*Yalla*, get down out of the truck now!"

Everyone complied in silence, except baby Lina who continued crying. All were acutely aware of their vulnerability, with no control over what would happen to them. Abu Bayda was pushing people along to make them move faster out of the truck's cabin. The father and son carefully dismounted the truck and walked to a large rock. Amer stood nearby, watching everyone dismount. He noticed the crying baby and he stroked his beard as if on the verge of a decision.

"Shut her mouth," Amer said angrily to Malika.

The little baby's face was like a cherry and her eyes were swollen with tears. Susan poured a little water into a cap for her and drizzled it in her mouth. The baby calmed a little and her breathing relaxed. Fatima and her little brother gripped their mother's clothes with their hands, bundling it in their fists as though they anticipated being torn away. Everyone assembled behind the big rock, crouching down into the black dirt as ants and flies scurried around in agitation at these unwanted intruders. This was a place where only venomous snakes and the carnivorous grey wolf were welcome.

The group of refugees clung tightly to one another, for a moment no longer separated by the social boundaries between strangers. They couldn't be sure if the truck had a flat tire or if they had been stopped by a criminal gang worse than the smugglers who now held their lives in the balance. In true form, Rima lit up a cigarette, exposing everyone to discovery and danger in order to satisfy herself. Susan admired her fearlessness but loathed the selfish way in which she wielded it.

One of the men couldn't hold himself any longer and he ran to another large rock a few meters away. Everyone turned their heads to follow him with their eyes, waiting to see why he had so brazenly run across the open dirt. The sound of his pants unzipping gave everyone their answer, causing the women to quickly look away to give him privacy he certainly seemed not to need. A few others joined him, taking the opportunity to empty their bladders at the risk of being captured by marauding Da'esh fighters or gangs that could be anywhere in this desert.

Susan stole a glance at the truck's tires, thinking the truck maybe had a flat. All the tires looked full and no one was near the truck. Heja noticed Susan's glances and seemed to share her concern. He edged himself toward her.

"Did you see anything? What are they doing?" he asked in fluent English with a tinge of a Kurdish accent. His choice of language caught Susan off guard. Somehow it worried her. She wondered why such an educated boy was escaping, and from whom. But that's what people must have thought about her too.

"It's not very clear," Susan said finally. "There are three guys standing some distance from the truck. One is on his phone."

Heja craned his neck to see over the rock, trying to get a better view.

"You're right," he said. "It's impossible to see what's going on." He stood up. "I'll go ask them. Maybe we can help."

"Are you out of your mind, Heja?" one of the men asked, tugging the boy's clothes to force him down. "Didn't you hear what Abu Bayda said? We are to wait here."

Heja immediately sat down. "Sorry, Hadi. I just wanted to help."

Amer whistled, then shouted. "Rima!" Rima stood immediately, dusted her pants off, shouldered her bag tightly and walked directly to him. Susan couldn't hear what they were saying to each other, but it seemed like an argument. Rima threw her hands up in protest at whatever Amer was trying to say. Abu Bayda joined the argument, pushing Rima by the shoulder and pointing at the group of refugees huddled by the rock. Headlights appeared over the horizon, quickly moving toward them.

Rima ran over to the group of worried refugees.

"*Yalla*," Rima shouted as she unzipped her bag. "Wear these." She started handing out black *abayas* to all the women older than thirteen. "Hurry up!"

The women quietly obeyed, pulling the black flowing cloth over their clothes. It didn't matter whether the women were Yazidi, Kurd, Assyrian, or any other minority. They were in Da'esh territory now, governed by an interpretation of Islam that forced all women to submit to men and cover themselves like unwanted slaves, treated as subhuman animals, regardless of their own beliefs. Rima put her finger to her nose to ensure everyone knew to be silent, especially the little ones. The sound of crunching sand and rocks grew louder as a new vehicle approached. No one could get a good look from where they hid. The boy grasped for his father's hands. All eyes darted about fearfully.

Ashwaq and Dalal gripped each other's hands tightly. It was clear they had been through a lot together already. Susan wondered if they were the same Yazidi girls that she had heard about on Kurdistan's *Rudaw* news channel right before she left Erbil. The story was about three Yazidi girls taken from Sinjar by Da'esh fighters and forced into sex slavery for a month before they bravely tried to mount an escape. One of the girls was shot in the head and killed before she could get away but the other two succeeded. They had to leave their sister's body behind as they fled to the mountains near Dohuk until the Peshmerga rescued them.

Da'esh spun intense propaganda against the Yazidi culture

because they lacked the capacity to understand any belief system different to their own narrative of death, rape and destruction. Da'esh seemed to conserve their worst animalistic tendencies for the Yazidis, they attempted to execute every Yazidi male they found in northern Iraq, while all captured Yazidi women were forced to convert to Islam and become Da'esh sex slaves. Thousands had already succumbed to this fate and thousands more were soon to follow as Da'esh expanded its grip across Syria and Iraq. Da'esh taught that Yazidis worshipped Satan because the Yazidis believed in a special angel called Melek Taus, a spirit in the form of a peacock that was sent to earth with a retinue of other angels to watch over mankind.

Susan craned her neck to see around the side of the stone she hid behind. A white Isuzu pickup truck pulled up to the smuggler's Bongo. The Isuzu looked older than Susan. The men standing in the back of the pickup moved a little and Susan could see the morning light glinting off the barrel of a PKM machine gun mounted on a spindle welded to the truck's body. Golden bullets in a long, wavy belt fed into the machine gun, patiently awaiting their resting place in human flesh. All the faces were wrapped beneath black scarves. Two men carried AK-47s and another had an M4 carbine with a brown strap over his shoulder, attached to an M79 grenade launcher with a wooden handle slung behind his back. The man with the M4 seemed to be in charge and he menacingly glared at the smugglers with his bandoliers of grenades crossed over another belt of 7.62 mm bullets shimmering across his chest like medals. One of the men hoisted a black flag up behind the truck's cabin. It had a white circle in the middle with some Arabic writing. Susan realised at once that today she'd meet a Da'esh fighter in person and she became paralyzed with fear.

One of the lackeys with an AK-47 jumped down from the truck. He had to be a teenager - he was too small to be an adult. Susan couldn't see his face, so it was hard to tell for sure. All the fighters looked dirty, ragged and agitated. It was as if their piety could only be expressed through how dirty they were willing to get.

Abu Bayda took the initiative. "*Salam aleykom*," he said, greeting the young Da'esh fighter. Ala and Amer glanced nervously back and forth from the Isuzu full of bloodthirsty religious fanatics to the Bongo that had just contained a dozen apostates.

"What are you doing here?" the young Da'esh fighter asked. He began walking around the perimeter of the Bongo truck, looking for something.

"*Wallah*. Our car broke down," Abu Bayda calmly assured them.

One of the Da'esh fighters still in the Isuzu kept a steady gaze on the smugglers while he flicked the ashes of a cigarette out the window. Susan thought it was ironic that these supposedly pious defenders of Islam who had banned cigarettes were now smoking them.

The rules must be flexible when you've got the guns, Susan thought to herself.

The young fighter stopped in front of the Bongo, reading the license plate. The Bongo had fake license plates for Ninawa Province in Iraq to help it blend in. It would be a death sentence to drive a car with Kurdistan plates into Da'esh territory.

"Where are you coming from?" the fighter demanded.

"Mosul," Abu Bayda replied.

"You're coming from Mosul, or you're going there?"

"We came from Mosul. We're heading to the border at Al Qaim to pick up our mother. She's waiting there. She went to Syria for medical treatment."

The young fighter stared at Abu Bayda and said nothing. The

Da'esh fighter smoking in the Isuzu decided to jump out and join in. He walked over and stood beside the young fighter. Looking around, he started walking toward the big rock where Susan and the rest were hiding. Amer immediately walked over to him and offered him a cigarette.

The man turned and stared at Amer. Amer continued holding his hand feebly in the air, though he clearly regretted offering it. Susan tightened the abaya around her head and crouched as low as she could. Everyone was silent. It seemed the Da'esh fighters, the smugglers and the refugees were all an audience now waiting for the drama to unfold between Amer and the Da'esh leader glaring at him.

Susan's heartbeat was rapidly increasing, and she was sure everyone else's was too. Rima glanced around at the refugees and put her finger to her lips again, ensuring everyone knew to stay absolutely silent. If Da'esh discovered them, all would be lost. The men would be killed, the women raped. Susan knew each person here had reason to be afraid, whether Christian, Yazidi or Muslim. She was also acutely aware that her Iranian nationality was only just less dangerous than being Yazidi. Da'esh was violently intolerant to Shi'a Muslims like Susan and she had heard many stories of fellow Shi'a captured by Da'esh and subjected to crucifixions, beheadings and death by stoning, a fate shared with the Yazidis and Muslims who had converted to Christianity. On Iran's state-run television channels that piped into Kurdistan, the Iranians fighting Da'esh in Iraq promised to rescue those captured but Susan knew they couldn't.

Looking down at Fatima sleeping peacefully in her arms, Susan silently brushed away a fly dancing on the little girl's face. Malika was watching them both and Susan realised that she carried not only the fate of her own life but that of this little child's until the danger passed.

The Da'esh leader plucked the cigarette from Amer's quivering hand. He crushed it slowly in his left hand, while he kept his right hand resting on the collapsible buttstock of his M4. After all the tobacco had floated to the ground, he threw the white wrapper at Amer's face. Amer winced.

"Do you know the penalty for smoking cigarettes?" asked the Da'esh leader who had been smoking not five minutes earlier.

"Forgive me," Amer said, shaking visibly. "I saw one in your hand, that's why I offered you one. I found it on the road and was going to give it to you. It wasn't mine."

The Da'esh leader yanked the charging handle back on his M4, chambering a round. Susan saw Amer freeze, as though petrified. Rima was shaking now too and was visibly worried about Amer. Suddenly it became clear that Rima was not a refugee after all but was one of the smugglers, probably Amer's sister. She must have been inserted into the group to keep an eye on everyone.

The Da'esh leader grabbed Amer by the shirt and shoved him to the ground. "Aren't you a Muslim?" he shouted angrily, his face mask billowing slightly with the pressure of his voice.

"Yes." Amer said weakly, his voice shaking. Abu Bayda and Ala ran to Amer.

The young Da'esh fighter that had been searching the car seemed to be growing frustrated. He kicked the tire and then tore some papers and cloth from the front seat, throwing it all onto the ground. He seemed to be looking for something valuable to steal rather than evidence of anything nefarious. Making his way to the back of the Bongo, he tore out the tools and jack, tossing them onto the ground.

"The three of you, kneel down," the Da'esh leader instructed Amer, Ala and Abu Bayda. His voice was devoid of emotion but full of authority. "Put your hands behind your heads. *Yalla!*" the Da'esh leader shouted. "Empty your pockets in front of you."

The three men obeyed, discarding pieces of paper, some money, keys, a lighter and their identification cards. The Da'esh leader kicked the items around on the ground with his foot, still clinging tightly to his rifle. One of the Da'esh fighters came over and picked up their identification cards. He tried bending them and he held them up to the light, then ran his fingers across them, trying to see if they were counterfeit.

The refugees' silent concentration was broken by an almost imperceptible whimper. Everyone hiding behind the rock looked at the young offender and then down at his feet. A brown snake was slithering past, evidently just as scared of these intruders as they were of Da'esh. Malika could see the fear in her son's eyes and she motioned to him to stay calm and not to move. Ashwaq and Dalal clung to each other and stared at Malika. Everyone feared the snake but they feared being caught by Da'esh even more.

Meanwhile, Abu Bayda reluctantly took a wad of money wrapped in an elastic from his pocket and placed it on the ground. The Da'esh leader bent over immediately and snatched it up. He stuffed it into his clothing and leaned back. It seemed this was what he had been looking for. He said something to the young Da'esh fighter and the boy went over to the Bongo to remove the plastic gas can that was strapped to the side. The boy carried the can over with both hands, trying to look strong but clearly struggling to carry the weight. The Da'esh fighter that had stayed beside the machine gun in the Isuzu jumped out and started filming with his phone.

"Pour it on this *kafir*," the leader said, pointing to Amer. The young Da'esh fighter quickly complied, as thought he was doing Amer a favour. Amer began pleading and praying and the other two smugglers started pleading along with him. They begged for forgiveness, for Amer's life, for mercy.

"He's so young," Abu Bayda pleaded. "Please, take me instead."

Amer was babbling a *zikr* prayer and crying, his tears mixing with the gas dripping from his head.

The Da'esh leader picked up the lighter Amer had placed on the ground in front of him. He lit it and threw it at Amer. Flames roared immediately, consuming Amer. Screams from all three smugglers blended together as if they were all burning alive. Amer began running blindly, trying in vain to extinguish himself. The Da'esh men proceeded to take all the tools from the Bongo, along with the rest of the gasoline and food that was in the back of the truck. They loaded their Isuzu as if oblivious to the fact that Amer was on fire and dying behind them.

The screams and wails became too much for Fatima and she began crying. Rima jumped on her immediately and covered her face with a cloth to silence her.

The Da'esh leader stopped loading the truck and motioned for everyone to be quiet. "Stop. Did you hear that?" He looked at the young Da'esh fighter. "Did you search everywhere?"

"Yes *sidi*," the boy said dutifully.

"Did you see anything strange?"

"No *sidi*." The boy thought he heard the crying too but his mind was hazy from the hashish and Captagon he had come to rely upon to make his job as a Da'esh rule enforcer bearable. He had thought that the crying wasn't real. It couldn't be real. He stared at Amer's motionless body, by now curled into the foetal position as the flames freed him from this life. The other two smugglers were still kneeling but were bent all the way forward, covering their faces and weeping. The Da'esh leader looked down at the two men burying their heads in their hands.

"You should thank Allah we are sending these *kuffars* to hell. You are lucky there are brave, strong men like us to fight *jihad* and save your souls. Allah sent us to cleanse this land of the apostates and non-believers. Everyone gets what they deserve. We will never stop our mission. Thanks to Allah," he said, kissing his prayer beads. "Allah is great, Allah is great."

He snapped his fingers and motioned with his head toward the Isuzu. All the fighters mounted the truck and prepared to leave. The members of Da'esh had been promised virgins in heaven and all the wealth they could ever want in the afterlife as long as they carried out God's will. It just so happened that God's will was dictated by men even more depraved than the ones carrying out the executions, rapes and destruction from Palmyra to Mosul. With a little Captagon in their systems, it was like God's spirit entered their bodies and made it easy to kill women, children, or even themselves. Today they had gotten what they came for. One more sinner was dead and the fighters had even gotten some cash for their troubles of liquidating his soul. The fighters all shut the Isuzu doors, the engine revved and they tore off into the desert toward their next opportunity.

As soon as the truck became a tiny dot on the horizon, the refugees and the other smugglers ran over to Amer's body, still smouldering, with his clothes having melted onto his skin. Everyone began weeping and crying. Some of the refugees helped to throw dirt on Amer's body to try to put the remaining flames out and cool him. The fire was extinguished, but so was Amer.

Rima collapsed beside the charred remains. No part of the body was untouched. She grasped at clods of dirt from the ground, throwing them on her head, weeping uncontrollably, striking the ground with her fist over and over.

"Why? Why should my brother die for a twisted fantasy? Da'esh has covered the earth in blood, my brother's blood." She continued weeping, while Ala tried to comfort her and Heja put a cloth over her shoulders.

Malika covered baby Lina's face but she couldn't look away. The group was in shock. For a moment there were no smugglers, no refugees, no different religions. At that moment, everyone grieved for another human being lost to the desert. Abu Bayda carefully picked Rima up and walked her away from the body while she continued sobbing. Ashwaq brought Rima some water, pouring a little on her parched lips and washing some of the dirt away from her cheeks. Rima stared listlessly at the men as they began digging a hasty grave with their bare hands.

"Rima," Abu Bayda said. "You know you can't return to bury him back in Kurdistan. If you do, they'll kill us all."

"There is nothing left," Rima said without moving her eyes. "There is barely a body left to bury."

The smugglers and the refugees stood together over the shallow grave. The Muslims in the group said *zikr* and *salat* prayers, while the Christians drew crosses over their chests and the Yazidis prayed his soul would be reborn into a better life. The men lowered the body into the grave and began covering it with fresh dirt. Rima kissed the necklace she had been carrying as a gift for Amer's birthday. She hadn't had the chance to give it to him and now she never would. Amer had died the same day he was born.

Chapter Fifteen

The smugglers were supposed to be taking the refugees from Erbil through Ninawa and Al Anbar into the vast desert of western Iraq. This area was now nominally under the governance of Da'esh's new caliphate but the western desert was too expansive for anyone to maintain real control, which Saddam Hussein had learned decades before. The smugglers would cross the Euphrates River near the Syrian border where Al Qaim and Abu Kamal met on opposite sides of the Iraq-Syria border. Then they'd head into the unforgiving Syrian Desert known as the Badiyat ash-Sham. Unlike the Iraqi desert, Da'esh had full and complete control over Al Qaim, Abu Kamal and nearly every population centre northward snaking along the Euphrates River in Syria, all the way to their Syrian capital in Raqqa. The refugees thought they'd be going to the Turkish border and then on to Greece and further into Europe. But the road seemed to be taking them deeper into Da'esh territory and everyone was asking themselves the same question, if Amer was the first casualty, who would be next?

Yet again, everyone was piled on top of one another in the back of the Bongo truck. This time it was a silent ride and everyone wore faces of stone. Ashwaq and Dalal sat on either side of Rima, trying to comfort her. It was quiet enough that Susan could just about overhear parts of a conversation between Abu Bayda and Ala sitting up front in the cab.

"We have to," Abu Bayda was saying to Ala.

"But Da'esh owns that area, they'll kill us."

"Listen to me. You know they captured one of our guys before we left. If they get him to talk, and you know they will, he'll tell Da'esh which checkpoints we were planning to pass through. We can't risk going through those same ones now. It's too dangerous. We've got to assume he talked. We must take a route they won't be expecting. And they definitely won't be expecting us to drive straight through their territory."

Susan was trying hard to listen, to understand what the smugglers were planning. They had the refugees' lives in their hands and they wanted to take them straight into the lion's den. At that moment, Susan noticed Heja also listening to the smugglers. Susan looked at him and he locked eyes with her while continuing to keep his ear to the fabric to pick up the conversation.

"Excuse me. Excuse me sir," Heja said through the fabric to the men in the front. "Can we please stop? I need to use the toilet."

"This isn't a tour bus," came Abu Bayda's voice. Heja sat back, disappointed. A few moments passed and the voice came through the curtain again. "Fine, we'll stop, but you get two minutes maximum."

The Bongo truck stopped and the fabric was pulled away from the rear of the cabin. Bright daylight flooded in. Heja made his way over the arms, legs and layers of people stacked tightly in the cabin. He jumped out and Abu Bayda put his hand on Heja's shoulder.

"You are going to have to do it under my supervision. We can't take any more risks."

Heja walked with him a little distance from the truck. He tried for a few moments to relieve himself but it was difficult with the man's hand firmly planted on his shoulder. Finally, he was able to go. After zipping his pants, he looked up at the man. "Where are you taking us?"

"What do you mean where?"

"I know you aren't taking us the right way. I heard you."

"You little rat. Don't you dare say another word."

"I promise I won't, but only if you tell me the truth."

"Fine. We're going to Turkey but we're going a different way than we planned. We have to go through some rough areas, but trust me, it's better than if we get caught at a checkpoint."

The smugglers were going to drag them into the most dangerous place on earth because they couldn't come up with a better plan. Heja blinked in disbelief.

"You lied to a dozen people! You promised us you'd take us to Europe. Now you're taking us into the fire. You put every one of our lives at risk! How could we expect Da'esh to let us be after what they just did? They killed one of your own people! The killed him in front of our eyes. Do you really think it's wise to go even deeper into their territory?"

"Shut up." Abu Bayda tapped his silver 45 calibre pistol menacingly. "You talk, you die. Don't say a word to anyone. Now get back to the Bongo. *Yalla!*"

Heja reluctantly walked back to the truck and climbed inside. He took his seat across from Susan and looked at her. Susan could tell something was wrong. Heja felt like he had a ton of bricks on his shoulders and he wanted desperately to tell someone what he knew. But sharing his secret could cost him his life. He didn't know what to do. He looked at Rima. He felt that maybe he could tell her but she was resting her head against Dalal's shoulder and he decided not to disturb her. Instead, he disappeared into his own thoughts. He learned a long time ago that this was the only way to truly escape.

The truck started moving again, rumbling down the road and jumbling everyone around. The *abayas* were all bouncing in unison as the truck picked up speed along the bumpy road. Susan suddenly became aware of her hunger. She decided it was time to try having her sandwich again. She reached over Fatima, sleeping again in her lap, and pulled the bagged sandwich out of her backpack. The sound of the plastic grabbed everyone's attention. A dozen hungry eyes zeroed in on her sandwich. She felt bad because she wanted to offer everyone something but she barely had enough to feed herself. The smell of the cold cuts hung in the air, overpowering the fumes for a moment. Mouths were watering. Rima snapped back to reality for a moment, back to the old Rima that had been a force to be reckoned with. But something had changed in her. Her brother's death made her show some empathy as she used her confidence to help others instead of herself.

"Let her eat her food!" Rima said angrily.

"She can eat it," Hadi said. "No one said anything."

"Your eyes say it all, you're practically drooling. Don't be an animal. You're making her uncomfortable."

Hadi looked down at his feet. "Sorry. Please, eat."

Susan nibbled at her sandwich, trying to keep it out of view as much as she could. Even though Rima stood up for her, she didn't want to make anyone suffer by watching her eat. Little Fatima opened her eyes and looked up at Susan. Susan gave her a corner of the sandwich and smiled. She felt for a moment like a mother taking care of her baby. The memory of her own mother flooded her mind. Where was she now? Did she miss her? She tried to remember her mother's voice but it was only an echo in her memory. The bites she took stuck in her throat. She pressed her eyes shut. Was she swallowing food, or her tears?

The faces of her brother, her sister, her father, her mother, all passed in front of her. She wondered what had become of them, whether her mother's illness had gotten the better of her. She longed to hug her mother, she missed her smell, her warmth, her voice. Susan looked at the mother sitting with her three children in the back of the truck, now heading to Syria. Susan's own mother had sent her away and this mother in front of her had taken all three of her children regardless of the danger, no matter the cost. Susan wanted to believe that her mother's prayers were keeping her safe, that her mother was thinking of her at all.

She looked at Hadi, who had yelled at Heja to sit down when they were hiding from the Da'esh fighters. He looked to be about thirty years old and he was probably someone's father. She thought about her own father, wondered where he was and if he was still sitting around on the floor with his friends, ordering her mother around. Susan wondered if her father slept well at night knowing he was torturing his own sick wife. He certainly seemed pleased with himself, unmoved by the black eyes and the bruises he had given her mother, all the while taking the money for her medicine to spend on drugs. The week before Susan had left Tehran forever, her father had taken forty thousand tomans from her mother, which was part of a donation meant for the whole family. Susan knew he would never change and she hoped to never waste another thought on him.

She put the unfinished sandwich back in her backpack. She had lost her appetite. Leaning back against the fabric, she closed her eyes. No one was speaking. Hadi continued staring at his feet. The man seated beside Hadi carefully took out a date and passed it to him quickly.

"Thank you, Ahmad. I'm so hungry," Hadi said as he took the date and began nibbling on it.

It seemed that no one dared show the others that they had food. Susan could feel the truck tilting upward, driving through what must have been steep hills. The road felt worse and worse beneath them as they continued. Susan heard the driver whispering nervous *zikr* prayers to himself. He seemed to slow a little, perhaps trying not to flip the truck over the side of an unseen hillside.

"Don't you dare fall asleep!" Abu Bayda snarled to the driver. "It may be six in the morning but it will be your last morning if this car goes off the road."

Susan opened her eyes. Heja was looking through the slit in the fabric, letting in the morning light. He was straining to hear the smugglers up front, just like Susan.

"They're bastards," he said. Susan looked at him without replying.

Heja could see the hills growing into mountains outside. They were almost certainly near the border. He looked at his watch and guessed that they reach Al Qaim in under two hours. He wanted to wake everyone up and shout to the ceiling that they were being led into a death trap. But he thought twice since telling them wouldn't change anything, except perhaps earning himself a bullet in the head. Still, Heja knew he would never forgive himself if something happened to all these innocent people stacked like livestock in a cattle car.

Susan saw the worry on Heja's face. She could tell he knew something, could tell he was battling with something. She knew because she often felt the same. She guessed Heja had made Abu Bayda stop the car so they could talk about something, something that couldn't be said near anyone else. Susan wanted to have the same talk with Abu Bayda. She wanted to find out what he told Heja that had made Heja so concerned. She pulled the fabric back that separated them from the cabin. Aghast, she saw both the men's heads bobbing. They were falling asleep while everyone in the back was oblivious.

"Oh my God!" Susan shouted. She banged the cab frame with her hand to try to get Ala's attention before he went off the road.

They had been lucky they were going slow and that the road was straight enough that the truck hadn't flipped and killed them all. "*Sidi*! *Sidi*! Wake up!"

All the other refugees roused to attention, thinking Da'esh had returned. Malika knew what was happening and she started banging on the cab too, until Ala awakened fully. He came to his senses and stopped the car. Everyone was cursing and shouting in confusion. One by one, everyone jumped out of the truck. By now they realised Ala had been asleep and had almost killed them all. They were livid, shouting and clamouring to get at him.

Abu Bayda was furious at their brazen confidence, which threatened his position of power. "Shut up you bastards! All of you, shut up!" He pulled his gun out and fired three shots into the air and then levelled his gun, moving it horizontally in front each frozen face in front of him. He had his power back.

The father who had been helping his blind son suddenly stepped forward. "That woman's brother is dead, and now you want to kill us? Better you stayed asleep and we'd all be dead, including you. Did we pay you to take our lives?"

"You better watch yourself!"

The father and Abu Bayda continued shouting back and forth at one another. The rest of the group stood behind the father, supporting him with their presence but saying and doing nothing else.

The man's son stood beside Susan. He was shaking and staring at an invisible point far away.

Susan gently touched the boy's shoulders to let him know he had a friend beside him.

"What's your name?" Susan asked in the best Arabic she could muster. The boy said nothing but shook a little less. He was looking around to find the voice. Susan held his hands in hers and asked, "Can you see me?" The boy shook his head. Susan started to feel worried.

"Where is my dad?" the boy asked finally.

"That's your father? The one that's been next to you this whole time?"

"Yes. Look, please don't tell anyone I'm blind. If the smugglers know, they'll throw me out for sure. I'm dead weight."

"Don't worry, I won't," Susan said calmly, still holding his hands. The boy's father continued arguing with Abu Bayda.

Ala jumped out of the car. He looked fearsome, just like the Da'esh fighters they were escaping from. He walked right up to the father arguing with Abu Bayda and pushed him. "That's it!" Spittle flying from his mouth landing on the father's shirt. "Get back in the car or we're leaving your ass here!"

The father lost his balance and fell on the ground, bracing himself with both palms. Some of the other men helped him stand. He was furious. "You have no right to treat us like animals!" He turned to the refugees standing in a half circle around him and the smugglers. "Look! They've been lying to you!" He pointed west, toward the hills. "Do you see those hills? That's the border. That's where they're taking us. That's Da'esh territory." He turned and fearlessly faced Abu Bayda. "In fact, you are Da'esh. You are taking us to be leverage for your own lives!"

The group was silent and so were the smugglers. Everyone was shocked. Abu Bayda grimaced, staring at the man who had just questioned his honour. Without hesitation, he raised the gun, held his arm steady and pulled the trigger. The father's head caved, his body slackened and pink mist exploded backward, as droplets of blood splattered those standing around him. His body collapsed to the ground into an unnatural position only achieved in the moment of an unexpected death.

The blind son ran immediately towards the sound of the gunshot. He could tell what happened. He didn't need to see to know. "Dad, daddy," he cried.

Susan collapsed in tears. She couldn't see anything around her. What was happening to her? What was happening to all of them?

Abu Bayda slowly pointed the gun at each person standing paralyzed before him. "Will you be silent now or do I need to silence you forever? That's right. We're going to Syria. If you have a problem, tell me. I will make things very easy for you. Otherwise, the questions stop here. Do you understand?" No one said a word. The boy was holding his father's limp body in his arms as he rocked back and forth, sobbing. "I asked if you understood!" Abu Bayda shouted. Everyone slowly nodded. "Good! Get back in the truck, *yalla!*" He shoved shoulders and backs and heads, furiously stuffing them into the truck.

Susan tried to help the blind boy back to the car, but he remained crouched on the ground beside his father's body. Before getting in, she turned to look back at the body lying there, a crumpled mess of blood, clothes and flesh. This corpse would not get the honour of a shallow grave like Rima's brother had.

"What about him?" Susan asked meekly.

"You get in the truck!" Abu Bayda shouted. "He's dead. It's none of your business now." He shoved Susan toward the truck and she bumped her head against the side of the metal frame. She felt blood trickle down her temple. Ashwaq saw the blood coming down Susan's cheek and neck. Her eyes widened and she shrieked, slapping her hands over her face. Head wounds always bled profusely even if they were minor. Susan wiped her wound with the *abaya* and put pressure on it to try to stop the bleeding, more for the people around her than for herself.

Malika's children were in complete shock. Within hours they

had witnessed a boy only a few years older than themselves burned alive, then a father shot in the head right before their eyes and now a woman beaten with impunity, bleeding in silence. Their faces were white with fear and horror. Tears trickled down some cheeks but others had no tears left. Instead, dry dirt stains were caked on their skin where their last tears had fallen hours ago. The blind boy crouched beside his father, clutching his knees tightly to his chest, rocking side to side, silently sobbing. Though blind, his life hadn't been in total darkness until this moment.

Abu Bayda and Ala were arguing with one another outside the Bongo. They were both cruel but the driver was unprepared for this level of violence. In between yelling and cursing at the refugees, the two smugglers fiercely debated how their cargo should be handled from then on. They were losing their grip on the situation, rapidly reducing their control over the group to the simplicity of the bullet.

Malika was struggling to get up into the Bongo's cabin, with the unsteady swaddling wrapped around her keeping baby Lina against her chest. Abu Bayda broke from his argument momentarily in order to shove her violently into the cabin. Her baby nearly fell from the force of it and her little son cursed at the smuggler and ran toward him. The man parried the boy with his hip, knocking the boy off his feet. Malika shrieked and some of the others went to help the boy up. Dalal sat and cried, staring up at the sky. Complaints and words were futile now, as they had all long ago put their trust in the hands of those who now betrayed them.

Heja stretched his arms to pull himself into the Bongo but Abu Bayda was growing impatient. He grabbed Heja's jacket by the shoulder, trying to push him forward. "I can do it myself!" Heja insisted.

The Bongo's engine roared to life but Susan noticed the blind boy was still sitting beside his father's corpse on the roadside.

"Excuse me, sir?" Susan asked Abu Bayda.

"Yea? What?"

"We're going to take the boy with us, right?"

"*La hawla wa-la quwwata illa bi-llah*, it's none of your business," he said, turning his head forward. "Sluts," he muttered under his breath. No one opposed the man with the gun. They had all decided their own survival was more important than a stranger's honour, or even a stranger's life. All except Susan.

"Please, I'm begging you. I'll take responsibility for him."

"How can you take responsibility for someone when you need someone to take care of you, *Irani*?" He was trying to insult her but instead, Susan was heartened by the mention of her nationality. At least Iranians weren't joining Da'esh.

Abu Bayda turned in his seat and shouted at the refugees. "This is my car. If you're coming with us, stay. If not, get the hell out." He drew his pistol and placed it on the separator between the front seat and the back cabin. "I'll count to five."

Everyone knew their lives would be over if they left. There was nowhere to go and they were surrounded by groups that would have clamoured over each other for the prize of capturing a fleeing refugee. The little boy sat alone outside, weeping for the only person who loved him, unaware of the battle raging in the Bongo over his survival.

"One, two," Abu Bayda counted slowly, testing the obedience of his human cargo.

His furrowed brow, dirty face and deformed ears burned an image in everyone's mind of the one they should fear the most. The threat of Da'esh, starvation and the desert all became abstractions.

The only immediate danger was Abu Bayda and his menacing pistol, hungry for obedience. This, the man they'd entrusted with their lives not a few days before.

"Three." Everyone carefully glanced around, morbidly curious who would make their pact with death. "Four."

Suddenly a voice broke the standoff, but it came from outside. "Me!" It was the little blind boy, still outside. "I will stay with my father!"

"No!" Susan screamed. "You must come with us."

"No. I'll stay with him. I can't leave him. He never left me and he died to look out for me. Go, leave me."

"It's desert all around us," Susan continued. "We're almost to Syria. We're practically at the border. There's danger in every direction. Every person out there is an enemy." Susan feared the boy would be killed, maimed or tortured because he had a disability. Da'esh was already well known for this kind of depravity and who knew what other men were waiting in the desert to satisfy their insecurities through cruelty and violence.

The boy clutched his knees tighter, rocking more forcefully. "My father will be alright. He will wake up and hold my hands again. He'll take me with him." He placed his hands on his father's chest, finding the centre near his heart. He laid his head there, as if waiting for the heartbeat to begin again. "Don't worry, Daddy. I'll stay with you until you can continue on. You promised me you'd take me to the sea and that we'd meet mommy again. She's watching over us now; she's praying for us from heaven. You promised you'd never leave me alone and so I promise I'll never leave you alone either. I'll wait until you can stand again. I will wait forever."

The boy kissed his father's lifeless hands and pressed his head against his father's chest, burying himself there, unmoved by the smuggler's threats. His hope rested with his father. He would not abandon hope.

Heja looked at Susan. "He's blind?" Susan nodded, brushing away a teardrop from her cheek.

"So," Abu Bayda said. "Only the blind boy is strong enough to defy me and stay behind? No more takers? Don't say I didn't give you the chance to leave. You better not jump out the back like goats once the truck starts moving again. Now, be good and shut your mouths. We'll be at the border soon." His idea of being good was obedience, silence and submission. In his world, life consisted of two paths: dying now or dying slowly. It wasn't just his appearance that made him look like a member of Da'esh.

Heja quickly leaned forward. "Let me talk to the boy for a minute. Just one minute."

"No, you had your chance. Stay in your place." Abu Bayda made up his mind. The boy would be left behind, left to the unforgiving desert.

"His father paid you to take him and his son," Heja continued. "He paid you to take him and now it's your responsibility, one human to another, to take him to the end. Take him to the destination you promised us all."

"Boy, you talk too much. Your words will end your life."

"He's blind. Don't you get it? He won't survive without us."

The boy was staring in the direction of the Bongo, waiting for someone to reach out and take his hands like his father used to.

"I know he's blind. That's not my problem. It's his problem." With that, Abu Bayda shut the fabric separating the front of the truck with the back, tying a little string to seal it.

The van lurched forward and the refugees stared out the back as the little blind boy sat there, growing smaller and smaller, his arms outstretched, waiting for the hands that would never come.

Susan began crying uncontrollably. Ashwaq leaned over and

comforted her, hugging her and stroking her head. The Dalal girl cried quietly, her past bubbling up through her tears. Not everyone shared in their compassion.

"Good," said one of the men beside the two Yazidis. "There is more room to stretch my legs now." He unabashedly brushed his knee against Ashwaq's leg. She grimaced and pulled herself away from his unwanted advance.

It became obvious to Susan that since the smugglers had their money, there really was no reason to keep anyone alive. First it was Amer and now a man and his son. Two killed, one left for dead. Still, the groups lurking out beyond the highway promised a fate worse than a simple gunshot. The smugglers were the best worst option. Susan once had a strong hope for the future but that was long ago, before her mother had forced her out of her home, before she became the object of her manager's desire, before she had put her life into a murderer's hands. Hope had long since been replaced by fear, despair and loneliness. She had to keep moving in order to survive. What other option did she have?

Chapter Sixteen

"Where are we going?" Malika looked at Susan, as if she somehow knew the future.

"I have no idea." The fumes from the Bongo's struggling engine were filling the cabin and making Susan light-headed. "These bastards have been lying to us all along. There is no way to know now where we're going or even who's really got us."

"But God will save us. Be sure to cover your face. Where we're headed now, there are groups worse than Da'esh." Malika shook her head and tightened her *abaya*.

Susan stared at her. "What are you talking about?"

"Don't you know anything about the war in Syria?"

"Yes, a little." She remembered Farah, who had nothing but still managed to house her, care for her and protect her. And Susan had abandoned her without thanks or farewells.

"The country is split between different factions," Malika continued. "You've got the pro-regime forces, Turkish-backed opposition, American-backed opposition, Kurds supporting both sides and then there is Russia and Iran. And those are just the big ones. There are a bunch of groups in the northwest that are leftovers from when al-Qaeda was still big and then you've got Shi'a militias running around fighting against Jordan's militias near the southern borders, not to mention Lebanese Hezbollah and the Syrian military itself. And in the middle of it all, there are huge areas under Da'esh administration. They control more oilfields in Syria than the Syrian government. We'll pass through checkpoints after checkpoints and there will be no way to know who's who or if they'll want to rape us, kill us, or just take our money." She paused, looking at Susan from head to toe. "You're Iranian, right?"

Susan shifted uncomfortably, then nodded her head. "Yes, I am."

"Well, to cross into Syria we'll have to go through Al Qaim into Abu Kamal. You know who controls that area?"

Susan had no idea. She stared at Malika, listening to her, unsure who could be worse than Da'esh.

"It's Hezbollah." She stopped, pursing her lips a moment. "Hezbollah and Iran. They'll stop us, no doubt. They will search the car and all of us. They will be thorough."

Susan's face flushed. She tried to stay calm. Now she knew what would be worse than being captured by Da'esh, at least for her. "If they find out I'm Iranian, they'll take me and God only knows what they'll do to me. Death would be an escape." Rima was listening to the conversation and glared at her as though choosing death was an insult to Amer, who never got to choose. But Susan meant it.

"Yea, and at the Syrian checkpoints, you can't claim you're Kurdish. They'll take you and hand you over to one of the pro-regime groups or to the opposition, depending who is running the checkpoint. Either way, it's a death sentence for all of us."

"What can I do then?" Susan asked desperately. "I don't even speak enough Arabic to get beyond basic questions."

"See, this is the problem. They'll know immediately you're not Arabic anyway. You have a Farsi accent. There is no way to hide that." Malika tightened her *abaya* and looked at the floor, thinking for a moment. If the opposition stopped them, they'd take Susan and do something terrible to her, no doubt. But the other refugees would be punished for harbouring her in the first place. Malika couldn't let her children be harmed because of Susan. At the same time, Susan was innocent so she couldn't just abandon her.

"Listen," she said, leaning closer to Susan. "Can you not talk?"

"Excuse me? I wasn't talking."

"No, I mean, can you be mute? Can you pretend you can't talk?"

"What? No, I can't do that. What if I accidentally make a noise? What if they hit me and I shriek in pain? It would be the end of us all."

Malika was unmoved. "Everyone, listen up." All heads turned toward her. The refugees were surprised to hear such a strength coming from someone who had said almost nothing up to this point. "These bastards are taking us to Syria. Everyone knows what's going on there. Only God knows if we will arrive at the seashore alive or as corpses."

"Shut your mouth!" Ahmad yelled. "Don't talk about death. If the smugglers don't kill us, your miserable pessimism will."

Rima kicked him. "Shut up you idiot. She has the balls to speak up. That's more than I can say for you." Rima's action made Ahmad even more upset, but his objections were now limited to his contorted face and crossed arms. After all, he had nothing to offer.

Malika continued. "As we all know, this woman is Iranian." She pointed at Susan and some of the men smirked. "And you all know Iraq is like a paradise compared to the situation in Syria. These people are driving us straight into the heart of it all. There will be many groups, many checkpoints, many chances for one of you to destroy us all. However, there is one thing we can do. It's to support this Iranian girl by keeping up a ruse. She is going to pretend to be mute so that she doesn't have to reveal her nationality to anyone outside of this vehicle. This will make all of your lives easier, so it's in your best interest to play along."

Some of the men were chuckling amongst each other. "I wish her government was mute, too," one of them said. He was picking at his fingernail with a knife. Ashwaq glared at him, and he didn't dare look up.

"Why are you talking like idiots?" Ashwaq asked. "What does the government have to do with anyone in here? Don't you see her trying to help us? She's suffering, just like the rest of us. She's not on vacation. She's running somewhere, just like all of you. The road behind us is soaked in blood." She looked directly at the one picking his nails. "Don't make the way ahead the same, or it will be your blood soaking it."

Malika smiled at Ashwaq, grateful to have an ally in this stranger. "Did you all get it?" she asked with new strength. The men nodded their heads reluctantly, some still trying to rebel with rolling eyes. Keeping a secret that would protect them all was a burden only because none of them had come up with the idea.

Susan held Malika's hand. "Thank you." She looked at Malika and the two Yazidi women beside her.

"Don't worry," Malika said, smiling kindly. "I'm here. I'll answer questions for you if they ask, as if I'm your mother. There won't be a problem, *inshallah*."

What else could Susan fear? Her situation couldn't get any worse than it was now. She was in the utmost danger. Looking forward to her goal was the only method she could use to overcome the terror. She had some allies around her, and of course a few enemies. But no one would follow her to the end except herself. Who would fight for humanity? Who would fight these smugglers-turned-captors? Susan was certain some would prostrate themselves on the road to certain death, giving no resistance. Susan knew others would stand and fight and some might even survive.

Susan was pulled out of her thoughts by the sound of Ashwaq heaving uncontrollably. It seemed she needed to vomit but she couldn't. Dalal massaged her shoulders and her back.

"Are you alright, Ashwaq?" she asked.

Ashwaq nodded. "Yes, but I really need to get some fresh air."

Three Syrian men were sitting across from Susan and the Yazidi women, staring in disgust. The youngest looking one grimaced. "Don't throw up in our faces."

Ashwaq ignored him but Dalal glared at him and he shut his mouth. Dalal banged on the fabric separating the front from the back of the Bongo. "Hey! Pull over," she shouted to the driver. The roar of the overheated engine drowned her voice, or maybe the smugglers were just ignoring her pleas. She started kicking the lower part of the cab, which was metal and made a sound that couldn't be ignored. The truck made a hard stop, thrusting everyone forward into one another. The fabric covering the back of the cabin suddenly tore open, flooding the inside with light. Abu Bayda stood there, framed in the sun, his dark figure contrasting against the shades of colour stretching out into the hills behind him. No one wanted their eyes to adjust enough to see his face.

"What's the problem? Who's having a seizure back here?"

"This woman needs to wash," Dalal said bravely, while Ashwaq covered her mouth and face with both hands.

"You think you'll find a toilet in this desert? Puke in a cup and toss it out the back."

Rima couldn't take her compatriot's utter disregard for human life. "Can't you see her face? She's white like a ghost. She's really sick. She looks like she's about to puke blood. Do you want that in your Bongo?"

Abu Bayda put his hands on his hips and spat on the ground. "Fine. You get five minutes. Hurry up."

No sooner had the words exited his mouth did the refugees burst out of their mobile prison. Everyone needed the break but only

Ashwaq and Dalal had been brave enough to demand it. Ashwaq only took a few steps out of the truck before she vomited. Dalal wet some fabric and wiped her face carefully. Rima stood nearby but lit a cigarette instead of helping the two Yazidi women. The three Syrian men who hadn't offered a word of help were using the stop to go off on their own and stretch their legs. Susan walked over to Ashwaq, holding Fatima against her chest.

"Are you feeling better?" Ashwaq nodded meekly. "I think maybe your blood pressure is low or maybe it's your blood sugar, I haven't seen you eat anything in more than a day." Ashwaq focused carefully on Susan's words but said nothing. "Did you bring anything with you? Water? Food? I have some dates if you need some. Just tell me." She gently patted Ashwaq on the shoulder. "Don't worry, God is with us. Just stay strong. This road is making us all sick." Susan looked at Ashwaq sitting there, her innocent face, her hands clasped between her legs, a prisoner to an unseen jailer.

Ashwaq looked up at Susan and began to cry quietly. Susan hugged her and didn't let go. She could feel the sadness radiating out of Ashwaq's body and into her own. Dalal stood nearby, watching. She couldn't hold in her own past and her pain came through in a stream of tears. Susan looked up at Dalal, then back at young Ashwaq, still young. She could guess the source of their despair. These women had been Da'esh brides, stolen from their families, then married to jihadis and made into sex slaves for the very men who had murdered their families in Sinjar. Thousands had died. Many of the survivors wished they could join the departed. The Da'esh animals contented themselves with a few moments of pleasure at the cost of these women's lives and their honour. Ashwaq was pregnant with a nameless, faceless Da'esh fighter's baby. Susan wondered how Ashwaq would go on, knowing she was carrying the child of a terrorist in her belly.

Susan noticed the three Syrian men moving away from the rest of the group. It seemed their pace was increasing. They were running. How had they planned an escape? They had barely spoken a word so far, except to ridicule Ashwaq and complain. Susan looked quickly at Ala and Abu Bayda. They were patrolling around on the other side of the Bongo, unable to see the men fleeing. The oldest of the three Syrians came around the Bongo and came in front of the smugglers to distract them.

"How much further until we're out of Iraq?"

"Not sure," Abu Bayda answered absent-mindedly. "We'll go a little more way in the truck and then we'll have to walk across the border south of the official Al Qaim crossing." Susan overheard this but she couldn't be sure if what he was saying was true, or if it was another ruse.

"Ah," the Syrian man said nervously. Without thinking, he glanced over his shoulder to see if the other two had made it out yet. The smugglers both followed his gaze, making out the two figures dashing away over the hills.

"Stop!" Ala yelled, running after them with his pistol glinting in the sunlight, waving it above his head like a flag. Abu Bayda was much calmer. He put his elbow on the front of the truck to steady his aim, took a breath and fired.

The shell casing bounced off the windshield and landed at Susan's feet. She reached down and picked it up. It was scalding hot and there was black carbon burnt around the opening. She turned it over and looked at the back. The words "Federal 45 Auto" were pressed into it in a ring around the silver primer. She put the casing in her pocket and looked out over the hills. One of the boys was clutching his leg, limping but they were still both running for their lives. They became little figures dancing on the horizon as the heat broke up their silhouettes into horizontal mirages.

Abu Bayda was now staring at the older Syrian man. "You did this to yourself." The Syrian man stood motionless, neither fleeing nor fighting.

"Do what you must. I did what I had to do. These boys couldn't cross into Syria in this area. If they did, they'd be sent to fight in the Syrian army. I had to help them. They made the right choice. So did I." Susan admired his courage. This man knew he would pay with his life to help the boys escape and he did it anyway. Maybe there was still some hope left for mankind.

Rima paced around in her *abaya*, a cigarette hanging loosely from her lips. The cigarette and the *abaya* were such a strong juxtaposition for Susan that it made her smile involuntarily. In a way she admired Rima's strange freedom, caught between virtue and vice.

Ashwaq was sitting on a rock, oblivious to the summary death sentence Abu Bayda was meting out upon the Syrian man. She nibbled a piece of bread with cheese on it that Malika had given her. Susan touched her shoulder to catch her attention.

Abu Bayda was turning from red to purple. Susan could see the rise and fall of his chest as his rage built inside. He was about to explode. The gun in his hand was shaking, tapping rapidly against his thigh, waiting for its master's call. The women came closer together, forming a mass. The Syrian man stood alone, his chin still up.

"Bastards," Abu Bayda muttered under his breath. Suddenly he raised the pistol level with the man's face. The gasps and screams of the refugees witnessing another tragedy could not penetrate the focused rage pulsing through the smuggler's blood, blocking all sound and all sight except the whistle of the air forcing itself in and out of the Syrian man's nostrils like the breathing of a dying horse.

"You told them to run," seethed Abu Bayda. In a flash he struck the man's clenched jaw with the side of his pistol and then grabbed him by the neck. He held the man's throat for a moment, observing his face, looking for his remorse. Unsatisfied, the smuggler threw the man to the ground and kicked him in the stomach. The man gasped but found no air.

The sound of children crying seemed to be miles away. Susan thought she heard a raven cawing behind her but she wasn't sure if it was real. She hugged Fatima, covering her face with the cloth around her shoulders. She realised she was holding the little boy's hand tightly, too. Ashwaq stared listlessly through the events unfolding before her, while Dalal laid both hands on Ashwaq's head, steadying an unbound soul.

Abu Bayda stood over the Syrian man, imposing his authority through the memory of violence. He had regained his power over the group but that was not enough, not for him. Two members of the group had run away and were gone forever. They had defied him. Someone had to give their soul to Abu Bayda in exchange for those two little Syrian sheep. He looked down at the man laying at his feet. His eyes were clenched shut, blood oozing from his mouth and nostrils. He gripped his knees in a foetal position, clearly in pain but suffering silently so as not to gratify the wolf hovering above him.

Ala returned from his chase empty handed, breathing heavily. "They're gone." These were the words Abu Bayda was waiting for.

"Ahh! Bastards!" he shouted, unleashing a flurry of kicks into the Syrian man's chest so hard that he began rolling across the ground toward the group. Everyone backed up but each felt powerless to intervene. How many witnesses stood by in this contest of good and evil, like vultures waiting for the jackal to subdue its prey?

The man's face was a twisted grimace. The two smugglers

continued kicking him, balancing themselves with their arms outstretched, the momentum of their blows causing a fearsome torque in their bodies. The man flopped on the ground. He was a fish unhooked but left suffocating on the dock. There was a sea of blood around his head, mixing with the dirt and creating a terracotta halo around his skull. The smell of blood, clay and saliva entered Susan's nostrils. A dry heave rumbled up from her diaphragm and she could hear Ashwaq vomiting again too. Abu Bayda wiped his mouth as though he had just finished a meal. He looked around at everything but the body writhing before him, scanning for something. His eyes rested on a large rock nearby. He stormed over, picked it up, raised it above his head and threw it down with hellish force onto the Syrian man's skull, crushing it, blending flesh with granite, exacting his fee from humanity. The man's legs ceased writhing and only the twitches of his feet and hands showed that this body was recently alive.

Abu Bayda let his hands fall to his sides. He was breathing heavily but seemed to be calming down, satiated by his revenge. He walked back to the truck and lit a cigarette. The refugees stood in silence, unmoving, afraid. The growing symphony of flies became audible. They arrived late for the show but just in time. The raven swooped down from its pulpit, waddling confidently to the body, cocking its head to one side, observing the humans nearby.

The body on the ground was an unfinished story. He was killed for helping someone live. His crime was humanity. Who was he? A father waiting to meet his children or a sick mother's son? A stranger, a friend, a brother? There would be no eulogy for his heroic act, no memory of his name. He was another body in the desert, joining countless others. The weight of their loss seemed almost too heavy for those remaining to carry.

Chapter Seventeen

The Bongo lurched onward across the disintegrating road toward Syria. Susan felt dizzy, placing her palms on the truck bed trying to steady herself.

"Are you ok?" Malika asked.

"No. I feel trapped, I feel like we're all going to die. They are killing us so easily. What is life even worth?" She couldn't keep her emotions in anymore and she began to cry. "We can't ask anything, we're surrounded by Da'esh and God knows what deal these smugglers made with them or with someone else. We aren't even going where we're supposed to." She wiped her cheeks, sniffling a little.

"You're right. I have this feeling, too. They promised us freedom but gave us captivity instead." Malika's voice shook but she tried to stay strong for her children and for Susan. Rima was watching their exchange suspiciously, trying to listen to their conversation.

Susan lowered her voice. "They're killing the men one by one." She was doubly afraid. Not only was she a vulnerable woman in the hands of merciless smugglers but she was also Iranian. Before she left Erbil, Anas had told her not to trust Arabs. She hadn't told Anas her plan, her decision to put her life in the hands of Arab smugglers probably from the same tribes as the Da'esh leaders in control of Mosul, Ramadi and Fallujah. No one knew where Susan was except the people in this Bongo truck and only two of them really knew where she would be next.

Susan estimated that they had been driving for seven hours since they left the Syrian man for dead. She racked her brain to craft an escape plan but she had no idea where she was or who she could trust. She looked around at the refugees remaining with her there in the back of the Bongo truck. Dalal sat with her head against the metal frame, her eyes closed, her face so innocent. Ashwaq held a plastic cup in case she needed to vomit again, while Rima steadily watched Susan and Malika. Rima had become more human after she lost her brother but Susan was unconvinced that her transformation was either permanent or sincere. Hadi, Ahmad and Heja all looked like they were waiting for their number to be called. Everyone seemed to notice the pattern hanging over their group: they were being picked off one by one.

Susan leaned over to Malika and whispered. "If we tell Rima that we regret our decision to go to Europe, what do you think she'd say?" She knew that if she tried to escape and got caught it meant certain death but she didn't know what their destination was now either. She was only certain of one thing, that the road they were heading down stretched from Iraq to Syria and was only safe for drug smugglers, arms dealers and human traffickers.

Malika waited for Rima to look away before she answered. "They'll never let us go, not after what we've seen. They know we'd go straight to the Asayish or Parastin in Kurdistan and report them. Plus, we'd never get our money back either. I don't know about you but I gave them everything I had." She patted Fatima gently on the head. Susan tried to imagine how a mother must feel in this situation. Susan was alone; Malika had her children and they were sharing in her danger. "Anyway, we would be locked up as criminals if we went back. We paid smugglers to move us illegally out of the country. That was our decision and there is nothing we can do to change it."

Susan's brow furrowed. "There must be a way."

"What way? You're not from this place, from this life. You have no idea where you are. Where do you plan to go in this desert once you jump out with no food and no water? The only living things out there are things that want you dead." Susan knew she was right and she tried to think carefully about her choices. Malika looked Susan in the eye. "Worse than death, this area has people who are thirsty for a woman like you."

Susan looked over at Heja, who was staring out the slit in the fabric and watching the hills roll by. "Hey, Heja. Come look here." She motioned with her hand. "Can you see outside? Can you tell where we are?" Susan noticed Rima straining herself trying to hear what Susan was saying but it was clear she couldn't make out the words.

"Uh, yeah. It's the desert."

"I know." Susan rolled her eyes. "I mean, do you think we're in Iraq still, or Syria?"

"Well we've been on the way for hours." He looked at his watch. "Yeah, we've got to be in Syria by now." He shifted uncomfortably; his leg having fallen asleep. "We're heading straight for the heart of evil, straight to Da'esh. I don't know if you can see from where you are but we aren't on the road anymore. Haven't been for a while. We're driving across the open desert. Looks like we're heading straight west."

Susan stared intently at Heja. She wasn't sure if she should share her idea with him. "Do you want to escape together?" She blurted it out without thinking.

"Escape?" Heja breathed deeply as though the utterance itself was a crime. "That word has the same definition as capture right now."

"Well, I'm certain that if they take us into Raqqa, Idlib, Homs, Manbij, you name it, I'll be dead for sure anyway."

"Girl, you don't know where you're at. This place is dangerous even for smugglers who act like Da'esh. Imagine what it would be like out there for regular people, an Iranian woman and a Kurdish boy." He looked out the slit in the fabric. "I wish we could afford the classy smugglers. We'd be out of here on an airplane instead of this old Bongo."

They both smiled a little but Susan wished Heja would be more hopeful. This wasn't the end of the world, and Susan knew there must be multiple ways out. She just needed to find the right one at the right moment. She could see the hopelessness in everyone's eyes. It seemed these refugees had begun accepting their fate.

The car seemed to be reducing speed, gradually slowing until the engine sputtered. They were out of fuel. Everyone looked at each other, waiting for something to happen. Heja closed his eyes. "It can't get any worse, right?"

Suddenly the fabric covering the back was ripped away. Abu Bayda stood there, sneering. Somehow, he looked angrier each time he saw the refugees. Malika's children clung to her, trying to hide their faces from his seething glare.

"Everyone out!" he shouted. "*Yalla*! Hurry up!"

Heja was right. There was nothing in any direction except brown dirt and sand. The earth looked scorched by some unseen catastrophe. A sharp wind whipped across the plain and bit Susan's cheeks, catching her by surprise since the ground was so hot. She shivered, handing Fatima back to her mother so that she could tighten her shawl. She began walking around, feeling like she was on an expedition to Mars. She knew she couldn't escape now. There was nowhere to go. There were no buildings, no trees, no people, nothing.

Susan looked around at the other refugees. Some were stretching their legs, others sitting on the dirt, staring into the distance. Not one of them was overweight, their faces were bony, lips dry and white. They all seemed to have been underfed for years. Some hadn't had water for almost a day. They looked like prisoners of war.

Ala went back to the truck and closed the door. He bent the side mirror so no one could see what he was doing. He pulled out a little black kit from his clothes. He looked around once more and then tied a rope around his arm. He took a little syringe from the kit and found a good vein in his arm. He leaned his head back, letting the heroin transport him away from this desert. He hadn't flipped the mirror on the other side and Susan had seen what he was doing. She didn't dare say a word.

Abu Bayda made his way over to Ashwaq. "Hey, Yazidi." Ashwaq looked up at him with silent anger. He was standing so close she could smell his unwashed teeth and the scent of dried blood on his menacing *dishdasha*. He stared at her for a moment. "If you want, you can sit in the front of the car while we figure out this fuel problem. Are you feeling better?"

"I'm fine." Her voice was weak. After a moment she decided to go to the front anyway. She hadn't sat on something soft in days.

Abu Bayda turned and looked around at the group of refugees sprawled in a rough semi-circle around the back of the truck. "Listen up, everyone! We're twenty minutes from our next destination. We have no fuel. Everyone knows what happened to the extra fuel we had." He looked at Rima, who was staring at the ground. Everyone else was looking at him intently, hoping he'd finally have some information to offer.

Heja stood up. "How are we going to get fuel in this desert?"

Abu Bayda walked up to Heja, grabbing the boy's chin with one hand and tilting his head up as though he was inspecting a goat for the *Eid al Adha* sacrifice. "A very good question, little boy." He broke away from Heja and casually pulled the pistol out of his belt. He spun it lazily on his finger as he walked around to each of the refugees. Each person braced themselves, bristling as he approached. He seemed to revel in the fear and hate that he conjured in their minds. "Not to worry, we'll wait here for a little while in case a car passes by. No need to waste our energy if we don't have to. No more questions."

Rima ran up to him. She whispered something in his ear and he immediately turned to face Susan. Susan froze. He tapped his gun on her shoulder, then turned to address the group.

"One more thing, if anyone else is thinking to escape, tell me now so I can use less bullets later." He looked at Heja and shook his head. "Otherwise, if you need to pee or touch yourself or whatever you need to do, hurry up." He looked at Susan, grinning. "*Yalla!*" His words chaffed at Susan. He sounded like a farmer yelling at his livestock.

Malika ran to Susan with Fatima and her brother clinging to her *abaya*, and her infant Lina wrapped against her chest. "See? I told you Rima is still one of them. She was trying to listen to us to report us if we tried to escape."

"I know but we can't give up." Susan looked up, watching Rima light another cigarette. Suddenly a girl's scream caught everyone's attention. It was coming from the front of the truck. Abu Bayda ran over first, followed by Susan. Malika came too, her children in tow. Ala was on top of Ashwaq's body, moving with heavy, groping motions, trying in vain to tear away her *abaya*. He was too drugged up, his body too heavy. Malika reached in with her free hand, tearing at Ala's face, trying to stop him. Little Lina was now between Malika and Ala. Ala's behaviour reminded Susan of her own father and she stepped back in fear. Ala threw his hands up, finding his strength, pushing Malika back so violently that the toddler wrapped against her chest came loose, banging her tiny skull against the doorframe. The baby vomited immediately. Her eyes lost their muscular control, rolling back in her head.

"Stop! Stop!" Susan shouted, running back into the fray and pulling Malika away from the flailing man. Ashwaq ran out of the truck and rushed to Dalal. Malika saw the baby laying limp before her. She shrieked and beat her own head with the palms of her hands, falling to her knees in the sand. The baby was silent, motionless. Fatima looked on, wide-eyed and with her mouth slightly open, unsure what to do.

Heja ran over and picked up the lifeless little body. Malika stayed kneeling, gripping her hair with her hands but now totally silent. Her eyes were wide, her skin a shade lighter. Strangely, a smile appeared on her face. She couldn't move or speak. Heja crouched down and laid the baby carefully on the dirt, examining the bleeding gash on the back of her little head. He leaned close to her face, looking for a rise and fall of the chest, a pulse, anything. He wiped her face gently and looked up at Malika, who still sat in shock nearby. He gathered the limp body into his arms, stood and walked slowly over to her. She reached her arms out, ready to take her child. Tears were coming down Heja's cheeks. He placed the baby in Malika's arms. Everyone was silent, even Abu Bayda.

Malika became delirious. She switched back and forth from tears to that strange smile, staring wide-eyed at her unmoving child. Susan sat on the ground nearby, clasping both hands on top of her head, exasperated. The other refugees sat silently, motionless, fused to the earth as if God had cursed them all. No one could believe what they saw. The refugees were innocent but it was they who suffered while the smugglers seemed to carry the blessings of heaven.

"Susan," Malika called out. "Come, come see." She waved

excitedly. Susan couldn't hold her tears. She found the strength to stand but she felt gravity pulling her down. Malika rocked baby Lina slowly in her arms. "Come Susan, come see my baby. She's my life, my other half. She's sleeping now, you can see." She smiled. "She's sleeping forever." She moved her finger across the baby's face, then held the baby's colourless hand. "Sleep mama," Malika said, kissing the baby's hand.

Abu Bayda stood there, staring. Finally, he broke away and walked back to the truck to talk with Ala and find out what happened. Ala was still sprawled in the front seat, one arm hanging out the window. He looked at Abu Bayda without turning his head. "I didn't want to kill it," he said, his voice labouring. Abu Bayda handed him a water bottle.

"Drink this. You didn't kill anyone. It was God's will. It was *ajal*, it was her time. No one can escape their appointed time."

"I need to pray," Ala said, taking the water bottle.

"Pray for me too. You have a pure heart. These animals don't know you, but I do. You wouldn't hurt a fly. God knows that the suffering those creatures endure is a result of the wrongs they've done in their life. You are only a vehicle. These sluts want to go to Europe, the land of the *kuffars*. It's no wonder God wants them to die. It's better we make ourselves God's instrument than try to fight their fate."

Ala nodded slowly, comforted by his mentor. "I said *zikr* prayers before I touched her, so it was *halal*. I didn't want to force her."

"Don't worry brother, I understand you. These sluts in their *abayas* think they are pure like Mary. They deserve what happens to them. It isn't rape. They invite this upon themselves by their behaviour and their desires. We can't stop God from teaching them a lesson. They're hypocrites hiding under black shawls, trying to trick us. They've escaped from their families, dishonoured their tribes, their fathers and their lineages. That little Yazidi woman is alone with her baby. She abandoned her husband. You were God's tool for teaching her a lesson. You did the right thing my brother."

Behind the truck, Malika sat and held her daughter's body in her arms, adjusting the cloth around her. Her other two children sat in front of her, staring at their little sister's colourless face. "It's okay, my children. Listen, I'll tell you a story. One night, a cat was searching for food. He was in the back yard of a house, sniffing and checking every corner. Suddenly, the cat heard a noise. She went to investigate and found a pile of discarded fruit stuffed in a trash bin. The fruits were crying out. The cat asked the fruits, 'Why are you in the trash bin? Who could bite you only once and toss you away?' A big peach with barely a tooth mark in her glowing skin looked up at the cat and asked, 'Do you want to know? Listen and I'll tell you. Last night there was a birthday party, many children came and brought huge plates full of apples, pears, oranges, cherries, and peaches.'"

The two children were totally focused on their mother's story. The other refugees were listening too, some shocked that the mother was ignoring the tiny corpse in her arms, others eager to know what happened to the peach in the story. Malika looked around at her audience and continued her tale.

"...My friends and I were on one of those plates. Then someone put us in a nice bowl of water to wash our skin. It was so joyful. I can't describe it. But then, a pear with a big gash on his face interrupted the peach. 'Look at us, how ugly we've become. I was desired by everyone in the party but now I'm trash.' The pear wept but the peach continued her story. 'Someone put us back on the plate but now our skin was glistening in the afternoon sunlight and the breeze was so refreshing. Then someone picked me up and started to dry me off,' the peach trailed off, beginning to cry again. The cucumber spoke up, telling the cat, 'They were cruel, taking only a bite and then discarding us. They swept us outside with the broom as though we were trash, but we still had value.' Then the cat was ashamed for trying to nibble these noble fruits. Despite his hunger, the cat left the fruits in peace. You see, we are like these fruits. No one wants us, though we have value. But we have been thrown away."

Susan was watching Malika become more detached from reality, totally out of her mind. She was gesturing dramatically as she told her story, moving her hands up and down, shifting her body side to side. She periodically stared down at the motionless baby in her lap, as if her gestures would bring the life back into her daughter. She looked at her other two children, sitting frozen in front of her.

"Do you know why your sister is so calm?" Her son swallowed hard and then began to cry. "Don't cry my son. You're just thirsty, like your little sister." She took a bottle of water out of her bag and put it to her daughter's lifeless lips, pushing against her mouth. "My daughter, you must drink. You told me you were thirsty."

Susan couldn't take it anymore. She got up and ran over to them but Malika didn't notice. "Stop it!" Susan shouted. "The baby is dead. She's dead!"

Malika looked up at Susan, frowning. "No. My baby is alive. My daughter is alive!" She pushed Susan away and began to walk towards Heja, swaying slightly under the effects of her delirium. "She told me she's thirsty," she said to Heja. Heja stood before her, bewildered, unsure how to respond. She grabbed Heja's hand. "Come," she walked Heja to the spot on the ground where the baby had first started bleeding. "Can you wash the blood?" She asked, looking down at the halo of red soaked into the brown sand. Heja looked at the ground, wiping away tears. He shook his head. "I beg you to wash it." Finally, Heja knelt and began covering the blood stains with fresh dirt. Malika smiled. "Thank you, brother."

Fatima looked up, unsure what to do. "Hold your brother's hand," Malika said. "Come." The three of them began walking together, away from the Bongo. Malika carried the dead baby in her left arm and her son's hand in her right. Malika was going to walk until she found her daughter alive again. How much could a mother have lost already to walk her surviving children toward the abyss?

Susan ran to her, grabbing hold of her shawl. "Please. Please don't. We can take your baby, we can take her to the first hospital inside Syria." Malika only smiled. Susan dropped to her knees and looked at the little boy standing beside his mother. "Ask your mum. Tell her to continue with us. You've got to tell her. This road is so dangerous."

The boy began crying and covered his eyes with his hands. Susan looked at his hands, covered in dirt, peeling, dry, cracked. His face was covered in a thin layer of dirt, and the tears were making little dark rivers down his cheeks. His shoes were ripped, his knees bent, he was exhausted enough already.

"No, that's it," Susan said, standing up. "You can't go. Look at your children. They can barely take another step. They're dehydrated and starving. They'll die out here."

Malika said nothing, grabbed her son's hand and continued walking away. The strange smile was back on her face as she walked toward the unknown. Heja ran over to try to help.

"Stop, please," he said. "You're in shock. Look around you." He waved his hand, sweeping across the desert's great expanse. "I promise we'll take her to a hospital. Give me the baby and I'll hold her for you until we get to Syria." He knew his offer was made in vain but he had no choice. He had to try to save three people's lives, since they had lost more than that on their journey together already. He reached out to take the body out of Malika's arms. To his surprise, she didn't resist. To his even greater surprise, he felt a pulse in the baby's little body.

"Be careful not to wake her up," Malika said, still smiling. She kissed baby Lina on the cheek.

Abu Bayda ran over to them and grabbed the baby from Heja's arms. "What decisions do you think you're making for yourself?" he demanded.

"Give the baby back, murderer!" Susan shouted at him. The back of Abu Bayda's fist cracked across her face, knocking her backward. She lost her balance and fell to the ground, grabbing her face and crying out. She could feel warm blood oozing down her cheek near her ear and her face was throbbing, but she could only see pricks of light.

Hadi and Ahmad ran to Susan but they stopped short of intervening. They knew they'd be punished if they tried to stop Abu Bayda. Their good intentions weren't strong enough to put themselves at risk. Someone wiped Susan's face with a piece of cloth. She groaned in pain but was thankful at least one person was willing to step forward to help her.

Abu Bayda looked around at the semi-circle of refugees gathering around him while Susan sat in the dirt nearby. "Listen to me!" he shouted, with the baby in one hand and his pistol in the other. "You'll bury your baby here." He paused for a moment, his eyes widening as he felt the baby's heartbeat. His eyes darted to Malika but then he continued his speech. "I'll take you and your other two children but not this dead thing."

He was acting as though Malika had been caring for a plastic doll all along, burdening the rest of the group with her fantasy. He refused to accept that the baby he now held was alive. He couldn't see Malika's heart and he couldn't bring himself to accept his mistake for fear of further losing his grip of power over the group.

Ala came sauntering over, having finished his prayer. "I won't let anyone bring a dead body into my truck." He spat on the ground and adjusted his pants.

What could a man have asked his god that had absolved him so thoroughly of his sins that he could replace all wrongdoing with confidence such as this? His words stabbed Malika's heart, as if he killed her child twice.

Rima was not participating in Ala's show. She stood at a distance in silence. She finally came over to the group and took a cigarette from the driver without saying a word.

She sat in front of the truck, away from everyone else, smoking her cigarette slowly. The cigarette was Rima's only friend now. She could find any reason to smoke one, whether upon witnessing her brother's death or standing by while her comrade killed an innocent woman's baby and left her for dead. Nicotine flowed into her body, while her connection to humanity flowed out of it in puffs of gray smoke.

Heja was glaring at Abu Bayda. "You're inhuman!" he shouted, unable to bear the cruelty occurring before him. "How could you leave a baby in the desert? You know better than anyone else here what kind of people there are along this road! It's thieves, smugglers and murderers. You know better, because you're all of these!" Ala took a step toward Heja as he spoke. Heja turned his gaze toward him and then back to Abu Bayda. "You and your stupid friend."

Abu Bayda was grinding his teeth, staring at Heja. Hadi and Ahmad sensed the danger Heja was in and they stood off to the side, out of Abu Bayda's way. They acted as though they didn't share the same fate as Heja, even though everyone standing on this patch of earth was headed to the same destination. The only difference was that Heja was brave enough to stand up for someone else without expecting anything in return.

"How can she bury a baby whose heart still beats?" Heja asked, looking around at each face, addressing the whole group. "Are you Muslim?"

Abu Bayda stood silently, listening to the noise while plotting Heja's death. Without a word, he handed the baby back to her mother. Malika began crying tears of joy the moment her daughter was back in her arms. She was speechless, so full of joy to have all three of her children back around her. A mother should never outlive her child.

"Listen," Abu Bayda said. "I will only take you and your two puppies." He pointed with his chin in disdain at Malika's two children standing beside her. Susan remained on the ground nearby, gripping the side of her head.

Malika decided not to subject herself to the devil she knew. She looked down at Susan, smiled in thanks for a stranger's kindness and then gently tapped her children on the shoulders. The remnants of this family began walking slowly away from the group, away from the Bongo, away from one kind of abuse and into another untold fate where Da'esh camps bustled only 30 kilometres away. After a few steps, she paused, turning toward the group. Her eyes were full of the tears that could only be shed by an innocent. Her gaze lingered on Susan and Heja for a moment. "God be with you all." She started walking.

Everyone watched them depart but said nothing. Then, Hadi stood up and began making half-hearted steps toward Malika and her children, perhaps waiting to see if others would join him. Abu

Bayda leveled his gun at him.

"If you take one more step, I'll send you quickly to the same place they're going."

The group was now half the size of that mass of strangers whose lives had all intersected on the cold floor of that compound only a few days before. The smugglers seemed to be more and more satiated with each stop, culling the weak as they saw fit. It seemed so easy for them to take a life. For them, each living flame was extinguished as easily as a candle. The group of refugees sat in a little group on the dirt, waiting for their master's next command. Abu Bayda had his power back.

The smugglers went back to the front seat of the Bongo, putting some fabric on the windshield to keep the sun out. It seemed they were prepared to wait until a car passed carrying some extra fuel. Susan felt that this was not their first time running out of gas in the desert. Rima walked calmly around the Bongo, alone in her thoughts, perhaps transporting herself somewhere else. She was no longer drinking the people's water, no longer smoking their cigarettes, no longer making demands. She was slowly becoming one of the refugees. Maybe she could hear the chorus of growling stomachs around her or maybe she had too much humanity left to remain attached to the other two smugglers. Or maybe her devotion to them died with her brother.

A few hours passed while Susan sat with the rest of the group on the dirt. Their group huddled in little mountains of black, brown and burgundy fabrics. The beginning of the sunset began to melt away what hopes they had of rescue. Ashwaq and Dalal sat beside Susan. Susan continued holding a fabric compress against her head all afternoon and into the dusk. She could feel her eyes reddened by tears, blood and frustration. The *abaya* she was commanded to wear on her head now rested around her shoulders to protect her from the elements. Susan thought it was a much more practical use for fabric than for hiding a woman's face. Rima approached Susan, holding a cigarette butt in her hand.

"Come on," she said, half-heartedly. "You need to put the shawl all the way over your hair. You need to cover up."

Susan and her two Yazidi companions looked up at Rima, disgusted that she still found the words to betray her own sisters after what she'd seen her religion do to her brother. Somehow the visibility of Susan's hair was more dangerous than the gash on the side of her head. It wasn't just Da'esh who justified their subjugation of women. Da'esh was just an expression of what many who believed they were less extreme were prepared deep in their consciences to accept. The most twisted form of this subjugation of women was using other women to enforce these injustices upon their own sisters through the Quranic teaching of *amr wa nahy*, commanding good and forbidding vice. The morality police were not just a creation of the Taliban, al-Qaeda or Da'esh. Some governments enforced these terms of social slavery over women. Rima embraced her role as a *hisbah* enforcer, hoping her obedience would bring her blessings in heaven. How misguided she was, Susan thought to herself as she reluctantly tightened her *abaya* just enough to make Rima leave her alone.

A cold wind began rolling across the desert, settling equally over everyone. Two of the men were scavenging the desolation for a few pieces of kindling. There weren't enough jackets to go around, so they were shared among two and three individuals as little tents covering a shoulder here, a leg there, half a back there. The cold sapped the energy from the soul and no one was immune. Susan longed for the comforting warmth of a glass teacup in her hands.

Each person felt the cold entering first their skin, then their bones and finally their minds. The men wearing sandals lost feeling in their toes, while all began shivering uncontrollably. The desert was like two worlds: blazing in the day, freezing at night. Either way, the desert had a way of sucking the life out of the human body.

Hadi and Ahmad returned with kindling to make a small fire. It was difficult, not only because the wind competed with their little flame but also because their hands were too cold to hold anything tightly. Ahmad kept dropping the lighter as it slipped from his hands each time he tried sparking a flame. As the fire eventually danced into existence, Susan could a see a little sea of faces all turned toward it. Everyone was equal before the fire.

Those who sat a little further away decided to get up and move towards the heat. They groaned and grimaced as they were forced to feel the soreness in their joints and the hunger in their bellies awakened by their sudden movements. Abu Bayda and Ala remained in the Bongo, screened from the wind, separated from the refugees like wardens watching the prison yard from their post.

"Didn't you hide a few litres of fuel in the car?" Abu Bayda asked. He was flicking his lighter absent-mindedly, his right foot on the dashboard and his arm over the top of his head. It looked like he had fallen out of the sky and landed in the seat.

"How should I know we'd be stuck out here like this? I did bring extra but your wild friends spent my fuel supply. And forget about these animals we've got with us. They're dropping like flies anyway. Plus, it's getting colder by the minute."

"Then pray to *Allah* that someone drives by soon. It's in *Allah's* hands."

Abu Bayda closed his eyes for a moment, remembering his own captivity. Long before he joined Da'esh, and even longer before he left it to pursue his own entrepreneurial ambitions by smuggling anyone who'd pay enough, he had been a prisoner in a cement hell called Abu Ghraib. This prison had been built by Saddam Hussein and then used by the Americans when they replaced him. This was where he had met the men who would lead him down the path of the *Salafiya*, a way of justifying violence, greed and vice through the thinly veiled mantle of a religion that they claimed would bring peace, charity and good deeds. After he was released, he moved drugs, weapons and people for the newly formed al-Qaeda in Iraq led by Abu Musab al-Zarqawi, a Jordanian jihadist who thirsted for blood more than water. He was captured by the Americans again, this time put into Camp Bucca where many acolytes of the future Da'esh organisation were incubated. Of course, Rima couldn't know that Abu Bayda and Ala had agreed with their old Da'esh friends ahead of time to come and purge Amer from the group in order to increase the pay out between the surviving smugglers. Suddenly, yellow lights washed into the truck's cab, rousing Abu Bayda from his thoughts. He jumped out of the car and rubbed his eyes to see the moving lights more clearly. A car was approaching.

"Get in the car!" he yelled. "*Yalla, yalla*, let's go."

The refugees jumped up as quickly as their tired, hungry bodies would allow and made their way into the back of the Bongo. There was a lot more space now, so they were able to cram inside much faster than before. Ala carefully folded his syringe and its accessories into a leather folding wallet, hiding the kit under the seat. Then he got out and kicked dirt over the fire to conceal the flame and make it look like there wasn't a group of refugees warming themselves there moments before.

"Don't move a muscle," he shouted into the back of the Bongo. "No one make a noise. Be mute."

Susan felt the emptiness in the truck embracing her. The woman with her three children was gone. They used to sit right by Susan. She felt a lump growing in her throat and the pain on the side of her skull was dulled by the creeping feeling of loss that ate away at her heart. She tried to keep the lump from erupting into tears but her heart wasn't made of stone. She bit her lip to distract herself.

She began to realise that any moment on this journey could be her final one alive. Would she know which breath would be her last? Susan remembered the faces of the people about to be beheaded in the Da'esh videos her manager in Erbil used to watch. Sometimes they smiled, sometimes they had no emotion at all. She began to understand how these people became so broken that they could no longer resist death.

The sound of tires crackling over dry dirt became louder. The two smugglers stood beside the truck, trying their best to appear like innocent drivers stranded in the desert. A white Toyota Hilux pulled up, illuminating the Bongo with its yellow headlights. The Hilux slowed and pulled up alongside the Bongo. Susan looked out the crack in the fabric. There were two men in the front and three in the back. There wasn't a big machine gun bolted into the truck bed this time but there was still no way to know who these people were. Susan hoped they could help get them out of this desert.

The two smugglers walked toward the Hilux, apparently without fear. Was this another part of the plan they had for them? The men in the front of the truck got out and greeted the smugglers in a friendly way. The refugees kept silent but some, like Susan, could see the disconcerting situation unfolding outside. Laughter and greetings filtered through the fabric into the back of the Bongo. The refugees stirred uncomfortably.

Chapter Eighteen

The dirty fabric covering the back of the Bongo moved aside and a halo of yellow light coalesced around the figure of a man. "Put on your *hijab!*" The voice came again, stronger. "Wear your *abaya!*"

Susan felt that she had no energy. She was ready to pretend to be mute to save energy and, maybe, her life. The halo faded away as everyone's eyes adjusted. Before them stood a man with messy hair and bloodshot eyes and a beard so wild it seemed a razor had never met his face. His light khaki uniform was the colour of mustard in the yellow glare of the Hilux headlights. Susan had no idea which group he belonged to. There were more than fifty different militias controlling the territory in this area of the desert between Rif Dimashq in Syria and Al Anbar in Iraq. The man grinned, revealing brownish gums and teeth like corn kernels. Susan felt a chill come over her as the smell his breath entered her nostrils.

He looked at each face before him, smiling all the while. "You," he said, pointing at Heja. "What's your name, boy?"

"My name is Heja." He spoke with a special confidence more suited for receiving an award than for standing at the rocky shore of his own demise.

"Good. Come down here, little Heja. Bring all your stuff."

Rima grimaced. Susan could tell she was frustrated that she was no longer included in the plan. But there was nothing she could do. Her brother was dead and she was now just another woman alone among smugglers.

Heja grabbed his bag and jumped out the back of the Bongo. He landed inches from another frowning, leathery face. It was Abu

Bayda. He held his prayer beads in his hand, worryingly flipping bead after bead over his finger, quietly murmuring his *zikr* prayers. The strange man stared at Heja a moment, while Heja tried to straighten himself and keep his dignity despite the penetrating fear that grasped at his gut.

"Take off your shawls," the man said loudly, speaking over Heja's head to the women inside the Bongo as if Heja wasn't standing there in front of him. The man smiled, looking directly through Heja, his eyes resting on the frightened women slowly removing their *abaya* and *hijab*. Ashwaq helped Susan remove the fabric from her head, which had fused to her face with the sticky dried blood caked around her wound. Susan winced and she looked up at Abu Bayda while the fabric made a little tearing sound as it was freed from her bloodied skin. His face was emotionless, perhaps deliberately so now that he saw his handiwork exposed to the light. His brow furrowed involuntarily, a momentary flash of pity or perhaps regret. He quickly coughed and rubbed his forehead, wiping away his feeling. He couldn't risk being human in front of these refugees.

Heja still stood there, holding his bag in his hand. He helped each of the men climb down out of the truck. The smugglers and the soldiers stood off to the side, evidently having a great conversation. One of the men put a little propane tank on the hood of the Hilux, lit it and then put a little metal teapot on top. Soon they began handing out sweets to one another. Each refugee's mouth watered as the little white Turkish delights were doled out among the smugglers and the soldiers but not to them. The smugglers excitedly nibbled the sweets and took some sugar from a little plastic bag like schoolchildren at recess. Susan decided schoolchildren had more brainpower than these animals and far more honour.

A man in military clothes walked over to the refugees. "Get in two lines, men here, women there." He motioned to his sides with his hands. "Good, now I want all of you to take your bags and drop them on the ground in front of you." Ala and Abu Bayda stayed by the teapot, enjoying the show.

The other men in the Hilux got out, right on cue. They grabbed up all the bags and began placing rectangular blocks of something wrapped in layers of plastic into each bag. Each block looked to weigh about a kilogram and each bag got four or five of them. The men put different coloured *keffiyeh*, prayer rugs and religious photos on top of the bricks to conceal them in the bags. Susan looked at Heja. He was growing visibly uncomfortable with these people putting bricks of drugs into each refugee's bag. They all knew that one kilogram of heroin was a death sentence. Each bag was worth four of their lives.

Heja knew they'd be killed or tortured if they were caught, whether by Hezbollah, Syrian soldiers, or whoever else happened to be in control of whatever part of the Baghdad- Damascus Highway they were on at the time. Heja took the drugs out of his bag and marched angrily over to the Hilux. "Isn't it enough that we apparently paid you to kill us? Now you want us to be your drug mules, too," throwing the drugs onto the hood of the truck.

The man in uniform said nothing. He looked at Heja and then poured some tea for himself into the little glass cup. The tea leaves swirled inside as the hot liquid mixed with the cold. He seemed to be in charge, even having more power than the smugglers. His men continued packing drugs into the bags belonging to the other refugees behind Heja.

"I regret my decision," Heja exclaimed. "I don't want to go to Europe."

The man came close to Heja. His breath smelled like mouldy tea leaves. He stared deeply into Heja's eyes, searching for resistance so that he might crush it. Heja tried to remain steadfast, tried to hold the man's gaze.

"I'm not continuing with the group," Heja continued, perhaps more to convince himself. "Keep the five thousand euros I paid. I don't want it." He stepped back, feeling the pressure of the man's unwavering gaze over his body. The man lunged his hand out, grabbed Heja's shirt tightly at his chest and smashed his knee into Heja's groin. He let go and Heja crumpled to the ground in pain, gripping his knees and tightly closing his eyes as tears silently poured out onto his cheeks and into the dirt. The other men all winced, smugglers and refugees alike. Heja tried to mutter curses at the man but his words were caught in his stomach.

The man took the boiling pot of tea and emptied it slowly on Heja's face. His skin turned burgundy and he screamed in pain. The smugglers turned and laughed as Heja writhed in pain. They handed out more sweets to nibble on while they revelled in his suffering. The man kicked dirt in Heja's face and walked back to his compatriots.

"Burn their clothes. Leave no traces behind."

The men stopped watching the poor boy weeping in pain and dutifully turned their attention to collecting up all the belongings that had to be displaced from the bags in order to fit the drugs. Susan was watching in horror as Heja sat up, poured water on his face and writhed again in pain as his burns became visible. Susan began to stand but a hand grabbed her wrist. Susan looked down to see Rima staring up at her in desperation.

"God knows what they'll do to you if you go," Rima said. "It's not worth it. Sit and be quiet."

By now everyone had turned their attention from Heja, as if noticing him would make them guilty and worthy of punishment. Two of the soldier's men came around the Bongo, each carrying a big plastic ten-litre jug of fuel. They filled the car's gas tank with a siphon and then brought the empty jugs back to the Hilux. Susan wondered if the smugglers had planned to run out of fuel on purpose. Then the men searched the refugees and their pocket litter on the ground in front of each of them, taking the cigarettes, lighters, money and anything else they felt was worth anything. They distributed the refugees' valuables amongst themselves, smiling and laughing the whole time.

Susan strained to overhear their conversation, which was partially drowned out by the sound of the running motor coming from the Hilux.

"—a real beauty under that *abaya*..."

"Shame she had three puppies with her."

"We took care of them, don't worry."

"What did you do with them?"

"Well, we couldn't keep them, that's for sure."

They all laughed and one of the men poured more tea for all of them.

"So how did her little puppy die?" asked Abu Bayda.

"She fell down while her mother misbehaved," the man in the uniform replied. "It was good. One less loose end for us to worry about when we finished with the mother."

Susan was disgusted. That innocent family was discarded into the desert to starve to death or to suffer a continuous cycle of abuse and torture.

Abu Bayda came over to the huddled refugees, his black *dishdasha* flowing around him in the wind. "Whose bag is this?" he demanded, holding up one of the bags full of drugs.

"It's mine," Ahmad said sheepishly. Abu Bayda stared at him, waiting for a more confident answer. Ahmad understood. "This is my bag," he said, this time with conviction.

"Good, good boy." He gently slapped Ahmad's face twice, giving him the gentlest abuse he could muster in a show of acceptance. He began patrolling the line of refugees. "Did you understand? These are your bags now. No one gave you these drugs. These are yours and you're carrying them because you want to. Do you get it?"

The refugees stared up at him blankly, exhaustion competing with this man for control over their behaviour.

"I can't hear you!" He slapped Hadi, who was standing before him, knocking him over. He stood over Hadi's body but looked down the line of fearful faces. "Now, is there any more misunderstanding?"

Heads shook from side to side slowly in grudging compliance.

"Good. Now listen up. These bags are worth four, five time more than your life. Care for them like your own babies. If I find out that any is missing, I will take your flesh in compensation. For a gram, you'll lose a finger. Any more than that and you'll lose your life." He turned his back on them and walked over to the Hilux for a final glass of tea. He looked over his shoulder at the cowering refugees. "Keep your eyes on your prize," he shouted gleefully. "Now get back in the Bongo!"

Abu Bayda called the man in the soldier's uniform over and whispered something in his ear. Susan saw them look at her. The man in the uniform nodded and smiled as he stared at Susan. Nearby, a few of the soldier's men were digging a human-sized hole in the ground. Abu Bayda was filling his magazine with fresh bullets. One of the other men was leaning against the Hilux, nibbling on a toothpick while cleaning his AK-47 with a dirty towel.

Heja was still writhing on the ground near the front of the Hilux. He was trying to open his eyes but he couldn't. They were too swollen and his skin had melted grotesquely. Susan could barely recognize the face of the only male in this group of strangers willing to stand up for any of them. The men walking around him seemed to ignore his existence. The hole was now quite deep, with fresh soil piled up around it having a lighter brown colour than the wind-beaten and crackled surface of the desert. Three of the soldier's men suddenly focused their attention on Heja. The stood around him in a little circle, staring down at him. The man in the uniform nodded his head and the men dragged Heja by his legs toward the hole in the ground. Heja screamed and clawed at the ground but he was too weak and he couldn't see anything. He tried to cling to life, resisting. He promised himself his last breath would exit his body in defiance of these men.

The smugglers needed to get rid of their only barrier to their little operation. Heja was too risky to keep alive. He threatened their fragile religious justification for their behaviours, challenging their message with rationality and logic. They dumped his books onto his body and tossed his little notebook beside him. They feared his knowledge, his ability to read books, his desire to speak up. Like a book to be burned, they needed to purge him. Clods of earth covered his body as they silenced their only opposition. The gun was mightier than the pen. Here in the desert, it had to be.

The Hilux was first to depart, heading north. Susan sat close to Ashwaq and Dalal in the back of the Bongo. They all watched the Hilux get smaller through the little slit in the fabric. Suddenly the Bongo rumbled back to life, ready to take the refugees deeper into the heart of the Syrian desert and toward an uncertain future. As the vehicle started moving, everyone in the back looked around at one another.

"Who were they?" Ashwaq asked.

Hadi unzipped his bag and rifled around inside to see exactly what they'd put in there. "Whoever they were, they've got a lot of support to move these of drugs so easily." He took one of this plastic-wrapped bricks out of his bag. Ashwaq's mouth dropped as she saw the amount held before her.

"God have mercy on you. And on all of us. God knows what will happen to us if we get caught with this."

The others unzipped their bags and began looking with horror at their fates tucked carefully inside.

"We are all going to die," Ashwaq whispered, quietly wiping away her tears. "They're going to catch us and we're going to be blamed. We'd be lucky only to be put away forever in Tadmur Prison. We'll be killed for sure." Susan patted her gently, trying to console her. It was no use, because Susan, like all the rest, felt the same concern. Ashwaq was the only one brave enough to put their fear into words.

Rima grabbed the brick out of Hadi's hand. She held the corner to her nose, breathing in deeply. Her calmness showed it was not her first time being around this quantity of drugs. The boy quickly snatched it back.

"Give it back," he said. "I don't want to be the next casualty. And who knows, maybe you're one of them." He glared at Rima.

"So what?" Rima said, smirking.

"Then I'll kill you myself. We still have a long way. I don't need any more danger than I've already got."

The smugglers had by now turned the music up in the front of the truck. It seemed they were in range of a radio station, which was both comforting and horrifying to Susan. Who owned that station? Were people out patrolling the roads? What if they were caught?

The smugglers were singing along with the music cheerfully. It seemed their moods had improved since meeting the other men. They were trying to match each other's voices, singing in unison like a family on the way to the annual *Sizdahbedar* picnic. It was ironic, because the singer was Salima, a Jewish woman who had lived in Iraq for many years. Salima's voice was otherworldly, transporting the smugglers to a time before they had devoted their lives to an idea that justified rapine and exploitation. Somehow this Jewish woman's voice was pure for them but the Muslim sisters these men kept as prisoners in the back of the Bongo were the worst of humankind. What were these men celebrating? Everything they had was taken from someone else.

The cruelty of it all was driving Susan mad. She grabbed a part of the metal frame, balancing herself to stand in the moving truck. After some difficulty, she was up on her knees and started removing her *abaya*. She decided she would die sooner or later and she refused to die covered against her will. She crawled on her knees toward the back of the truck cabin, trying to reach the big opening in the fabric buffeting in the breeze. Hadi stared at the gash on Susan's face. Susan was having a hard time focusing because only her left eye would open all the way. The right was too swollen. Some moved out of her way, but none offered help.

"Where is she going?" Rima whispered.

Susan pulled the fabric back, letting cool air gush in. It was refreshing to feel that breeze, to feel a hint of freedom. She stared out at the empty desert behind them and the snaking pair of tire tracks blooming behind the Bongo as it headed into the desolate expanse. Susan could see the stars twinkling above, shining with a clarity only possible in the emptiest places on earth. She saw the moon looking back at her. She addressed it directly.

"It's not fair for me. I learned how to become the master of my life despite being beaten, exploited, extorted and abused. I stayed quiet; I was mute. It didn't matter that it was in Iran or somewhere else. It's the people themselves. Their nationality is meaningless. They are swift to be cruel, calling it defence. God, it isn't fair for me to die here. Are you really watching us from up there? What seeds of evil did you plant in us that we race with fate to send our brothers and sisters to heaven far sooner than they're meant to be? Why did I have to leave my mother's arms and enter this cruel world? It's been years since I've had a family. At least let me die in my mother's arms. Isn't it my right?" Susan stared up at the sky, wiping tears and wincing from the salt entering the cuts around her eyes.

Clouds on the horizon were gathering closer at she looked up at the sky. Maybe rain would bring new life. A flash of light illuminated the desert, casting everything for a moment in a blue-white hue. The thunderclap roused everyone and some joined Susan looking out the back. Rain came down in sheets. Susan stretched her hand out the back to catch some of the raindrops. The feel of the innocent rain made her smile. The rain could penetrate all borders, all peoples, all mentalities.

The Bongo slowed a bit as the rain intensified and Ala turned the music down so he could concentrate. Susan continued watching everything moving out behind the Bongo, widening the view as the truck sped away. She saw an old woman wearing a black dress covered in dirt, supporting herself with a wooden cane as she walked to nowhere in the desert. An old dog dutifully trailed behind her. His ribs were showing but he seemed to value loyalty over food. Susan blinked a few times to ensure she wasn't hallucinating. The truck was turning closer to the woman and her dog, the vehicle moving slowly enough now that Susan could see the woman's expression, she seemed just as surprised to see a truck in such a place as Susan was to see the woman there. The dog quickly came in front of the woman, placing itself between his owner and the truck, giving his last energies to protect his master. He mustered a few laboured barks. Susan made eye contact with the woman and they held each other's gaze for what seemed like a long time. The rain became so heavy that Susan couldn't see the woman anymore. The only visible thing now was the clay turning to mud in the tire tracks behind the Bongo, all illuminated with the faint red glow of the brake lights.

Ala was checking his mirrors to ensure the old woman didn't see the refugees he was carrying in the back of the truck. He sped up a bit to get as far from any potential witnesses as he could. Susan got a little more rain on her hand and licked her palm to taste the freedom falling from the sky. Some of the other refugees copied Susan, though they may not have understood why she did it. They were thirsty and dirty, and the rain washed both away. A single drop of rainwater was a blessing in this desert, since these refugees had lost everything else. There was no more food, no more water. Susan looked up at the sky and silently thanked God for giving her those raindrops.

Hadi jerked awake. "Hey. This is Syria, we're definitely in Syria now."

The passengers edged towards the opening to look outside. Susan could hear Hadi flicking his prayer beads and whispering, "God save us."

Susan turned to Hadi, and grabbed his sleeve, pulling him away from his prayer. "Why did you say that?"

"Why? Don't you understand? This is Syria, not Iraq. There are checkpoints everywhere. We'll be lucky if these bastards even know to which militia base they're taking us. If not, we're entering the lion's den."

The Yazidi women were listening to him and they knew he was right. Dalal handed Susan the *abaya* she'd discarded. "I know you don't want to wear it. God knows I don't either. But you need to here. It's for all our safety. Remember what that precious mother Malika said before we lost her in the desert? She recommended you to be mute. Can you do that?"

Susan nodded, reluctantly taking the *abaya* back. Dalal and Ashwaq both helped Susan to get the fabric over her head. Ashwaq jumped a little when she saw the extent of the damage to the side of Susan's face. There was white pus and some yellowish liquid gathering around her eye. It was most definitely becoming infected and it was happening very quickly. Ashwaq's mother had been a nurse before Da'esh came and enslaved all the women in her family. Her mother had taught her a few things when she was younger and Ashwaq was grateful she knew what to do to help Susan. She looked in her fanny pack and found an antibiotic in an old white tube and a little container of betadine. Susan looked on but was too tired to say anything. Ashwaq poured some betadine on a piece of fabric and gently wiped Susan's wound. Susan groaned a little as the fabric touched the bruised and open flesh near her eye socket.

"Don't worry," Ashwaq said. "It'll make you feel better, I promise. If we don't do this now, it'll be much worse. Stay strong."

Susan gritted her teeth and squeezed her eyes shut.

"Give me some of those pills," Ashwaq said to Dalal. Dalal gave her two of the antibiotic tablets and Ashwaq put them in between Susan's lips. "Water?"

"We don't have any more."

Ashwaq motioned to Susan to swallow it anyway. She knew Rima was hiding a water bottle under her *abaya*. So often the *abaya* concealed a person's true character. Ashwaq knew better than to say anything but gave Rima a knowing look. Rima pulled the bottle tightly against herself, feeling as though Ashwaq could see through the *abaya*.

Chapter Nineteen

Abu Kamal in Syria shared the banks of the Euphrates River with Al Qaim in Iraq, which was its sister city on the other side of the border. This was where the smugglers planned to hand the refugees over to another group, who would supposedly take them onwards to Europe. Some of the refugees looked out the slits in the fabric to watch the city growing closer. All seemed agitated and nervous, except Hadi, who was nonchalantly cleaning his nails.

Hadi sat in the truck as though nothing out of the ordinary had happened since they left Erbil. Some of the others were anxious, afraid, but not him. Susan felt a huge valley between her own hope for the future and his fatalistic attitude toward life. Hadi was from Syria originally and had fought in the Free Syrian Army in the early years of the civil war against Bashar Al Assad's Syrian Arab Army. He had lost a leg in the war but Susan didn't know how it happened. All she knew was he rarely stood up and he limped on a prosthetic wherever he went. He was probably twenty-five years old now but he couldn't have been a day over twenty when he decided to pick up a weapon and try to take the power back from the brutal Assad regime. He seemed to mask his fear with indifference but Susan knew there was some humanity deep within him. No one fights for nothing.

Hadi remained seated even as the Bongo met real pavement and started heading toward the city. They were now near enough to civilization for militias, police and the military to be patrolling. The Hilux appeared in front of the Bongo and its passengers began keeping watch. Susan realised this little convoy was designed to secure the drugs, not the people carrying them. They passed through an area dotted with tents, coming to a stop near a loose gathering of about ten tents.

Around each of the little camps sat huddled groups of five, ten, fifteen refugees. They all had a token man in a black outfit walking around, patrolling their existence. It seemed each group had an overseer very similar to Abu Bayda in his black *dishdasha*. The area was a crowded mess of people, bags, trash and colourful fabric remnants leftover from others who had passed through this shantytown. Susan counted at least eighty men, women and children, all separated into their little islands. Abu Bayda jumped out of the Bongo and went over to greet the man in uniform. They walked together to another group of smugglers, cheerfully embracing them.

The women in each little group were totally covered by their *abayas* and their children were shrouded beneath them as well. It was like a robin protecting her chicks under her wing. Susan heard varying forms of sobs, babies crying and prayers, all mixing together as they floated over the smell of damp ashes. Some of the women were walking around and trying to bounce their child on a knee or in the air to cheer them up but it was no use.

Abu Bayda snapped his fingers and pointed to the Bongo. A few younger smugglers, no older than fifteen, looked up from where they sat and sprang up, shouldering their AK-47s. They came over to keep watch over the Bongo, while Abu Bayda and the man in uniform went into the nicest tent in the area, nestled away from the crowd. Susan figured this tent was their base of operations. A few moments later Abu Bayda came out of the tent alone, wading through the crowd of little families as he made his way back to the truck. He was holding a piece of plastic over his head to keep the rain from hitting his face. He pulled the cloth all the way back.

"*Yalla*," he said. "Leave your bags in the car and get out."

Everyone obeyed instantly. There was no one left to object. Abu Bayda had made sure of that. Ashwaq and Dalal helped Susan down out of the truck. Abu Bayda seemed irritated by the rain. He pushed the two Yazidi women away from Susan.

"Leave this slut! Let her walk herself."

The moment they let go of her, Susan fell to the ground. The pain became stronger, her head was throbbing. She tried to swallow the groans she so wanted to make. She needed to look strong. She pulled herself up off the ground and followed behind the group. Her *abaya* was covered in muddy dirt. She looked at the refugees sitting in the little groups around her. Their eyes were turned upward, seeking help. The sound of the crying children took Susan's attention. Maybe the mother they left behind in the desert had found her way here. She looked at the sea of destitute faces around her. Who were they?

Where had they come from? What were their stories? They all shared one thing in common: the desire for freedom.

Susan wondered how long these people had been sitting in the cold, wet mud. No one seemed to be speaking. She could feel their despair covering her like a dark blanket. Her hair had stuck to her face after only a few minutes of walking in the rain. She couldn't imagine how these people were feeling, after being here for what looked like weeks or months. Near one tent, a man vomited, while a boy lay on his back nearby in the mud. A mother was trying to wake him but his eyes remained shut. Across the way, a woman was resting her head on a man's shoulder, both were staring a thousand miles into the distance.

Another woman was trying to dry her soaked hair with her hijab, using it like a towel after a shower, something none of these people had the luxury of experiencing, perhaps ever. A teenaged boy crossed in front of Susan, carrying his disabled brother on his back. Some children ran by, trying to catch raindrops in their mouths.

Just as Susan felt like giving up, she saw a young boy watching her from the side of the pathway. He held a red teddy bear against his chest and covered the teddy's head with his hand to protect it from the rain. In this place full of the remnants of societies their governments rejected, the boy stood with his innocence and hope somehow still intact. Susan had to be strong like this young boy.

Abu Bayda stopped near one of the tents and motioned for everyone to sit down. He walked away without a word and Susan slumped down to the ground against the side of the tent. A little girl covering her head with a plastic bowl walked up to Susan. At first, she looked at Susan fearlessly, not smiling but not sad. She was about five years old.

Her curly hair stuck to her forehead and she was trying to search for a face behind Susan's *abaya*. Susan smiled, but the little girl couldn't see it easily because of the fabric covering her face. She reached out, moving Susan's *abaya* away so she could see the fellow human sitting on the ground in front of her. Susan was surprised the little girl was so bold but she was glad the girl knew there was a harmless person forced to hide under the black cloth.

"No, you don't have to do that," Susan said quietly. The little girl jumped back, startled. She must have been surprised to hear a voice come out of the cloth, like a mummy telling a child at the museum to step back. The girl shook off her uncertainty, stepping back toward Susan. She put the plastic bowl over Susan's head to save her from the rain. Then she ran away. Susan felt the lump in her throat growing. The poor little girl, having nothing at all, gave away her only possession to help a stranger. Susan adjusted the bowl on her head, handling it with care like a gold tiara.

The sky darkened as the storm gathered. The smugglers were all inside their tents, enjoying their hot tea, sweets and stories. The refugees all had to stay there on the ground. They were stuck outside, with no water, no piece of dry bread, starving slowly. The thunderclaps started getting closer together.

Children hid beneath the folds of the *abayas* flowing around them. Hail began to fall and the little ice balls plinked loudly off the bowl on Susan's head. There were so many heads with nothing covering them and Susan could feel the pain of each individual piece of hail striking these families left to wither away in the desert while the smugglers prepared themselves for the next round of torment.

The wind whipped through the makeshift camp, tearing at clothes, battering the sides of the tents and carrying away loose items into the desert. Everyone seemed to be bent over, grasping children, belongings and each other, as if all of them could be blown away into the night. Susan felt lethargic from the painkiller Ashwaq had given her. Her legs felt like they were rooted to the mud beneath her. She felt again like giving up but she thought about the little boy with the teddy and the girl who had just given her the only possession she had. There was still hope, despite the reality that those suffering most were the most likely to suffer more.

The storm subsided after about twenty minutes. God was letting the refugees catch their collective breath. Ashwaq took the lull as an opportunity to go and check on Susan while Abu Bayda was out of sight.

"Where is your bag?" Ashwaq asked.

Susan couldn't hear very well, with the medicine damping her ears and the crowd moving around her drowning out Ashwaq's gentle voice.

"Susan," she said, touching Susan's shoulder lightly. She put the back of her hand near Susan's nose to feel for respiration. She looked over at Dalal, who was watching with worry. "Can you go see if her bag is in the truck?" Dalal got up and came over, kneeling beside Ashwaq.

"What if the smugglers see me?" They both looked around nervously, taking in their surroundings, seeing if they could feel any danger lurking around the corner. Some young refugee boys stood off to the side, half naked in their shorts, trying to wring out their clothes.

"Go," Ashwaq said. "Go now. Bring her some dry clothes."

Dalal ran to the truck and jumped inside. She opened each bag, one by one, looking for something to give her. She found some dry pants and a shirt, hopped out of the truck and ran back over. She handed Ashwaq the clothes, and then opened her *abaya* to hide Susan from sight while Ashwaq helped to change Susan's clothes. They could hear the voices of the smugglers growing louder. They must have finished their little joyful gathering, refreshed and ready to resume their show of force over the weakened refugees.

"Susan," Ashwaq said. "Open your mouth, have some water." Dalal had given her a bottle of water she found in the Bongo. Susan opened her mouth a millimetre, trying to take a sip. Ashwaq helped her open a little more, then gave her some water. The water felt like pure energy entering her body. Her face brightened just a little. "Listen," Ashwaq said. "You need to find your strength. You have to be able to stand." She looked around nervously, knowing the smugglers would be back barking commands very soon. "If you don't rescue yourself, no one will. They aren't going to let us help you." Susan nodded.

Dalal and Ashwaq grabbed each of Susan's arms, helping her stand. The blood rushed to her head but she stood firm. The two Yazidi women quickly went back to re-join the rest of the refugees from their group. One of the young smugglers guarding the area came near Susan. "*Yalla!*" he shouted at her. "What the hell are you doing here?" He shoved her mercilessly and Susan almost lost her balance. "It's time to go! Move!" He pointed at the Bongo with this AK-47. To her dismay, Abu Bayda returned, jumping energetically into the front seat of the truck. Everyone got back into the Bongo and the two Yazidi women helped Susan climb in.

The truck started moving again, this time with several other vehicles trailing behind in a convoy. There were some new people in the Bongo with them this time. An elderly couple, both perhaps eighty years old, sat in a corner and the rest was a family of eight, of all ages. It was hard to tell if they were a single nuclear family, or if they were cousins, aunts and uncles. The rain started coming down outside again. Susan thanked God for the moment of reprieve earlier that had allowed Ashwaq and Dalal to help her change into dry clothes and have some water.

Rima leaned her head back against the fabric, her eyes half open. Her head fell to the side and came to rest on a man's shoulder beside her. This elderly couple had only just now joined them all, as the smugglers made their convoy from the camp. The man's wife watched Rima with horror. She pointed angrily at Rima and the man pulled away. Rima didn't move, her head stayed there, neck half bent, eyes motionless. Susan realised Rima must have taken some of the drugs.

Susan looked away, trying to get that ghostly face out of her mind. She noticed Ahmad rifling through his bag, moving the bricks of drugs to the side. He seemed far too skinny for his height but Susan could tell it was lack of food rather than an affliction like Rima's that had made him this way. He was looking for something else. Suddenly he smiled and pulled a shiny object halfway out of the bag to ensure the thing he held was real. It was a silver semi-automatic pistol with a black handguard. He pushed it back under the bricks of drugs but kept his hand on it.

"Hey, brother," he said, nudging Hadi. Hadi leaned over.

"What's in your bag?" Hadi asked.

"What do you mean? Same thing that's in yours. Give it another look."

Hadi smirked as he unzipped his bag. He moved some of the bricks around, and then stopped for a moment. His eyes lit up and he looked up at Ahmad, who was waiting expectantly for Hadi's reaction. Hadi pulled his hand up slightly from the bag, revealing a black pistol that looked like it had never been used. The two looked at each other and smiled.

Susan's heart leapt into her throat and she could feel her pulse in her ears. Someone had left weapons for these men in their bags. Did someone want revenge against the smugglers? Would these men become cruel, just like Abu Bayda, now that they held the power over life and death in their hands?

Hadi and Ahmad were no doubt thinking of escape. Susan was worried that the guns were placed there as a trap, one that could bring collective punishment for them all. Hadi slipped the gun quickly out of his bag and into the old woman's bag beside him.

This elderly couple had dozed off soon after the truck started moving. It seemed this experience was nothing new to them. As Hadi buried the gun deeper, a miniature Quran fell out of the bag and landed beside him. This little book had kept this woman safe by God's grace until now. Would the gun change her luck?

The Bongo picked up speed and the vibrations Susan felt changed from an unimproved dirt road to flat asphalt. The truck went faster and started to swerve. Rima fell over onto the man's shoulder again but this time the car was moving so violently that the man's wife decided to cling to her husband's shoulder instead of complaining. It felt like the driver was racing on a track. One of the refugees pulled the fabric aside slightly and Susan heard him gasp. She shuffled forward to get a better look. Two tan Ford Ranger pickups were chasing after them. Each truck had a huge yellow flag with green writing, fluttering from a pole stuck on the back. The flag had a green fist holding an AK-47 beside the outline of a globe. It was clear now: the people chasing them were from Hezbollah.

"They'll stop us for sure," Hadi said, zipping his bag shut. Susan looked around at everyone nervously. They were bumping into one another as the driver tried to out manoeuvre the much newer, more powerful trucks chasing after them. "Either they'll kill us when they stop us, or the driver will kill us when he crashes," Hadi continued.

The Bongo stopped abruptly, throwing everyone forward on top of one another. The passengers were so tired and shocked that for a moment they remained in a big pile, saving their energy, unsure of the next trial.

The cloth tore open. Abu Bayda stood there, facing the two Ford Rangers that had pulled up behind the Bongo.

"Look all you want, feel free to search them," he shouted to the men in the trucks.

One man exited from each truck, almost on cue. They wore green fatigues, green hats with a yellow Hezbollah emblem on the front and both had carefully trimmed beards. They even wore the same watch. The only difference was that one was taller than the other. The shorter man walked toward Abu Bayda, while the taller man walked around the Bongo, slowly taking in the scene in front of him. It looked more like he was looking at a painting in a museum than a truck full of refugees in the middle of the desert. As he came around the side, he noticed the old woman sitting there.

"*Salam Aleykom*," he said to her.

"*Waleykum salam*," she replied cordially, as if they had just met at the market.

The tall man walked back around and came to stand beside the shorter one, both of them facing Abu Bayda with the Bongo behind him. They looked directly inside at the sea of faces staring back at them.

"I told you they're our family," Abu Bayda said.

The taller man whisked his moustache with his finger, flicking away a fly. "Where are you coming from?"

"Abu Kamal." He got no reply and it made him nervous. "We're going to Damascus," he added without prompting.

"Hm," the tall man said, continuing to stare into the back of the Bongo. He looked at the short man. "Check their ID cards."

Abu Bayda forced a smile and turned to the huddled refugees inside the Bongo. "Brothers, sisters, get your identification cards ready. Show them to the nice men."

Two other men exited the Ford Rangers. They were dressed exactly the same as the first two. They walked up to the side of the Bongo without a word and dropped down on their backs to roll underneath the truck, probably looking for contraband.

"Who are these people?" Susan whispered to Ashwaq.

Ashwaq remained frozen in place, speaking out of the side of her mouth. "Hezbollah. They're with the Syrian government. Now is the time to be mute."

Susan looked at the shorter man checking the identification cards. His face was strangely familiar, too familiar. She was sure she had seen him before. She felt dizzy. She knew him. The blood rushed to her head and she felt herself falling onto Ashwaq's shoulder. The man looked up quickly, surprised to see the woman falling over in front of him. Ashwaq smiled and hugged Susan.

"It's normal for a pregnant girl," Ashwaq said to the man, smiling innocently.

He nodded and returned to checking the stack of identification cards in front of him. He was making two piles of cards. One pile for fakes, one pile for authentic cards. The pile of fakes was getting bigger than the pile of real cards and Abu Bayda was getting anxious.

Ashwaq tucked a bottle of water under Susan's *abaya*. Susan drank a little and once again she felt refreshed. She opened her eyes and looked at the man's face again. She couldn't shake the familiarity she felt when she looked at him. She sipped some more water and then felt a bump under the truck. The Hezbollah men must have been searching more vigorously now that they knew the identification cards were mostly fake. The man gathered the two stacks of cards in his hands and took them back to one of the Ford Rangers. Abu Bayda quickly shut the fabric but not before he gave a menacing glare to the faces looking back at him.

The refugees were all alone together in the dim truck cabin, waiting for something to happen. Ahmad was considering his options. He looked at Hadi, who was looking straight back at him, communicating without speaking. The best way to save their lives would be to escape now, before the truck started again. Who knew what danger the truck would drive them to next? The two men looked at Ashwaq and Dalal, who seemed to understand what was going on. Ashwaq turned to Susan, and Susan knew it, too. Hadi beckoned to Ahmad.

"What do you have in mind, Hadi?" Ahmad whispered.

"We can take these women with us. We'll look like a family. It'll be easy to avoid attention."

"What about Rima?"

"She's high as a kite. She won't know what's going on." They both looked at her. "She can't even open her eyes. We can take the extra *abaya* and other stuff from her bag. The Yazidi girls can help us. They hate Rima anyway."

"And the Iranian?" Ahmad asked, glancing at Susan.

"I'm not sure to be honest," Hadi said. "She looks pretty bad. We'd probably have to carry her eventually. She could get worse, too." Ahmad nodded in agreement and Hadi continued. "We should leave her."

Hadi shuffled over to Ashwaq and Dalal. Rima mumbled something incoherently and stirred a little but her eyes stayed shut. Hadi proceeded to share his plan with the two Yazidi women. After he was done, Dalal looked at his bag and then back to him.

"Where did you get the guns?" she asked.

"They were left for us."

"Oh yeah. What if it's a trap and they're going to kill you?"

"Nah," he replied, shaking his head. "Take the *abayas* and put them over the ones you're already wearing. We're going to need them later."

The women looked at each other. Ashwaq turned back to face Hadi. "Ok. On one condition."

"What condition?" He didn't like that a woman was trying to negotiate with him in his moment of power.

"Susan comes with us."

He rolled his eyes. "*Ya Allah!*" He exhaled in frustration. "She's dying! We can't take her. She's dead weight. She can't even walk on her own."

"You lost your sisters and brother in the war, right?"

"Yeah, so?" He was growing impatient. "What's that got to do with this girl?"

"This girl right here has a family, too. She needs our help. She's injured because of me. She tried to help us. We need to help her, too. You're out of your mind if you think I'll let her be left alone with these animals. If you have any shred of religion in your heart, you'll help a fellow human being."

While they were talking, they heard truck doors slamming shut and engines starting. They looked out the fabric to see the Hezbollah fighters driving away. A few other trucks full of refugees were visible behind their own Bongo. The drivers and other smugglers were ordering people out of the trucks and telling them to sit on the cold ground. Sure enough, Abu Bayda came around the back and pulled the fabric open.

"All of you! Out!" he shouted. "Sit on the ground and wait for our friends to join us."

They all obeyed dutifully, quietly bearing their injuries, exhaustion and fear. The two Yazidi women helped Susan down while Ahmad and Hadi followed them to the place they chose to sit and wait, which was a shady area behind a large plastic water cistern. It seemed the smugglers had arranged for someone to pick up the drugs and some of the people from this location. They could see a village about three kilometres away. There were flags and antennas sticking out of almost every roof. If they disguised themselves properly, they could probably slip into that village and remain unnoticed, hiding until they found somewhere else to go. For now, they were sitting on the hardened clay floor like sheep waiting for their shepherd. This would be the best time to escape and they all knew it.

One of the smugglers from another truck was moving some of the bags around, probably preparing them for transfer. Hadi and Ahmad watched the guard carefully. He came near their bags, picking one up. The two looked at each other, relieved that it wasn't one of the bags with a gun inside. Hadi nodded and they both jumped up and cornered the young guard behind the nearby truck. The guard was in his teens and he had the immortal confidence of youth. He glared fearlessly at the two men pinning him against the truck, his left hand clasped around a pistol hidden under his jacket.

"Listen to me," the young guard said. "You don't understand. I did it for Susan."

"Oh yeah? You did what? Who's that?" Hadi demanded, surprised by the guard's confidence.

"I put those guns in your bags earlier for Susan, the Iranian girl. Those guns are there so you can rescue her and yourselves."

Hadi and Ahmad loosened their grip on the guard and looked over at Susan in disbelief. She sat alone on a piece of granite sticking out of the brown earth nearby, twirling a piece of grass in her fingers, oblivious to what the guard had just said.

"So, what's your plan?" The guard looked at the two of them expectantly.

They weren't sure if they could trust him. He could be bluffing. Maybe he saw them handling the guns earlier. It didn't matter, they were dead if they stayed with the smugglers anyway. It was worth the risk.

"How far are we from the city?" Hadi asked.

"Well, there are a few cities along the way from here. There is Palmyra, which they call Tadmur here. But that place is very dangerous. You could get caught by Da'esh or the Syrian army or anyone else who happens to be in control of the road when you pass by. And if they caught you with Susan—," he trailed off, looking over at her.

"Wait, how do you know her anyway?"

"Look, you're wasting time. This is the best time to escape. Go hide yourselves somewhere and wait for the right moment to make your move. These trucks will all be gone soon enough."

"Oh yeah, great idea," Hadi said sarcastically. "How do we know you aren't planning with the other smugglers to force us into a corner so they can kill us all for trying to escape?"

"Listen to me, I asked you to help Susan. You barely knew her name before I said it. And if they see me talking to you like this, they'll kill me, too." He looked deep in Hadi's eyes, clenching his jaw. "And I know you, too," he said to Hadi. "I know your face. You used to be in the Syrian Arab Army. You're a defector. You joined the opposition forces after the Arab Spring got out of control and you couldn't bring yourself to do what Assad tried to make you do to your own people."

Hadi looked at the guard in disbelief. He was right. Maybe he had seen a picture of him throwing Molotov cocktails at the Syrian Army's T-54 tanks that were demolishing the buildings in his childhood village. Or maybe he saw him in one of the camps where the Syrian opposition recruited defectors. Maybe he had made it all up. Hadi couldn't be sure.

"Keep along the desert road, heading northwest. The entrances to the cities are usually heavily guarded and have checkpoints. You will get stopped every kilometre along the way if you try to go through the main road."

"What if we continue with these smugglers? Do you think they'll bring at least some of us to our destination in Europe like they promised?"

"Are you kidding? There is no destination, there never was. Look, try to reach Homs. There are real smugglers there who will send you to Turkey or Cyprus by boat. They won't pick you off one by one or make you into drug mules like these ones will."

"Alright. We're doing it. We're going."

The guard nodded only once and then walked away to one of the other trucks. He told a few of the women wearing *abayas* that were sitting together to get up and go over near the truck owned by Abu Bayda. The two men went back to Susan and the Yazidi women to explain the plan. But they didn't tell Susan that the guard knew her, nor did they tell anyone that he had given them the guns.

Susan and the Yazidi women, having received their instructions, dashed back behind a muddy water cistern off the side of the road. At the same time, the two men donned *abayas* to disguise themselves as women, and ran toward the village using the mud huts at the edge of the farmland as cover. The men found a mud hut with a good vantage point to observe the smuggler caravan. They entered and came face to face with a very surprised old man. He thought they were women and, too shocked to react, said nothing. Meanwhile, the two men went over to the square window in the wall and observed the smugglers. The trucks were all started up and it looked like the smugglers were preparing to move. They were shouting and throwing up their arms, putting everyone in a rush to get back in the trucks.

Susan and the Yazidi women overheard the smugglers in front of the water tank.

"Did you check every truck?"

"Yes, *sidi*,"

"Dead or alive, none left behind?"

"None, *sidi*. We looked everywhere."

The women kept their eyes shut from fear, wishing the smugglers would just go away. Susan could hardly stand, overwhelmed by the pain in her leg and head. She lost her balance and slid to the ground. Ashwaq and Dalal looked at each other, afraid to move in case they would make even more noise. Then, Abu Bayda fired a single shot into the air.

"*Ya Allah*, we've been caught," Dalal said.

Susan kept her eyes shut. They could hear the gravel crunching beneath the feet of a smuggler coming near their water tank. Susan covered her mouth, trying to silence her heavy breathing. Suddenly a thunderclap interrupted their tension. The sky opened up, dumping heavy rain on smuggler and refugee alike. The smuggler ran back to the truck as fast as he could, covering his head with his shirt. The women couldn't even hear the truck motors anymore as the intensity of the storm increased. They used their backpacks to shield their heads. Susan started to lose feeling in her fingers from the cold. But she had to stay strong. The smugglers would be gone soon. They looked out at the caravan. The trucks were lining up, headlights sending tubes of light ahead of them, windshield wipers furiously fighting with the rain on the glass. The trucks started moving and the huddled group watched as their captors disappeared. The smugglers were gone. For the first time, the desert had been kind to Susan.

Chapter Twenty

"Did they leave?" Hadi asked.

"Yes," Ahmad answered.

The old man's jaw dropped. He thought God had sent him two *houris* but their voices showed that they were men hidden under that black fabric. The tea boiling in the samovar was squealing, sending an angled jet of steam toward the ceiling. Forgetting the non sequitur before him for a moment, he rushed over to fix the temperature on the burner.

"What if he reports us to someone?" Hadi asked. "We need to get out of here."

He looked over at the teapot with forlorn eyes. He had never wanted the comfort of warm tea as he did at that moment. He opened the small refrigerator in the corner near the window. There was nothing inside but a half-empty platter of dates and a few shrivelled olives. He took a few dates out and closed the refrigerator door and gave one to his companion. The old man stood there motionless except to periodically sip his tea as he watched them move about his home.

Hadi began searching the house, looking for anything useful. He grabbed a blanket and wrapped it over his arm. The old man had no weapons, no phone and nobody. He walked around the other mostly empty rooms, whistling periodically in a pattern they had agreed on during their escape plan. It let the others know the whistler was alright. Ahmad kept watch on the old man and the world outside the window. A few moments later, the Yazidi women and Susan entered the home after they too heard the periodic whistles.

The women looked at each other giddily, each feeling the lightness of freedom from the constant watch of the smugglers. They hugged each other, their tears wetting their *abayas*. Ashwaq started to pull her *abaya* back, ready to experience true freedom.

"No," Ahmad said. "Keep it on for now. We don't know if we're really in the clear yet." Ashwaq reluctantly pulled the fabric back up over her head, once again hiding herself from the world. He was right but she wanted her freedom.

Hadi came back into the main room, beckoning to the group.

"Follow me. I've actually been in this area before. I can get us through here safely." He turned and walked out of the mud hut into the field. The women exchanged glances with Ahmad in hesitation but then they all moved as one after Hadi. They had to trust each other for now, it was all they had.

They moved westward toward the sinking sun, which was peeking through the shifting rain clouds. The long shadows of buildings, palm trees and electrical poles stretched out across the muddy fields ahead of them. Gray clouds gathered on the horizon as the evening rain prepared for its nightly show, teasing the refugees with occasional tiny raindrops that turned into big globs of water. Then the sky opened completely and the five runaways were washed in cool rain. Mud gathered around each of their footsteps, turning the bottom of the women's *abayas* into heavy rings of soaked dirt. Ahmad and Hadi had taken shoes from the mud hut before they left, so they were able to walk more easily across the soaked fields. Visibility became shorter and shorter as the dark clouds blocked the last of the daylight. Dalal pulled a flashlight out from under her *abaya* and lit the way in front of her.

"Turn off that flashlight!" Hadi snapped. "People will be able to see us."

Suddenly a distant voice shouted to them through the rain. "They'll find you! They'll chop off your head and send you straight to hell!" It was the angry voice of the old man; he must have been looking for them and the flashlight gave them away in that sea of rain.

"Keep moving," Hadi said, keeping his head down as he looked at the ground before each step. "Don't look at him."

The elderly man chased after them but he was too weak and aged to catch up. His ragged clothes stuck to his body and he shook his cane in the air as if to invoke the storm clouds to strike these criminals to dust.

The group kept on walking, covering field after field for hours. The old man was long gone. Susan felt cramps in her thighs but she told herself to keep pushing forward. They were heading toward a crest of light blurred against the horizon. There was a city a few kilometres away. Their thirst and dizziness clawed at each of them. While they would regularly fall to the ground in exhaustion, they helped each other up and stayed close together, marching forward as a family toward a forgotten homeland.

"Where the hell are you taking us?" Ahmad asked Hadi. "Now you aren't telling us anything, just like the smugglers."

Hadi stopped dead in his tracks. "I did what they'd never do for you! I accepted the plan without question. I'm leading us all to freedom."

"You did it for yourself, just as much or more than for any of us. Are you saying you hadn't wanted to escape? That you are coming along to lead us out of the kindness of your heart? Come on, admit it. You are just as thirsty for—."

Hadi grabbed Ahmad's throat, cutting his words in half. The two Yazidi women jumped back and clutched each other's arms in fear.

"Listen to me and listen good. I was man enough to come up with an escape plan and now I'm leading it for you because you're too weak. I could've ignored you and gone out alone, or just with you instead of with these women, too. I can easily find my way out in this desert. God knows I've been here before. Respect the risk I've taken for you." He looked at Susan, Ashwaq and Dalal, all huddling nervously together in the rain. "I've taken this risk for all of you. Don't make me cash in on your disrespect with your own blood."

Dalal knew this fight was not really with the women. She relaxed a little and bent to adjust her shoes that had by now suctioned themselves to her wet feet. Susan and Ashwaq took comfort in Dalal's calmness and they pulled her *abaya* back and helped her to steady herself as she put her shoes back on.

The two men seemed to calm down, too. Ahmad begrudgingly submitted to Hadi's leadership. He flipped his *abaya* up over his shoulder, then over the other shoulder. He adjusted the part covering his face, transferring his frustration from Hadi to his *abaya*.

"How do you women wear this damn fabric all the time?" Ahmad huffed. "I feel like a prisoner carrying my jail cell on my body. I can't breathe with this thing." He was grasping at the fabric clinging to his body, trying to walk while avoiding tripping over his own feet. "Look what we men have done to you, to make you have to wear this terrible thing."

Ashwaq and Dalal chuckled to themselves. They would never normally wear an *abaya*, since they were Yazidis, not Muslims. Susan, on the other hand, knew very well what he meant. The shawl, the *hijab*, the *chadoor*, these were devices designed to assist men from sinning with their hungry eyes. Women had to bear the burden of it all. Men got to wear whatever they wanted and look at whomever they wanted. If a woman was being stared at, it was her own fault for not being covered enough. Somehow men had rationalised all of this to ensure they didn't have to change their behaviour, at the expense of half the world.

Susan spent many years under that mobile prison that Iran's religious elites claim is for the woman's own protection. Who were they to decide what Susan could or could not wear?

Such a question would be enough to make her disappear if she was still in Tehran. The *hijab* made her feel decrepit, untouchable, a pariah, from the moment she woke up until the moment she slept. She was not worthy of being seen in public. Her body was a problem and it was her fault if it was abused. The moment the *hijab* fell over her hair, her power was transferred to the men who forced her to wear it, along with the women who foolishly thought they were performing some kind of religious duty by arresting those women who refused it. In reality, those women who worked for the religious police to enforce the *hijab* were just ignorant, working against their own gender at the behest of men who couldn't control their own impulses. Either way, it was women like Susan who had to suffer for all their misguided and oppressive ideas about how a woman should exist in the world. The *hijab* was a reminder that someone else controlled the wearer and that the wearer was a slave to society.

Susan looked at Ashwaq, walking proudly with her *abaya* off her head, her hair settled around her shoulders. Susan wanted to speak to her but she was so hungry and tired that the only words she could muster were about food. She took Ashwaq's hand.

"Do you have anything to eat?"

They slowed their pace a moment so Ashwaq could check both bags for a little something. She had been carrying Susan's bag along with her own the whole time. She rustled through the bags a bit and looked up at Susan. She shook her head.

"I'm sorry, Susan. There's nothing left for us." Ashwaq was

secretly relieved that her own hunger was sapping her body of its ability to go on, because that meant perhaps she'd miscarry and she wouldn't be forced to bring a Da'esh terrorist's child into the world. At the same time, she didn't want Susan to suffer.

Susan nodded once and continued walking. Her stomach was in a knot and her vision was failing her. Still, she forced herself to keep moving. Ahmad overheard them and looked Susan up and down disapprovingly. Hadi had heard them too but he pretended he hadn't. He was keeping his food for himself. Although he wasn't going to share his food, he felt that he could give them a break.

"Let's stop here a moment. I'm going to observe the road and check where we are, make sure there aren't any surprises."

Everyone was grateful for the rest, sitting on the ground, stretching their legs and massaging their arms and thighs. Susan felt the blood in her feet and she hoped this break would be long enough for her body's circulation to normalize. Dalal was fingering a blister on her heel. Ashwaq rubbed her toes to bring the warmth back to her feet. Ahmad man was touching his lips thoughtfully, feeling the chapped and broken skin around his mouth.

"I need your knife," Susan said to him. He stretched his hand out for her to take the knife but Susan's fingers couldn't close all the way around the handle because the rain had sucked away her warmth and lowered her circulation.

"Here, let me help you," Ashwaq said. She took Susan's hands and blew on them, then rubbed them quickly with her own palms.

"Thanks." She removed her *abaya* and grabbed her long, black hair in her hand. She looked at it, marveling at how ratty and matted it had become in such a short time. Without pause, she grabbed the knife and began cutting the hair away in big clumps.

"What are you doing?" Ashwaq asked, flustered. "Why are you

doing that?" She began to cry as she watched Susan chop and discard her hair onto the ground.

Susan looked up at Ashwaq with tears in her eyes. "I used to put my head on my mother's lap. She would braid my hair, telling me how she loved me. She would say, 'Susan, my daughter, promise you'll never cut the flow of this velvet waterfall, never.' I kept that promise for years, even though she made me homeless when I was young. I don't know where she is. She's not even in my dreams anymore. She's gone."

Ashwaq and Dalal stared at Susan, fixated on the tragedy falling to the ground before them in big clumps.

"I kept my hair long for her. I tried to take care of it until today. It was something my mum loved and it reminded me of her. She would smile when she saw me running with the wind in my hair when I was a little kid. She cursed the earth and sky the day I had to wear the *hijab* to school for the first time. I was seven years old." Susan wiped a tear from her cheek. "If I never see my mother again, I don't want to see my hair either. It reminds me of her every time I feel it around my shoulders, as though it was the memory of her embrace. It's been almost twenty years since I was free. I can't carry this with me."

Ashwaq picked up some of Susan's cut hair from the ground. She held it in her hands for a moment and then set it back down delicately. She looked up at Ahmad. "Please," she said to him, sobbing quietly. "Take the knife back, she's done with it."

Susan exhaled, feeling the lightness in her head and shoulders. Her breath quivered as she fought hard to hold back tears. This was the last step toward freeing herself from her family, her promises and her past, but she wished she didn't have to. She felt totally alone, a body with no past and no future.

"How are my wounds?" Susan asked, trying to ground herself in the present. She peeled the bandage from the side of her face so the Yazidi women could get a better look.

Ashwaq and Dalal exchanged glances. "Much better," Ashwaq said quickly as she reached for some more antibiotics to give Susan. Ashwaq didn't want to make Susan feel any worse but the wound was deteriorating into an infection that was now reaching its tendrils down Susan's neck. The rain and cold were everyone's enemies right now but Susan was the most visibly battered. The white of Susan's eyes was now like cherry tomatoes with a little black dot in the middle. Blood pooled beneath the skin around her eye socket and the swelling made a purple crescent moon to frame the whole mess.

"Thank you," Susan said, trying her best to smile.

When Hadi returned, they all stood back up together and pressed onward, walking for several more hours without stopping. By now, each member of their little ragged group carried a wooden stick to balance their steps and thrust them forward. The darkness and clouds were competing with the sun, which finally won out and began to rise. The rays of dawn illuminated rooftops of a nearby village. Hadi slowed, then stopped.

"Lay on the ground," Hadi instructed.

"What is it?" Dalal asked. "Tell us what happened."

Ahmad glared at Hadi too, wanting to know what was going on. "Come on, don't be suddenly mute," he said. "Tell us why we're hiding."

"Be quiet," Hadi whispered. "We're near a village that I know. There are some people here working for Da'esh. We don't want them to see us."

His hurried Arabic was difficult for Susan to understand. Ashwaq could tell Susan was straining to make sense of it so she whispered a translation to Susan.

Ahmad eyed Hadi sceptically. "This is just one of a thousand tiny villages across this desert." It's odd you know the composition of this one particular village." He scoffed and looked out over the field toward the rooftops. "We're starving, we need water and we can get these in this village. It's hard to believe you really know there is Da'esh in this village, unless—," he went on, until he felt the steel of Hadi's pistol against his temple.

"What are you trying to say, huh? Are you trying to say I'm with Da'esh?" Hadi's eyes were wide and his teeth glistened in the dawn light.

"Maybe."

"I swear to God!" Hadi pushed his pistol harder against Ahmad's head, leaving a pink ring impression on his temple from the cold barrel.

"Stop it!" Ashwaq said, pushing her arms between them to create some distance. "You're both acting like children. What's wrong with you? No one here belongs to any group but our own right now. Your pasts all died along the road, far behind us. We're all walking together now. We are in hell, all of us. We trusted you both, you two men. Our lives are in your hands. You think these guns make you powerful? They only make you cruel. Are you proud to threaten to murder one another? Get it together."

The two men stared in stunned silence at Ashwaq, forgetting their argument for a moment. It took courage for a woman to stand up to armed men. Her strength alone silenced them.

"He's right," Dalal said. "We can't continue like this without finding something to eat and getting some water. We go from cold to hot and back to cold again, our clothes are a mess, our feet are numb. We're near a village and we need to take advantage of that now before it's too late." The group was silent, but all were nodding in agreement. They were so close to other human beings, people with food, shelter, water. "One of us needs to volunteer to go into the village to get help." Still, no one stood.

After a few moments of silence from the group, Susan raised her feeble hand. "What?" Dalal said. "No way you're going, this is not on you. You won't be able to get by in there anyway. They speak Syrian Arabic. They'll kill you or give you up to some armed group." She looked at Ashwaq, Hadi and Ahmad. "It's got to be one of us. We just need to get close enough to get food and water."

Hadi crossed his arms. "You don't get it; these people won't let you stay alive if they catch a stranger like you in their village."

"Get over yourself," Dalal said. "Come on, we can all move together. Just be careful."

They pulled themselves forward, crouching low to the ground to get closer to the group of little mud houses clustered together. Hadi led the way. They were close enough now that they could hear families talking inside the different homes. The muddy soil was clinging to their feet, slowing their movement and making it difficult to sneak onward effectively.

Hadi raised his hand, motioning for the group to stop for a moment. He was breathing hard, spooked by something.

"What is it?" Ahmad asked. Hadi motioned with his chin and they all followed his gaze a dozen meters down the path leading to the village centre. The voices in the homes all suddenly ceased, as if one cue. The group looked with horror as two pickup trucks drove into the middle of the village. They were full of fighters swinging their rifles in the air over their heads. The flags stuck out of the back of the trucks were unmistakable. Black background, white circle in the middle, child-like Arabic writing. It was Da'esh, come to terrorise another unnamed village.

Another truck appeared, this time a Bongo very similar to the smuggler's truck. The men hopped out from each vehicle and went to embrace one another with hugs, kisses and laughter.

Susan counted at least twenty men, all carrying AK-47s, M16s and pistols, covering their heads in *keffiyehs* of different shades of red and black. She could hear the different accents, too. These weren't just Iraqis or Syrians. There were foreigners among them. They lit each other's cigarettes and some shot into the air, as if celebrating something. None of the villagers made a sound, hiding deep in their homes, hoping the Da'esh fighters would leave them quickly.

The Da'esh fighters surrounded the Bongo. They tore the fabric back and Susan and the Yazidi women gasped at what they saw. A dozen women in black *abayas* were shackled to one another with heavy chains. The men hurried them off the truck, kicking and shouting angrily at them like cattle to the slaughter. The women were chained together in order from shortest to tallest, the tow at the front much shorter than the rest. They must have been barely teenagers, if that.

Ashwaq vomited but kept it in her mouth to avoid being heard by the Da'esh fighters. Susan hung her head, unable to watch the women being divided up among the men. They could do nothing to fight back against two dozen armed jackals. Dalal covered her ears to block the out the screams from the enslaved women suffering only a few meters away. She began shaking her head quickly and then reached for Hadi's gun. She bolted upward, ready to die as long as she could take some of these men with her. Hadi looked at her for a moment in shock and then grabbed her wrist, pulling her back to a crouch.

"Are you crazy? You think you can stop them with just one pistol? They have automatic weapons. You wouldn't even hit one before they tore you in half."

Hadi took his gun out of Dalal's hands and tucked it back into his pants. "Keep calm." He looked at Susan and Ashwaq. "We all need to remain calm or else we won't make it out of here. Pick your battles."

They stayed there crouching in the dirt for what felt like hours. The Da'esh fighters had by now taken all their enslaved women into some of the mud huts and none had come outside. The little group huddled together, waiting for the right moment.

Then, one of the Da'esh fighters burst out of a hut, dragging a half-naked woman behind him, kicking and screaming. Her hands were bound and her clothes had been torn to pieces. She was cursing the man, spitting on his face and rubbing dirt on her own body. The man was groping her and trying to force her head to the dirt.

"You bastard!" she shouted. "You're not Muslims! You're animals who believe in nothing but your own greed and hatred of the rest of us! You are godless animals!" Another Da'esh fighter had come outside by now and he laughed at her. He grabbed her breast and the other man laughed along with him.

"Kill me now! *Ya Allah*, give me my relief." She was weeping now, kicking dirt towards the men who stood a meter away from her as she writhed on the ground. As she shrieked and cursed, a third Da'esh fighter exited another house and walked directly toward her. He pulled his pistol out and shot the woman point blank. Her body crumpled to the ground. The other two men cheered and clapped him on the back.

Susan gasped and then immediately covered her mouth. "Oh my God," she whispered through her hands. "God have mercy on us all. These creatures are worse than animals." It seemed that God heard no prayers since Da'esh came to Iraq and Syria.

"How long are we going to stay here like sitting ducks?" Ahmad asked to no one in particular. The weather was getting colder and their hands were all turning white.

"They'll stay here all night I think," Hadi replied. "Then they'll go to the city."

"Which city?" Ahmad asked.

"Raqqa probably." He motioned northwest with his index finger. "They'll take these women with them back to the city and sell them to another group."

At that moment they heard two men's voices very close to where they hid. They listened carefully, trying to make out the conversation. The language was totally foreign to all of them. Hadi touched his nose to drive the point home that they all needed to listen and be silent. The men were standing behind a building on the edge of the olive grove about ten meters from where the group hid. Both men had long black beards but no moustaches. The language they spoke sounded similar to Russian.

Susan tapped Ashwaq. "It's Uzbek I think." Ashwaq passed the information down the line to Hadi.

The men wore heavy black boots on their feet and wool gloves on their hands. Hadi looked enviously at these, since his fingers and toes were almost numb from the cold and wet. He looked down at the ripped sneakers he wore that he had taken from the old man's mud hut in the last village.

The Uzbek men's shouts pulled his attention back to them. It sounded as though they were shouting at one another. Other men exited the huts one by one, finishing their deeds and congratulating each other on their physical prowess. The men shouted at the women to get back into the Bongo. The women exited the houses, shoulders fallen, heads lowered, tears soaking their *abayas*. Susan and the Yazidi women hugged each other as they listened to the women weeping on their way back to the truck, forced to walk over the corpse of someone's sister, mother or daughter. Her naked body lay twisted and dark blood had soaked around her upper body like a misshapen crown. The two Uzbek men walked back to their pickup truck and jumped inside, putting a temporary strain on the truck's suspension.

The man breathed deeply as he watched the Da'esh fighters get back into their trucks. One of the younger fighters caught his attention.

"Bastard! I know that little Da'esh kid! His beard still hasn't grown out. He was our neighbour in Tal Afar, living with his mother and sister before Da'esh arrived. When they came, he killed his own mother for trying to escape and then he gave his sister as a gift to the Da'esh foreign fighters sweeping through the area. Then he joined." Hadi spat on the ground. "I'll never forget that little devil's face."

They all watched as the trucks circled into a convoy and departed, the wind whipping at their flags as they headed west. The Da'esh fighters were holding their guns up in the air and hooting. Susan wondered who they were trying to scare. Was it the enslaved women chained up in the back of their Bongo? Or the villagers here that were forced at gunpoint to allow the men into their homes to rape these innocents?

"Be careful," Hadi said. "We can move forward but there could be mines buried around here. Try to walk in footprints that are already there, or tire tracks." They walked together, crouching carefully along the walls of the mud huts on the outskirts of the village. Hadi looked into the kitchen window of one of the houses. "Everyone, sit here."

There was a boy inside the house sitting beside a radio. He appeared to be asleep. A woman's muffled shrieks came from inside the house. Hadi motioned for everyone to follow him. They had to find a better hiding area or else they'd be killed if the Da'esh convoy returned. Plus, they couldn't be sure that all the Da'esh fighters had actually left. After a few more steps, Hadi held his hand low, indicating they needed to stop and wait. He pointed to the front door of the next hut up ahead. There were two pairs of boots just like the ones the Uzbeks wore.

"Grab that piece of plastic wrap on the ground there," Hadi whispered to Ahmad. "You women wait here, come in after a minute or two." He looked up at Ahmad and motioned with his head for them to go inside.

Hadi went in first, then came Ahmad. Before them sat a Da'esh fighter asleep in a chair. Without pause, Hadi got behind the fighter and wrapped the plastic over his head, pulling it tightly around the neck. He used his foot to push against the back of the chair to increase the tightness of the seal. The fighter kicked his feet while the plastic suctioned itself into his mouth. The more he fought, the less oxygen he had. The inside of the bag was filling with condensation as Hadi kept holding the plastic down. The fighter's entire neck was a throbbing purple mass that hardly looked human. His feet started slipping on the floor, his kicks losing strength as his consciousness escaped him with his last breaths.

Ashwaq and Dalal came in, followed by Susan. Susan and Dalal backed up into the corner opposite the suffocating Da'esh fighter and crouched down. Ashwaq kept moving across the room and down the hall. In the next bedroom, Ashwaq could hear a man grunting and squealing in Arabic at a woman who was screaming in Kurdish between her sobs.

Ashwaq stood there a moment, unsure what to do. She wasn't noticed yet. The man was trying to cover the girl's mouth with his hand to silence her. Then the man turned, looking directly at Ashwaq, and she froze.

"Ah, you arrived. I've been waiting for you." He got up off the floor and stepped over the girl writhing on the ground. He turned to face Ashwaq, his hairy, naked body framing him like an animal who had just learned to speak and walk upright. Ashwaq couldn't control her breathing and she felt her heart pounding in her chest as the man took a step toward her. He crinkled his forehead, perhaps trying to make himself more endearing to the women he was about to rape. He motioned toward the girl on the floor and Ashwaq came closer, her hands shaking.

"Yes," he said. "Good, you know what to do. Lay beside her."

Ashwaq lay beside the girl, who couldn't have been more than fourteen. She looked into the girl's eyes, swollen from bruises and tears. Suddenly the man ripped Ashwaq's *abaya* off without warning. He was grinning wide, his yellowed teeth glistening in the light streaming in from the square cut hole in the wall separating the bedroom from the pasture outside. Something caught his attention and he looked outside. Suddenly, a single pop echoed in the room. He looked down at his chest as blood spurted out and quickly covered his belly. Then he looked at Ashwaq. She lay there, her back against the floor, her knees bent, feet flat on the ground. Between her legs, the glint of the pistol flashed in the light. Ashwaq and the gun were the last thing this Da'esh fighter would see. He fell to the floor in a pool of blood forming around him like an *abaya*.

The girl was shrieking beside Ashwaq, her fear so deep she felt everything around her could harm her.

"Stand up," Ashwaq said, pulling the girl to her feet. "Stay calm, we are here to help you. I am Yazidi, just like you. That man isn't going to hurt you anymore."

Hadi rushed in and quickly took in the situation. He was carrying the black push-to- talk radio that the other fighter had in the other room.

"*Hamoodi, Hamoodi*," a voice crackled over the radio.

The young girl was clutching her chest with both hands and babbling incoherently as she stared at the corpse swimming in its own blood in front of her.

The radio crackled and beeped once. Then a man's voice came on. "We're on our way back, *Hamoodi*. Make the girls ready for us. We'll be there in thirty."

"*Yalla*," Hadi barked. "Everyone up, we need to move." The young Yazidi girl was still sitting on the floor, looking at her hands. One of them was bleeding.

"We need to leave here or they'll kill you," Ashwaq told the girl.

"I think my hand is broken," the girl said. "It hurts so much."

"You need to handle it for now, ok?" Ashwaq told her. Dalal walked in and handed Ashwaq some fabric and a little stick so Ashwaq could splint the girl's hand. She pulled the fabric tight and then helped the girl stand up. Hadi and the man went to the other room while the two Yazidi women helped the girl get dressed.

As they walked out of the room, the girl broke away for a moment, ran up to the dead Da'esh fighter laying on the ground and kicked him in the groin. "Bastard. He wanted me to bring one of my cousins in here so he could have us both. He got what he deserved."

They searched the house to see if there was anything useful for their journey. Susan lifted a wood panel that was covering a pile of old Nokia and Motorola phones and she jumped back at what she saw. Beneath the phones were plastic oil containers full of fuses, mortars and bags of powder. The smell of ammonia wafted up and made her nose curl. She gently placed the wood panel back down over the explosives and stepped away.

Hadi came back into the main room with an armful of boots,

clothes and utility belts with holstered pistols and ammunition. Dalal brought in a handful of fake passports and identification cards and set them on the ground in a pile. Susan grabbed some fresh bread and a container of cooked rice from the counter.

Everyone tried on the different boots, shirts and socks, trying to find something that fit at least a little. Hadi clipped one of the utility belts around his waist and handed the other to Ahmad. He then put the radio into a little pocket on the side of the belt and attachedsome car keys he had found.

The Yazidi girl was looking out the window into the courtyard where the Da'esh fighter had shot the woman trying to flee. She was shaking but couldn't look away. Ashwaq put her arms around the girl and spoke to her quietly, trying to soothe her. The girl spoke softly to Ashwaq.

After a moment, Dalal called Hadi over to the window.

"Look, that girl who died out there is Ashwaq's niece," motioning out the window with her head while Ashwaq continued hugging the young Yazidi girl. "She'd been sold into slavery to one of those animals and they took the rest of the women, too. I don't think she realises the one laying out there is her niece."

"Are you sure?" Hadi asked.

"I swear it's her." Dalal looked determined. "We need to go out there and bury her quickly before Ashwaq discovers her niece is dead. They were like sisters."

Hadi nodded and walked over to Susan. "Listen, you need to kill some time in here." She looked at him inquisitively, not sure if she could trust him. She wondered if he was about to try to ditch them all in this village. Hadi grabbed her *abaya* from the side. "It's not what you think. That woman they killed? That's Ashwaq's family. We need to get her buried so she doesn't lose her mind and get us all killed." Susan opened her mouth to speak but Hadi stopped her. "This is not the time to argue. Please go over there and make sure Ashwaq stays inside. I need ten minutes."

Susan nodded and went to Ashwaq and the Yazidi girl, stepping over the suffocated Da'esh fighter. She wondered if he was in heaven now, with his *houris*, his river of wine and his cups of honey. Wherever he was, it was better than the hell Susan was in. Susan felt fearless or perhaps her emotions had run away from her. The sight of blood used to make her faint but now she stared at death and didn't flinch. She no longer fit into a society in which women were weak because of their gender. She used to fear judgement, what other people thought of her, freedom, taking a step. But no longer. She embraced risk, she believed in herself and she was determined to obtain her freedom.

Dalal was watching Susan standing over the body. She could tell there were thoughts of strength going through Susan's mind and she was proud of her. "You're a lion. You're a real woman," she said, smiling. She wanted Susan to feel strong and to feel like she was part of the group. Susan smiled back, proud to have another strong woman along with her on this journey. In this room, there were no nationalities or religions. Instead, there were just a few people who trusted each other and who had to look out for each other.

Susan decided to search the other rooms to help find useful items for the journey ahead. She looked under rags, wooden planks and blankets strewn about the bedrooms. She tried to look up onto the higher cement shelves in the walls but she wasn't tall enough. She took a wood broom shaft and swept it across the shelves to see if there was anything hidden up there. A woman's hair band and a pair of old, crumpled panties fell onto the floor. Susan wondered how many times Da'esh fighters had used this place to bring women and how many women hadn't made it out alive. The Yazidi girl's sobbing became so loud that Susan could hear it from the other room. She came over to make sure the girl was alright.

"We would say our last rites every time they were going to take us somewhere," the girl was saying to Ashwaq and Dalal. "We were sure we were going to die each time. It was a surprise whenever Da'esh allowed us to live. We wished they wouldn't. We'd rather not suffer on this earth, forced to endure these animals, day in and day out." The two Yazidi women hugged the girl, listening to her story with silent understanding as she sobbed.

Chapter Twenty-One

Ahmad came inside and looked around. "Hey, we need to go. Come on."

Everyone grabbed whatever useful items they'd found in the house and rushed outside. One of the old Hilux pickup trucks Da'esh had left behind was running now and Hadi was sitting in the driver's seat. Everyone piled into the truck, women in back, the two men in the front.

"Hadi, this is so dangerous. What if this car has GPS?" Ahmad asked nervously, pushing empty cans with his feet under the seat. "What if they find us?"

"There's no other way." He eyed the women in the back, glancing from face to face and noticing their fear. "Anyway, it's less than half an hour before they realise what happened. They'll be looking for us whether we're in this truck or running across the fields."

"I really wish we could just search the car to check for a GPS or a transmitter or something."

Hadi said nothing, mashing his foot on the accelerator. The dirt road fought with the truck's suspension, tossing everyone in the back around worse than the Bongo. The Yazidi girl grasped her hand and winced, smacking into the side of the door after they went over a big pothole.

"Do you even know where we are?" Ahmad asked. "Or where we're going?"

"Save your breath." Hadi handed Ahmad a rifle scope. "Here, take this. Look around and tell me if you see lights or people outside along the way."

Ahmad snatched it and started scanning the horizon. "*Ya Allah!*"

he exclaimed.

Hadi smashed the brakes and the girls all slid forward, bumping into each other and the seats in front. Hadi grabbed the scope and looked out into the same direction. Hadi brought the scope away from his eye for a moment, exchanging a worried glance with Ahmad. A truck was approaching, kicking up a tail of dust behind it, now visible to all.

"Wear your *abayas*!" Hadi shouted. "Hurry! And get your guns ready."

"Are you nuts?" Ahmad looked pale. "Are you going to smash us into that truck?"

Hadi glared at him with fiery eyes. "What else do you want me to do?" He didn't wait for an answer. He stuck a cigarette in his lips and snapped his lighter across it, lighting it expertly. He jammed his foot on the gas pedal and the Hilux twisted slightly as the torque rushed through the metal frame and launched them forward.

Ashwaq and Dalal held their pistols in their hands beneath a red blanket covering their legs. Hadi adjusted himself in the seat, anxious for action. A second truck was visible now, trailing behind the first. Susan hugged the Yazidi girl, who was clutching her hand and moaning quietly in pain. Hadi drove confidently, staying straight and not gripping the wheel too tight. Susan could tell it wasn't his first getaway.

The two cars were driving side-by-side and gaining on the Hilux. Condensation was building up inside and Hadi tried to flick on the defroster but his fingers were too cold to push the button. Ahmad glared at him and flicked it for him. Susan looked over her shoulder through the window above the seat. She could see the black flag whipping along behind each of the two Ford Rangers. There were several men visible in the front seats. Ahmad saw it too.

"God have mercy on us." Ahmad was gripping his knees.

"Stop being so hopeless!" Hadi snapped back, keeping one hand on the wheel and the other holding his gun in his lap. The two trucks were about twenty meters away now. Hadi reduced his speed slightly and cracked the window. He tossed the cigarette butt out the window and put another between his lips. He moved his head quickly from side to side, making his neck pop.

Ahmad was staring at the road in front of them, eyes wide. Maybe if he didn't turn his head, the Da'esh fighters in the two trucks beside them would just disappear. He turned the music down and the sound of an Arab singer was drowned out by the crackling dirt under the car and sound of blood pulsing in his ears. The trucks came alongside the Hilux.

The men in the closest truck were all staring into the Hilux, including the driver. Hadi said nothing and kept his head straight and his eyes on the road. It seemed the Da'esh fighters were waiting for these passengers to turn and acknowledge their greatness. The women clung to one another in the back, trying not to look at the men staring at them through the window. Hadi flipped on the hazard lights but as soon as he did, he questioned himself.

"You'll get their attention if you put those lights on!" Ahmad shouted through his teeth. He pushed the button to turn the hazards off.

Hadi glared at him, misplaced anger boiling up to his eyes. "They already see us, you idiot!" He wanted to release all his anguish and all his grief. All he knew was violence. He looked in the rearview at the two Ford Rangers, which had stopped now behind them. Hadi hit the gas, keeping an eye on the trucks as he accelerated. The men weren't getting out of their vehicles. Ahmad looked out the side mirror too and then back at Hadi.

"Be careful, for these women's sakes. Their lives are in your hands. They could get shot or we could crash. You have to think of them."

"*Ya Khuda*," Susan said, covering her mouth with her hands as she saw the two Ford Rangers making U-turns to move over a hill around to the Hilux. They came up alongside the Hilux again, this time with their weapons out.

"Get down!" Hadi shouted to everyone in the car. As soon as he spoke, the Da'esh fighters in the trucks began opening fire on the Hilux. Hadi swerved left and right, trying to dodge them as best he could.

Ashwaq and Dalal rolled their window down and began shooting at the two trucks racing beside them. While reloading her magazine, Ashwaq looked over at Susan. "Hold her." She motioned to the captive Yazidi girl with her head. She turned back to the window, racking a round into the chamber.

"Are you ready?" she asked Dalal. Dalal nodded, flicking the safety up. They pushed themselves against the window frame and started shooting.

"Bastards!" Dalal yelled, shooting out the glass on the passenger window of the first Ford Ranger.

The rain had started again but Susan couldn't tell if there was thunder too or if her ears were just ringing from the loud *pop-pop-pop* of the pistols near her head. Hadi flipped the truck into a J-turn. Ashwaq braced herself, then straightened her arm, holding the pistol out the window. She exhaled and pulled the slack out of the trigger. *Pop!* Only one shot cracked in all their ears but it was enough for one of the Da'esh fighters to live his last day on earth. His body crumpled forward in the truck bed. He fell over the side, rolling into the dirt. His friends in the front of the truck hadn't noticed he was dead yet, or maybe they had but they were too inhumane to care. Susan and Dalal stared at Ashwaq.

Suddenly one of the trucks whipped around and collided with theirs. The hoods of both crinkled and flew up, blocking the windshields. The other truck peeled away, fleeing. Hadi jumped out of the truck, fearlessly shooting as he made his way toward the disabled Ford Ranger. Steam was coming out of the engine and the smell of burning plastic and battery acid burned through the air. The Da'esh fighter in the driver's seat draped his hands over the wheel, his eyes half open. Blood covered his face while the window's blood stain made a screen between Hadi and those inside. The driver tried to get his bearings and exit the truck but his hands couldn't grasp the door handle. *Pop!* Hadi shot point blank through the glass and the man stopped struggling. *Pop! Pop!* Hadi fired again through the hole in the glass. The man in the passenger seat crumpled down into his seat.

The third fighter had been launched out of the back of the pickup by the crash. He was crawling on his elbows on the dirt, trying to get to cover. After he heard the third shot, he pulled his pistol out of his belt and threw it as far as his broken arm would allow. He put both hands on top of his head and lay on the ground with a look of absolute fear on his face. All his pain was pushed to the side for a moment while he plead for his life.

"Please, I'm unarmed, please don't kill me."

Hadi looked down at him, disgusted with how easily this Da'esh follower surrendered. Moments before, the man was ready to rape and pillage the innocent but as soon as his weapon was gone, he was impotent. Ashwaq threw the truck door open, jumped down and ran over to the man. She kicked his gut with her foot, flipping him over so his belly faced the sky like a dog submitting to its master. Dalal followed, kicking the man in the groin and spitting on his face. Hadi knelt over the man's head.

"Open your mouth, you dog!" Hadi shouted. The man started to cry. Hadi shoved the pistol between his lips.

"Please," the man protested, his words deforming around the barrel. "I made a mistake. I'll do whatever you want!"

Ashwaq kicked the air out of his chest. The man crumpled into a foetal position but was able to muster a dirty glare at Ashwaq. Despite all his supposed remorse and his apparent pain, he was able to disdain a woman touching his body with her feet. She spit on him. "Bastard."

Hadi pulled Ashwaq back. "I'll punish him. Don't worry." He pulled the man up to his knees and shoved the pistol into his cheek. Susan walked up to the man and faced him.

"Maybe we should see how he likes it," pulling her *abaya* off. "I want to see how he feels." She looked at the whimpering man. "Wear it!" She handed the crumpled fabric to Hadi, keeping her eyes on the man's pathetic face the whole time, feeling no sympathy for his quivering body. Hadi pulled the *abaya* down over the man's body.

"Give me your phone," Hadi demanded. The man reached into his pocket and handed it to him gingerly. Hadi snatched it and began to take pictures of the former Da'esh fighter, now just a whimpering man in *hijab*.

"It suits you, *afarin!*" Susan said, walking in a circle around the man. "You tell us all that wearing this will ensure we go to heaven. Now we're doing you a favour and making sure you are as religious as you want us to be. Do you feel freedom? Can you feel how good of a Muslim we've made you? Can you feel the purity hidden under your robes? What a good little boy you are, following our rules. Perhaps we should make a video of your piety and post it on social media so your brothers can all see. Let them know you've received a message from Allah instructing you that men should wear *hijab* too, especially *abaya*, *burka* and *chadoor*. It's for your own good of course. You say you are a soldier of Allah, so such a holy man should be protected from unwanted eyes, right? Seeing your hair is haram. So, we will protect you and protect ourselves by hiding you from the world, making your existence imaginary." She paused, looking down at the pathetic man writhing on the ground. "You don't know what Islam is."

Susan stood close to the man, his face tight with rage and fear. She showed him her wrist. "Does this arouse you? Are you losing control?" She twirled her hair around her fingers. The man glared angrily at her, gritting his teeth but staying silent under the shadow of the gun. "Hadi, it seems this obedient *hijabi* has nothing to say."

Hadi grabbed the front of the *abaya,* tightening it around the man's neck. The man coughed and his face turned purple. "You ran out of words?" Hadi asked. "You had so much to say in your videos. Doesn't Da'esh have all the answers? Where are your answers now?"

Ashwaq, Dalal and the Yazidi girl stood around Susan, staring at the symbol of their suffering. Susan started recording a video with the man's phone.

"Talk, you bastard," Ashwaq said. "Tell us your ideas are all made up, that you're a violent monster because you're selfish and perverted. Say it's easier to kill and steal than be a normal member of society." She put her pistol on the man's forehead, pressing the *abaya* fabric against his skin with the barrel. "Tell us the truth!"

Hadi put a hand on Ashwaq's shoulder. "We can use him. Let him live for now."

"Why should we let him live? He has done nothing to deserve this air, this sunlight, this world, for another minute. He was shooting at us just moments ago. And worse, who knows how many innocents he's killed, how many families he's destroyed, how many women he's raped?"

"He will have his day. Don't worry. But we do need someone who knows this area. We could be ambushed again, or caught at a checkpoint, or drive over a roadside bomb."

Ahmad by now had decided to get out of the truck. He walked up to Hadi after listening to the whole exchange. "Are you crazy?" he asked Hadi. "This is a Da'esh fighter. He'll either betray us, or we'll be killed for having him in our vehicle."

Hadi was unmoved. "We need him. We aren't from this area, we don't know the roads, we don't know which villages are friendly or which harbour hundreds of men just like him. Having one of them as a prisoner is better than having a hundred of them encircling us."

"Yeah sure. He does know the way. He knows the way straight to an ambush. He could easily lie to us and turn us over to his friends. They put men in cages and burn them alive. It's not worth the risk. We've made it this far. Why should we guarantee a violent death by putting our lives in enemy hands?"

By now Hadi was thinking carefully, considering what everyone was saying. They were right but there was a risk either way. He loosened his grip a bit on the *abaya* still constricting the fighter's throat. The fighter breathed deeply, his brain gaining more oxygen for the first time. His eyes darted around, taking in the faces of his captors arrayed around him in a semi-circle.

Hadi gathered up the headbands from the two dead Da'esh fighters in the truck. "Tie his hands with these," he said. "Let him wear his dead friends' headbands around his wrists to remind him how he got here." He looked in the fighter's eyes. "He knows what will happen to him if he tries to escape."

Hadi and Ahmad tied the fighter's wrists with the fabric. The fighter made a weak noise with his throat but couldn't find the strength to protest. His circulation was cut by the fabric and his fingers swelled. Hadi knocked him on the top of the head with the side of his pistol.

"The only way you'll be free is if you swallow a bullet from this gun, do you understand?" Hadi asked the fighter. The fighter nodded weakly.

The fighter hung his head and stared at the ground. "It's all a lie," he said to no one in particular.

Ashwaq pulled his chin up. "Hold your damn head up! What else should he say?"

Susan turned off the video and stared at the broken man before her. "Nothing. Continuing on this way makes us no better than them. We aren't like them. We want the truth but we aren't animals."

"Did you hear her?" Ashwaq asked him, tapping his cheek with her pistol.

The man looked up at Susan with repentant eyes. "They forced us, you have to understand." His voice quivered. "They tell us who to kill, it doesn't matter if it's a child, a grandmother, anybody. They tell us to rape the women to breed out their impurity. I regret what I did but it changes nothing. I was a coward. Instead of fighting back, I joined them. They would have killed me if I didn't. But now I have become one of them." He hung his head again, his face contorted in regret as the reality of his actions flooded his mind. "At first I was trying to earn money by doing their bidding so I could pay for my sister's medical treatments. I never thought I would have to kill anyone."

Hadi slapped him across the face. "You idiot! Even now, facing death and humiliation, you still have the strength to lie to our faces?"

"Please!" the man answered. "Take me with you. I know who

you are. You're the escaped refugees. Everyone is looking for you, it was all over the radio. They have a group looking for you in the desert." He paused, looking at all their faces. His eyes brightened for a moment. "I can help you evade them. It's already getting late. We need to head southwest from here, or else we'll hit ambushes and checkpoints in every other direction."

Ahmad shook his head disapprovingly. "I don't buy it. He's lying. He wants the bounty for our capture."

"If he's lying, how does he know we escaped from Abu Bayda?" Dalal asked.

Hadi helped the fighter up on his feet. "We have to take him with us. We're dead anyway if we don't. This is our only chance. Let's get back in the truck."

They stood for a moment, taking in the decision. The four women crammed into the back again, while Hadi sat the Da'esh fighter between himself and the other man. Hadi started the truck and then got out to push the hood down onto the engine, trying to keep it locked in place so it wouldn't fly up over the windshield when they started driving. Then he siphoned some of the gas out of the disabled Da'esh truck and put it into their own tank.

The women in the back looked out the windows in every direction as the truck started moving again. They kept watch over the horizon, their guns ready. The air was getting colder as they drove and the ground was slushy after the rains had washed over Rif Dimashq earlier in the day. Ahmad kept his pistol trained steadily on the Da'esh fighter as they drove.

"What if we get stopped at a Syrian government checkpoint?" Ahmad asked Hadi. "This Da'esh guy will be more a liability than a help, since they're enemies."

"The Syrian government has no control of the area from here to

Damascus," the Da'esh fighter said. Ahmad glared at him, annoyed he had answered a question meant for Hadi.

"Don't worry," Hadi said. "He's right."

"How much longer will we carry this trash with us?" Ahmad asked.

"Until I say."

Ahmad resented Hadi's assertiveness. "Don't forget we're a group and you're just a part of it. You aren't the boss. Do you understand?"

"Oh? So what if I don't?"

"Then I'll make you understand, boy!" Ahmad reached over the Da'esh prisoner between them to fix his gun on Hadi instead.

Hadi laughed maniacally and slammed his foot on the brake. He jumped up over the Da'esh prisoner, reaching for Ahmad's throat. They were tearing at each other, not really fighting for a purpose, releasing their frustration and anger on each other instead of on the enemy between them.

"Stop!" Ashwaq shouted, pushing them apart. "Stop fighting each other and focus on the task at hand! We need to get to freedom. Don't ruin it for all of us because you can't swallow your pride long enough to get us to safety." She leaned back. "Look at these two. We put our life in their hands and they're squabbling over nothing. We aren't giving up, and neither should you."

Susan noticed the Da'esh prisoner was enjoying the fight. Susan pushed his head toward Hadi. "See? He's the only one gaining from your arguments."

"This is all because of you!" Hadi let go of Ahmad's collar and smacked the Da'esh fighter upside his head with the pistol.

"Allah bless you," the fighter said, trying his best to sound innocent and meek.

"Let me sit next to him," Ashwaq offered eagerly.

"Absolutely not," both Hadi and Ahmad said at the same time.

"I'll free a bullet from this gun into your skull before I free you," Ashwaq whispered in his ear as she climbed up over the seat to sit beside him. The fighter shifted uncomfortably in his seat. Ashwaq tightened the knot on the fighter's bindings. She didn't want him to take advantage of the rift between the two refugee men. Ahmad was unhappy that Ashwaq had displaced him in the front of the truck and in their social hierarchy. He begrudgingly grabbed his bag and got into the back of the car with Susan, Dalal and the captive Yazidi.

They started driving, heading south as it began to drizzle again. Susan stretched her neck out of the truck to catch some raindrops on her tongue. She hadn't noticed how thirsty she was until the adrenaline started to subside. These days of fleeing, fighting and deprivation had transformed her. She felt strong in front of men who would have paralyzed her with fear just weeks before. Here in the desert, the truth began to take hold of Susan, teaching her that her strength, her confidence and her mind were her own and no one else's.

Chapter Twenty-Two

"Where do you want to go?" the Da'esh prisoner asked, his hands clasped together, tucked between his legs. He reminded Susan of a submissive dog now.

"Europe," Hadi said coldly. He was going through his cigarettes quickly and was now smoking Ahmad's pack.

"Why did you choose to escape this way?"

"The choice was made for us. We got here through lies and by force."

"You're lucky to be alive." The prisoner stared out the window, shaking his head. Ashwaq glared at him, cursing him with her eyes.

The sky was darkening as the rain came down more heavily. The headlights were two pillars of light in the desert, their reach shortening in the storm. Hadi tried to drive carefully, more so that he wouldn't hear any nagging from the older man or any complaints from the others than for any appreciation of safety. It was almost effective.

"Can you go slower?" the prisoner asked. Discs of light were visible on the horizon as they approached a village. "You've got to turn off your headlights and slow down."

"I won't be able to see if I do that," Hadi said, straining over the dash to see better out the windshield.

"We have to."

Hadi rolled his eyes but complied. "Tell the women to hide themselves in the back."

"Hide yourself," Ashwaq said, lifting her pistol out of her lap. The passengers in the back appreciated Ashwaq standing up for them but they knew they needed to hide regardless of who gave the order. They made themselves small, covering as much as they could with blankets and *abaya* fabric.

"Turn this way," the prisoner motioned left with his chin. Hadi turned the wheel on the prisoner's command.

"Now you're changing the route on orders from Da'esh?" Ashwaq asked, disgusted.

"What else can I do?" Hadi said. "I'm on your side but we don't have a choice. It's impossible to see. Even if I knew where to go, I wouldn't be able to navigate."

Their truck got closer to some buildings and they could see light inside through the windows. They were driving slowly enough that they could hear the everyday sounds of the village over the rain. Susan wondered if the chicken clucking nearby had any idea there was a war was going on around it. Hadi was praying he didn't hit a pothole or crash into a clothesline. Visibility was about a meter but sound still travelled. They could hear a family having an argument in one of the buildings and in another they could see a woman washing dishes, silhouetted in a bright yellow outline of light from inside a kitchen.

"Keep going this way," the prisoner said. "This area is controlled by these villagers, not by any outsiders like Da'esh or Hezbollah or anyone else. They can tell if someone is out of place very easily. They work with a lot of the armed factions but it's all opportunistic. They've reported movements to my Da'esh cell before in exchange for food and money. But they aren't fighters."

Hadi glanced down at the fuel gauge. It was down to half. He was relieved he had siphoned some gas from the disabled Ford Ranger but the remaining fuel wouldn't last forever. "How much longer until the city?"

"Not far," the prisoner answered. "If we get off this dirt road we'll be right outside the city." He looked out the window for a moment and then looked at Hadi. "You can turn your lights back on now." The lights came on and flooded the way ahead of them. Hadi exhaled, relaxing a little now that he could see what was in front of him. "Take another right here, and then go straight for a while," the prisoner instructed.

As the tires met the paved road, everyone sat back and let their guard down a bit. Susan rested her head against the window. She felt relieved they were out of that village and out of the desert. Pavement meant civilization.

The prisoner looked down at his feet. "I never thought I'd be in Da'esh," he said, to no one in particular. "I went to Turkey and fell in love. She introduced me to a group of guys who were volunteering to fight *jihad* in Syria against the apostate Assad regime. They offered better pay than any other work I'd find there as a refugee. I accepted it because I needed that money for my sister's medical bills. I went to a training camp where they taught us Religious Studies and prayers eight hours straight every day. In the beginning I knew this was not right for me but over time the ideas infected my mind and they have taken hold ever since. I can't shake what they taught me." He was crying, his voice full of regret. "That woman I loved, the one that introduced me to Da'esh, was taken by them and made a slave for one of the *mujahideen*. I was too new to the group to protest. I don't know where they took her, whether she's alive or dead. Allah only knows. I miss that smile, those eyes. Yet even these I begin to forget."

"How can you love the woman who introduced you to the devil?" Ashwaq asked. "She made you who you are, a Da'esh member."

"But I was in love with her. She said she'd marry me if I joined the *jihad*. I was blinded by love and I love her still. It doesn't matter what she did to me, or what I've become."

"See?" Ashwaq said, turning and looking at Susan, Dalal and the young Yazidi girl. "He'll never be sorry for his crimes. He justifies it to himself with words he barely understands, like love, regret and sorrow. He has no idea what these words mean. We are stupid to listen to him at all. His mouth should be taped shut." She turned back to the prisoner, who wouldn't look at her. "Better yet, we should've blown his brains out back there when we had the chance."

Hadi pulled a cigarette out of the pack with his lips and looked down at the empty carton. "Damn." He shook the carton, wishing it would refill itself magically. He tossed it out the window.

"You can have mine," the prisoner said. "I've some in my front pocket."

"You can take the packet out and put it on the dashboard for me to take," Hadi said. "Show some respect to your captor."

"But my hands are tied."

Hadi looked down at the prisoner's hands, weighing his desire for a cigarette over the necessity of keeping the prisoner tied up. Ashwaq watched him and raised her eyebrows. Hadi wished he wasn't addicted.

"I'll take one when the time is right," Hadi said, breathing deeply and resting his hand on his prosthetic leg. The pain was clear on his face but he didn't want to tell anyone how much pain his amputation continued to cause him. He took another deep breath and rolled the window up.

"How long have you guys been going through the Badia Desert?" the prisoner asked. Susan looked at him but said nothing.

"Two days," Hadi said.

"You came from Erbil?"

"Yeah, why?"

"Just curious. You came a long way. It was really unfortunate for you to sell yourselves to Omar."

"Who's Omar?" Ashwaq asked.

"The guy you paid to move you across the desert"

"You mean Abu Bayda? The man in the *dishdasha*?" Hadi asked quickly.

"Yes. He was a mid-level Da'esh commander earlier in the war but he decided to get into smuggling because he enjoys the whole business of trafficking. He was doing that when the Americans were in Iraq ten years ago and he went back to it after he got tired of being a regular Da'esh member. He uses the same old story with everyone, telling them he's taking them to Europe. He has actually gotten a few people there, don't get me wrong. But it's not his priority. He uses people to move drugs and weapons, then after the deliveries are made, he usually kills the men and sells the women to his friends in Da'esh. That was his plan for you. He has a crazy temper. And now you guys ran away from him. You have no idea how enraged he is. You did good to escape, because you probably wouldn't have made it out of the Rif alive but you'll be in danger from now on as long as you're in Syria."

He looked back up, checking each person's face for signs of emotion. No one said anything. He fingered the fabric on his wrists. "By the way," he said casually. "Which one of you girls is Susan?"

"Why would you ask that?" Hadi said angrily. "We've listened to enough of your bullshit. You're done talking. Don't forget who the prisoner is here."

"I didn't mean any harm. I just thought you'd want to know what I know."

Hadi slowed the car a bit and tightened his grip on the wheel. "What's that?"

"Omar wanted to sell her. She came with a very high price. Da'esh wanted her. They observed her for a year in Erbil, trying to entrap her somehow. They lured her with the promise of Europe and she took the bait."

"They sell women all the time," Ashwaq said. "High price, low price, it's not new."

"Are you jealous that Susan is worth more than you?" Hadi asked, smirking.

"Watch it," Ashwaq said, point the gun in Hadi's face. "She's my sister now. And not just Susan but any other woman made into an object to purchase for soulless animals."

Susan strained to hear the conversation but it was difficult to pick it up over the sound of the engine and the rain outside.

"So," Ashwaq asked the prisoner. "Why did they want her so badly?"

"I only know this much," he said. "Da'esh keeps secrets very well within the organisation. That's why it's so successful at evading the Americans and Assad."

Hadi remembered the young guard's words when they were making their escape. He had put those guns in their bags for Susan. He had told them to rescue themselves and made them promise to take care of Susan. Hadi was deep in thought as the prisoner brought him back to the truck.

"So do you guys have children?" he asked.

"Kids? What?" Hadi asked, annoyed. The Yazidi women stayed quiet. Ashwaq thought of the baby growing inside her. She said to herself, *I have one* and then swallowed the lump in her throat. She brushed a tear aside and looked out the window.

"What about you?" Hadi asked the prisoner.

"Yeah. I've got one but I never met him. The woman I loved disappeared when she was pregnant. I still dream about her and about the child I never met, going to the park as a family, watching our baby playing in the grass, living a normal life as mother and father to a normal child." He was crying again.

Hadi listened but didn't say anything. He was focusing on the road. The asphalt merged off into two directions, one way with much better surfacing than the other. He started going that way but the prisoner quickly got nervous.

"No, no, not this way. There are so many checkpoints on this road. They'll catch us."

"Shut up," Hadi said. "I know what I'm doing."

Ahmad spoke up from the back. "Hadi, where are we?"

"In the city, we can rest here."

"Can you pull over a second. I can't hear." Ahmad motioned in the rear-view for Hadi to stop the car. Hadi pulled off the road and put the car in park. Everyone looked out the windows to see where they were. There were crumbling piles of rubble that used to be houses, blasted away by airstrikes, bullet holes and rockets. It was clear this used to be a vibrant town but it was long dead. Hadi and the older man walked around to the front of the car to get a better look at their surroundings.

"We're in Homs. I'm pretty sure." It was too dark to make out any landmarks in the distance. Hadi walked back to the truck and stuck his head in the door. "Hey," he said to the prisoner. "Where are we?"

"You're right, we're almost to Homs. This is a very dangerous area. We need to get back on the other road. People around here have nothing to lose, there are dozens of different factions here."

Hadi wasn't sure if he could trust the prisoner. They could be in more danger just by having a Da'esh prisoner in their car, especially if the Syrian regime, a Shi'a militia group, or Quds Force stopped them. But if they got stopped at a Da'esh checkpoint or if Hayat

Tahrir al-Sham found them, they would need this prisoner to talk his way out of danger.

"It's been forty-eight hours since I slept," Hadi said. "Let's rest here a bit and then we'll continue on."

"Here? Where is here?" Ahmad asked. "We have no idea where we are or who controls this area." He gazed across the horizon. "People want us dead in every direction."

"I can't take another step, or keep my eyes open," Hadi gripped his prosthetic with both hands and limped to the truck to support himself against it.

"Let's vote," Ahmad man said. "Let's see how many people want to rest and how many think we should continue." He walked around to the truck's open door. "Everyone out! Women on this side, men stand over here." He pointed to two spots along the side of the truck. "We're taking a vote. Whoever wants to rest here, raise your hand."

A few seconds passed and no one moved. They could feel the tension in the air. Hadi raised his hand high. "Me," he said.

Susan raised her hand next. "Me."

Ashwaq and Dalal raised their hands. "We'll rest."

"Look," Hadi said. "That's four. That's enough. We're resting."

"Actually, you're wrong." Ahmad raised his pistol. "We're leaving now, no matter how many of you try to keep us in this death trap."

"Oh yeah?" Hadi asked, pointing his own gun at him. Ashwaq and Dalal followed suit. "Do you like this vote better?" He laughed dryly.

Ahmad pursed his lips and lowered his gun. He stepped back into the truck, defeated. Ashwaq took his pistol away and tucked it into her pants. She walked over to Hadi. "So, which hotel have you chosen for us Mr. Hadi?"

"It depends on the view you want. There is the sea, full of

American and Russian navy ships. There is the desert, full of Da'esh. Then there is Palmyra, destroyed but under Syrian government control. What'll it be ma'am?"

"Seems we should find a place here in these empty buildings."

The group walked a short distance and found a home that was still intact. There were bullet holes dotted through the walls, snaking in a pattern as if someone had sprayed their name in pointillist graffiti. Broken glass and splinters were strewn about but there were still some blankets and rags tucked against the walls. They walked carefully over the metal rods sticking out of the ground. Hadi kicked a used condom out of the way as he walked so the women wouldn't have to see it.

"The women can use this room and the men can go over here. Us men will sleep in the hallway near the street to stay close to the truck.

"Give me the keys," Ahmad demanded.

"Why?" Hadi asked, his hands on his hips.

"I need them."

Hadi looked him head to toe, sceptically. Finally, he tossed the keys. Ahmad caught them with his left hand and walked back to the truck.

"What's he doing?" Ashwaq asked.

"Maybe he's going to hide it?" Susan was guessing.

Sure enough, Ahmad started the truck and rolled it forward off the road and behind one of the houses. Moments later he reappeared, carrying the bag of food they had taken from the village. He put the bag down in the middle of the hallway. Hadi unfurled a blanket and dust flew into everyone's throats. They sat down on the blanket and grabbed at the food.

Ashwaq helped the captive Yazidi girl since her arm was too swollen to use. She mashed cooked rice into a piece of *shrak* bread and handed it to her. There wasn't enough food to feed them all but it was all they had. The prisoner sat in the corner, watching the group of refugees eating the food his friends had been squirreling away in the village. No one said a word. Everyone was too busy chewing and finding more to put in their bellies. When they were done, not even a crumb remained. The women took off their shawls and rolled them into little pillows. They laid beside each other and closed their eyes.

Hadi decided it was time to take that cigarette from the prisoner. He grabbed it and walked outside into the drizzling rain, sitting on a little mound of dirt to enjoy the cigarette he'd been dreaming about since his pack ran out. He inhaled deeply, closing his eyes. For a moment, he was the only human being on earth.

Ashwaq opened her bag and took out another pill for Susan's infection. There was only one left.

"You've got magic hands," Susan said. "Every time you take care of my wounds, I start to feel better." Ashwaq smiled at her with kind eyes and a hint of sadness. "Maybe I'm not really getting better but the feeling of another human being caring for me is medicine enough."

Ahwaq held Susan's hand. "We both suffer in our ways," she said. "You'd do the same for me, I know it. You rescued me before. I promise I'll take care of you until I can't anymore. I saw how they treated you before, when you and I were still strangers. You have always treated me fairly, like a sister. We are family now." Susan hugged Ashwaq, feeling tears dripping of her chin. The embrace ameliorated them both, as two strangers cared more for one another at that moment than anyone else in the world could.

Outside, Hadi walked around to see where they were. He kept his right hand on the pistol tucked into his waistband. Everywhere he looked, there was only rubble and destruction. Everything that wasn't bolted down had been looted. It was impossible to tell who was responsible for any of it, nor who had lived there before. It was just humans laying waste to other humans.

He walked back to the truck and opened the hood. He checked the fluid levels of the coolant and oil to ensure there weren't any leaks from the damage earlier. After he closed the hood he walked back into the house. Everyone was asleep, even the prisoner who was drooling, his mouth open and his hands tucked between his legs. He was laying in the foetal position. Hadi couldn't help but think how absurd this man was, laying like a baby on the ground as he slept, murdering the innocent while awake.

Hadi rolled an *abaya* into a pillow and placed it on the ground. He sat down and rested on it, taking his shoes off and checking his toes. The prosthetic was dirty but his real foot was swollen and the toes were deformed from wearing shoes that were too small for him. His sock was tattered and stuck to his skin. He peeled it off and threw the pieces to the side. He became aware of the prisoner's laboured snoring and he was surprised everyone else was able to sleep with such a noise. He laid down and stayed half asleep for a few hours, not letting his mind completely rest in case danger came without warning.

Soon it was getting light outside. Another night had passed and they were one step closer to their freedom. Suddenly the sound of a truck's engine woke everyone. Hadi jumped up and ran to the prisoner, pushing the pistol in his face.

"Who did you tell? Who did you call?"

"How can I call anyone? My hands and legs are bound."

Ahmad kept watch out the door, observing the area. A Bongo truck passed by, the same model and colour as the one Abu Bayda had. But there were a million Bongo trucks in Syria. Everyone crouched into the corner, staying out of view best they could. The Bongo came to a stop about fifty meters away near another building.

Hadi peered out one of the windows to see who was in the truck. They didn't look Syrian. They all had rifles, a mix of M16s and AK-47s. One of them had a PKM machine gun and was standing in the back of the Bongo, surveying the area. They were definitely Da'esh. They got out the truck and started walking around the other building. Hadi's blood was boiling as he watched these foreigners desecrating his Syrian homeland. He quietly pulled the slide back on his pistol, chambering a round. He was preparing himself to rush out and shoot them. He gritted his teeth, waiting for the right moment. A little boy came out of one of the buildings and said something to the men, then they all jumped into the truck along with the little boy. The truck revved its engine and drove away.

"We need to leave, right now," Hadi said, standing and brushing himself off. He was trying to contain himself. "Get to the truck. We're going." No one said a word, dutifully following him. Hadi started the engine and they were off again.

"How much longer are we going to drag this criminal with us?" Ahmad asked Hadi.

"Until he's no longer useful. By the way, you can kill him if you like. I'll tell you when though. If the government stops us, we can offer the Da'esh prisoner to them, saying we caught him and were trying to turn him in." Hadi looked at Ashwaq and Dalal. "What do you think?"

"Should he wrap him in paper and put a ribbon on him?" Ashwaq said, smirking. She quickly straightened her face. "They'd label us spies though and throw us in prison. They'd send you and Ahmad to serve in the military against your will. You know what kind of government we're talking about here in Syria. Susan knows, too. It's the same in Iran."

They all knew it was true. The people fighting in the Syrian army were all brainwashed after being forced into service and having their families threatened. They believed all the propaganda Assad pushed out on all the news channels, which were all controlled by the government. Assad had a way of turning his own people against themselves in order to distract them from the greater crimes for which he was the main culprit. It would take generations to wash this place of the Syrian regime.

"Once we reach Homs, we'll leave this car and find a way to Latakia," Hadi said.

"Will you take me with you?" the prisoner asked, his brow furrowed so deeply it made Susan uncomfortable. Hadi and Ashwaq couldn't hold back laughter.

"Do you think we're going on a field trip?" Ashwaq asked. "Did you forget who you are? Who you represent? People like you are the reason I am homeless, the reason my father and brothers were murdered and the reason I am who I am now."

"Please. My child and my woman may be in Europe. I saw many Da'esh fighters flee to Europe with their families. They're in Germany, Belgium, France. Maybe she's there with my child. I could leave this life behind, start a new one there."

"Sure, which date do you want to fly?" Hadi asked sarcastically. Ashwaq was grinning, enjoying the levity that had eluded her for so long.

Ahmad watched this exchange from the back seat of the truck. He began to wonder if Hadi and Ashwaq were somehow working with Da'esh, too. They were having too much fun with the prisoner. It didn't seem normal. He wondered if he had been fooled this whole time. He wished he'd killed Hadi the first chance he had.

The prisoner was still trying to convince them to take him. "I swear, I could change. I want a future just like you."

"Enough of your nonsense," Hadi said. "Start saying your *ashhad* prayers."

Ashwaq began to feel slightly uncomfortable with the way they were treating this man, even though Da'esh had ruined her life in so many ways. She felt empathy for him, knowing his child might be out there somewhere. She tried to push her feelings down. After all, men just like this one had killed or captured her entire family.

They finally entered Homs, the third largest city in western Syria and only two hours from Latakia, the port town that offered their best chance at boarding a vessel to Europe. They weren't safe yet. Homs was still cut in half between Syrian government forces and Da'esh. Much of the city was destroyed from airstrikes, house-to-house fighting and buried explosives.

"I can drive from here," the prisoner said, surprising everyone. Hadi looked at him and laughed. "Seriously, I know this area like the back of my hand. Trust me."

"Yeah," Hadi said with contempt. "You're the reason this city is destroyed. You probably fought my people here."

"Listen, this area is full of Da'esh. I know how to deal with them. We will most certainly hit their checkpoints before we make it out of the city."

Hadi thought for a moment, knowing the prisoner was right. "Ok but if you make the slightest mistake, you will be full of bullets before you have a chance to correct yourself." He pulled over and switched places with the prisoner, then loosened the fabric around his wrists. The man massaged his wrists for a moment, then placed his hands on the wheel. Everyone in the back put their *abayas* on as the truck started rolling forward.

They looked like a regular family under Da'esh rule just driving through the city. As they drove, they saw other people for the first time in days that weren't refugees, smugglers or captives. Now their lives were in this Da'esh fighter's hands. He took a few shortcuts down alleyways to avoid the main roads, clearly familiar with the area and avoiding checkpoints that he knew of. No one said a word, not even Ahmad. They were holding their breath, waiting to see if the prisoner would betray them.

The destruction around them was unavoidable. People were still living here, going about their daily lives but there were holes in almost every building, whether from bullets or bombs. It seemed that together the Syrian army and Da'esh had tried to purge this city of all human life, only to have it reoccupied as soon as the bombs stopped falling. One man sat in front of a shop with its windows blown out and all its shelves collapsed. Two men sat in front of a shuttered restaurant, playing backgammon on a little wooden table. They tossed the dice, trying their luck against one another, just like Da'esh and the Syrian army.

A bullet snapped by, clipping something near their truck. The young Yazidi girl shrieked and grabbed Susan. The prisoner stepped on the gas to try to get out of the area, turning down a side street. It was a bad turn. There were bodies laying on the side of the road, and they rolled over one like a speed bump before they knew what was happening. Snipers occupied the upper floors of the buildings around them. They had to be Da'esh based on the clothes of the dead laying in the street. The Syrian army must have been in the next set of buildings, firing in their direction. Everyone inside the truck was stuck in the middle of two opposing sides. They kept driving until they reached a roadblock of black tires piled high. Suddenly a *pop* cracked in the ally as the back window of the truck shattered. Ahmad slumped forward, his head caved outward through his face, now gone. The back of the driver's seat was covered in his blood, tissue and bone. The captive Yazidi girl screamed.

"We have to get out of this car, we're sitting ducks," the prisoner said. Everyone ran out and scurried into the next open building they saw. Everyone except Ahmad.

"Come on, follow me," the prisoner shouted.

"Shut up!" the Yazidi girl hissed. "It's your fault! You brought us here!"

"Where do you think we are? This is Syria. Everyone could be your enemy here. Bullets don't discriminate. Now come with me and live or stay and die. Your choice."

"But you said you knew the way, you lied to us!"

"I swear on my child's life, I didn't lie. I do know the way, but the way is dangerous. I am helping you; you have to follow me or you won't make it out of here." He crouched low and ran out, down the street. Everyone followed him. Hadi could barely continue, the pain in the stump of his leg shooting up into his femur while his prosthesis felt loose underneath. His face contorted and he struggled to keep his eyes open as the pain overtook his whole body. They made it to a collapsed building and took a moment to rest under the cover.

"Come here," the prisoner said. "I'll carry you. Give me your arm and I'll drape you over my shoulders."

Everyone exchanged uneasy glances. The prisoner knew Hadi had taken a risk to trust him since they captured him and he wanted to show him his gratitude. Hadi reached out his arm and the prisoner picked him up and draped him over his shoulders in a fireman's carry.

"Keep your hand on my back so I can stabilise my balance. Alright, let's go."

They bolted out into the kill zone as fast they could, running into the next open door they found, away from the sound of the gunfire. A woman was standing in the kitchen preparing some vegetables and she froze. She inhaled deeply, about to scream.

Ashwaq pointed her pistol at the woman's face.

"Shh! Don't think about it! We aren't the enemy. We won't bother you. We'll be gone in just a moment. Just don't get us all killed."

The woman backed up against the wall and raised her hands over her head. She was shaking. The prisoner looked out the window.

"Do you know anyone who can help us get out of here?" he asked the woman.

"N-n-no," the woman stammered as she gripped the chair beside her, her knuckles turning pure white.

The prisoner walked up to the woman and stood in her face. "Do you, or don't you?" he demanded.

Ashwaq walked over to the woman, trying to help her feel better. "Can you, please?"

The woman nodded her head. "You have to wait until tomorrow," she said finally.

"Do you think we're stupid?" the prisoner demanded. "You'll have us wait here only to have your people come and capture us!"

"If we stay here, we're dead," Hadi joined, taking a seat in the kitchen. Susan brought Hadi a glass of water from the sink. The glass was cracked and had a little floral design down the side of it. Its beauty in this chaos gave her pause. Hadi gratefully took the water and handed it back to Susan when he was finished. "We need to find someone to take us to Latakia."

He reached in his pocket and pulled out a little baggy of white pills. He threw them down on the floor in front of the woman. "Take this. We have no money, no valuables. Only this. You can barter it for money or give it to someone to help us."

The woman's eyes widened.

"You've got thirty minutes," Ashwaq told her.

"I've got to go outside to get someone for you," the woman said. "They took all our cell phones."

Everyone looked at each other, unsure what to do. "I'll come with you," the prisoner said finally.

"Where? I'll come with you," Hadi said, jumping on the prisoner's words. "Maybe you forgot. You're still a prisoner. You think you can take another prisoner for yourself, while you're still ours?"

"I can go alone," the woman said.

Hadi stood up. "Do you want us to bring you tea, too?" he said sarcastically. "Give me your phone."

"I told you I don't have one."

Hadi slammed his hand against the wall by her head. "I said give me the phone!" At that moment, a little boy came out of the closet in the hallway holding a gray Nokia in his hands. He shirt was tattered, his bare feet covered in dirt. Everyone stared at him in silence.

"Who told you to come out?" the woman shouted. "Back inside!"

Hadi snatched the phone angrily from the boy's hands. He checked the last calls quickly to ensure the boy hadn't called anyone while they were in the house. Then he held the phone in front of the woman's face.

"Make a phone call."

"Did you hear what he said?" the prisoner seethed, looking from her face to the phone and back again. The little boy ran back to the closet and closed the door. The woman dialled a number and put the phone to her ear.

Susan noticed the young Yazidi girl was crying quietly, holding her wrist. Susan went over to her. "How is it?"

The girl smiled up at her, her eyes full of pain and innocence. "I don't know, maybe better. But seeing these men yelling at a woman, these guns flashing in front of me, people dying around me. The pain is alive inside of me because of this."

Susan hugged the girl's head against her chest. "God is with us, we will survive."

Hadi snatched the phone back from the woman. "Who are you trying to call?"

"A smuggler." These words stabbed everyone in the room like a knife. Everyone glared at her as she looked back at them, confused. "Who else can I call? A tour leader? You're in the middle of a war zone."

The prisoner laughed bitterly. "Are you trying to make a joke? Take us to Latakia. That's it!" It seemed the prisoner now felt he was part of the group of refugees. Everyone exchanged glances, surprised at his determination to escape a life he chose.

"We can't take you with us all the way to Europe," Ashwaq said to him.

Hadi looked at his watch. "We are wasting time. We need to leave." He looked at the woman. "You're coming with us."

"Me? Why?" she asked, fear entering back into her voice.

"You know this place. If they see you with us, we have a higher chance of survival."

"What about my son?"

"Bring him. Tell him you're taking him on a holiday to the sea. Latakia is a beautiful beach. There are plenty of people there enjoying themselves as this war rages on. It's far enough from the main conflict areas. Now come on, it's safer there for you than it is here anyway. It would benefit you to leave."

"If they see me with you, they'll catch you for sure. Look, I can call my uncle. He's got a bus that runs a route between here and Latakia.

He can take you there. There are always little boats in Latakia that can ferry you into the Mediterranean. You can make your way on to Europe maybe, as many refugees do. You could get to Cyprus, even in a tiny boat."

Susan looked at Hadi and the prisoner, then at the three Yazidi women. "We don't need another woman with a dying child." They were reminded of what happened when they were still under Abu Bayda's control. The woman's phone lit up and after a quick glance at it, she reached down and picked up the packet of Hadi's narcotics.

"Uncle, it's me," the woman spoke hurriedly into the phone. "I need your help. I have some people here that need to get to safety, just like we used to help when the war started." After a few pleasantries and rushed words, she hung up and looked at the group of desperate refugees standing around her kitchen.

"Come with me." She knew exactly which way to go to avoid the snipers. After all, it was her cousins, brothers and family guarding these blocks in the city from Da'esh. She whistled and her son came out. She grabbed his hand and then motioned to the others to follow her. The little boy didn't say a word as his bare feet ran across the sharp gravel outside. The woman motioned for the group to move faster.

The prisoner noticed Hadi could barely move faster than a walking pace and picked him up again. Hadi was grateful but didn't want to say anything. The pain was too great. The sound of the explosions and gunfire was a little quieter now. They were all becoming deaf to them anyway, having been exposed to so much already. They ran through the streets as though those sounds were just a thunderstorm in spring. An old white bus pulled up on the main road as they emerged from the alley.

"Take this bus to Latakia. My uncle is the driver and he'll take you to a boat once you arrive." Everyone exchanged glances. The driver was an older man wearing a crisp white shirt, with his hair carefully parted on the side. His moustache was trimmed like the men in the photos of the Ba'ath Party after the Assad regime came to power. It was a strange sight to see a man so well dressed in the middle of a war between the Syrian regime and Da'esh.

"If you don't keep your promise and something happens, I'll come back for you myself," Hadi warned the woman.

The woman stood there, bouncing her son on her hip as she held him in her arms. "Go on. I have a child and you all have mothers."

After a pause, they all got in and sat down. The bus was empty except for them and the driver. Without a word, the man pulled the lever to close the door. Each of the refugees spread out in the bus, taking a seat for themselves. The bus started moving forward, gaining speed, causing all the different shades of brown on the buildings outside to blur together.

They could see columns of grey smoke rising throughout the city as it grew smaller behind them. A motorcycle passed the bus, carrying a family of three. The father was driving while the mother held the child in her lap. There was a big bag tied down to the front of the motorcycle. Flatbeds and box trucks passed by, all carrying people and cargo in the back. The passengers all looked very similar to the refugees in the bus. It seemed everyone was taking the M1 highway to freedom.

Susan saw two little boys on the side of the road struggling to fix the broken chain on their bicycle. Their faces were covered in dirt and their clothes were just different shades of brown. How far had they come already? It was hard to know for sure. Maybe they had taken that bike all the way Raqqah. Susan would not have been surprised. A young soldier was walking with a cane a little further down the road. He had his arm out, moving it up and down, hoping someone would stop to give him a ride to Hmeimim Air Base.

They drove down the exit ramp, which had a big flag of Bashar al-Assad's beaming face. Two speakers attached to the flagpole played patriotic music as if Assad thought he was the prophet and the refugees in their tents on the side of the road his worshippers. The tents lined the road as far as Susan could see ahead of the bus. Families stood outside each one, mostly families with small children. They stared at each passing vehicle, wishing there would be room for them. It seemed every person for miles around was just trying to escape Syria.

They drove another hour and the sea appeared on their left-hand side. Everyone looked at each other, energy returning to their faces. It seemed that the woman had been honest with them after all. They were too tired to talk but no one was brave enough to sleep.

Susan turned to the prisoner. One of them was prepared to sleep after all. The prisoner was snoring again, laying across the entire seat, his feet dangling in the aisle. Susan wondered what kind of man this prisoner was. The prisoner knew they wanted to kill him as soon as they reached safety but he slept like a baby. Ashwaq noticed Susan looking at the prisoner and she shook her head.

"Look, he's the only one here that's already in heaven."

Hadi smiled. He polished his pistol with the end of his shirt. He carefully released the catch so that he could clean the bolt and firing pin. Susan watched him thoughtfully. He cared for this pistol as though it had been handed down for generations.

The driver turned the knob on the radio. They had come close enough to civilization that music could be heard. The voice of Umm Kulthum washed over everyone, her song touching their ears like honey. Susan immediately felt calmer, closer to life. Dalal mouthed the words along with the song.

They passed Hmeimim Air Base on the right and the little town of Jableh on the left. Armoured vehicles with Russian flags flying passed them heading south. They were on the outskirts of Latakia now. They had finally made it. Susan felt like she was entering another world. Normal life became obvious on both sides of the street, as old men walked by and little children ran across the street. Women were walking around carrying produce they had just bought at the market, while battered Mercedes S600 sedans chugged along the side streets. It was as though the war was a million miles away.

The bus came to a roundabout and in the middle a huge Syrian flag fluttered in the Mediterranean breeze. The flag looked brand new, its brilliant white and reds catching Susan's eye. She had only seen black banners and yellow flags for what seemed like ages. She was shocked by the look of normalcy on the faces of pedestrians, at the somehow natural shouts between taxi drivers cutting each other off inside the traffic circle. A man was selling bottled honey while men and women sat on the terrace of a coffee shop. Palm trees lined the streets, carefully manicured with little bags under the branches to catch the dates. They drove by signs that read 'Apartment for Rent' and 'Office Available.'

By now everyone's faces were glued to the windows, looking out at the alien sights flowing past. It was as if none of the refugees had ever been in a city before this moment. The young Yazidi girl gasped each time she saw something that caught her attention. She was completely awed by the hustle and bustle of people oblivious to conflict going about their daily lives. If only they had seen what this girl had seen, lived through what she had lived through.

Susan had never imagined she would be a refugee, a fugitive

in Syria. Her head was pounding from the concussive force of explosions she had felt only a few hours before. The tendons in her hands were tight from the adrenaline subsiding back into the depths of her body. Her mouth was dry and her toes were numb. Everything seemed so bright outside. She couldn't control her hands from shaking as she watched a woman outside putting a piece of chocolate into a child's mouth.

The bus took a left turn and Susan could see the vast blue waters glistening in the sunlight in front of her. It was like a dream. Hadi turned and shook the prisoner to wake him. They were all staring at the white sandy beach stretching out before them. The old man stopped the bus near the water and pulled the lever to open the door. He looked briefly at his ragged group of passengers. Then he stood up and motioned with his head. They got out and followed him for about ten minutes. The air was so fresh and the only sound they could hear was the water lapping the shore. Susan wondered if this is what it felt like when the soul ascended to heaven.

They walked down a little goat trail to the shore. There was no one else around. The women took off their *abayas* and stuffed them in their bags. They didn't need to hide anymore. Susan could make out a little dinghy bobbing on the shoreline. A little shirtless boy wearing tattered blue jeans stood in the boat. He watched them approach as the old man smiled at him. The man stretched out his hand, as if he was revealing the boat from behind a curtain. Susan looked at Ashwaq and Dalal. Then they looked at Hadi and the prisoner. The prisoner held out his hand. Ashwaq and Dalal nodded to the younger Yazidi woman.

"Go ahead," Ashwaq said.

The girl took the prisoner's hand and climbed into the boat. Then Ashwaq got in and helped Dalal up. Susan walked up to the side of the boat, feeling her feet sinking in the sand. She hesitated, remembering the horror stories she'd heard of the many refugees who had gone before her in their tightly packed boats. Some had never arrived at another shore. She turned and looked at the city behind her, thinking of what lay beyond. Over those hills was Da'esh, smugglers, Erbil, Faisal, Farah, Haya, the manager, her mother. She turned back to the sea. She took a deep breath and stepped inside the boat. Hadi joined her and no one protested as the prisoner followed. The little boy flipped a rope up and into the boat, then he pulled the cord for the motor.

The old man waved to them as the boat went further and further. Soon the old bus driver became a small dot on the little white line of coast behind them as the sun set over the sea, casting a reddish hue on the shrinking hills.

Everyone sat in the boat in disbelief. Was this real? Were they really saved? They looked at one another not as strangers but as friends. Suddenly Hadi shouted happily, cheering at the top of his lungs. Susan hugged Ashwaq, Dalal and the Yazidi girl. The sun smiled down on them as they were washed in the light of the first sunset of their freedom. Susan looked at the red disc over the horizon, smiling, her face full of tears. She watched all the tired, joyous faces around her and hugged her knees, letting the gentle rocking of the sea embrace her. She began to hum the familiar sound of her consolation. It was her mother's lullaby, *La-la-yi, la-layi...*

BV - #0026 - 140521 - C0 - 203/127/17 - PB - 9781912092819 - Matt Lamination